Heroes
Wear
Stethoscopes

by JM Spade

Jean -
Thank you for
all your support!!

(signed)

Publisher: Independently published (December,
2019)

ISBN-10: 1701402882
ISBN-13: 978-1701402881

For more information, email: jmspade@mail.com

Thank you to Littmann® for allowing me to use my own
stethoscope on the cover.

Acknowledgements:

First, I give thanks to God.

Second, I give thanks to my family. Without their support, this would not be possible. My daughters (still young) have been helpful - allowing Mommy to write, while my husband has stepped up to help whenever possible!

Third, I have to give thanks to my friends and second family! These people that have gone above and beyond in their support for me as an author! They have listened to my non-stop chatter filled with excitement.

Specifically, I want to thank: Jessica Martin, Renee Uitto, Terri Ballard, & Kim Applebey.

A special shout-out to loved ones who are supporting me from Heaven: Charles Tackett, Bunny & Phil Hinderliter, Melody Ruggles, and Jan Applebey.

Lastly, I want to thank everyone for reading my books! From those that read "The Wish Lists" and now "Heroes Wear Stethoscopes"! Without you, none of this would be possible!

With love, JM Spade

Chapter 1

I entered my first room of the day. My watch showed 07:15 a.m. I'd barely had a chance to drink any coffee before the patient hit their call light, told the PCA that she wanted pain meds, and I was forced to abandon that coffee.

"I heard you're having some pain. Where are you hurting?" I asked as compassionately as I could muster.

"Ugh... My stomach feels like it's been stabbed with a knife," she groaned with a shrill voice.

"On a scale of one to Jesus being nailed to the cross, what would you rate your pain at?" she looked at me with confusion.

"Well... I guess it's a five?"

"Is that your pain score or are you asking me?" I asked sarcastically.

"Wow. Who pissed in your Wheaties?" she asked, irritated.

"Just trying to assess your pain," I responded sweetly.

"It's a five," she said with a straight face.

"Okay cool. Once you have your CT scan, the doctor will be able to prescribe some pain meds. I'll let him know you're at a five out of ten." I walked straight out of the room, curtain blowing in the breeze behind me.

I walked right back to my cup of coffee but was disappointed that it was only lukewarm at this point. I didn't give a shit and drank it anyway. My night shift work bestie, Sam, approached with his own cup of coffee and together we drank in silence, but he broke the silence first.

"Did you watch the game last night?"

"Of course. I stayed up to watch the end of it."

"Me too. I should have gone to bed."

I took the last drink from my coffee, tossed the cup in the garbage can, and bid him farewell as a new patient was brought to one of my empty rooms. The patient was a ninety-year-old woman with a chief complaint of increased confusion. The daughter was concerned she might have a urinary tract infection.

"How long has your mom been confused?"

"She's had some dementia for the last year, but the last day or so has been more confused than normal," the daughter replied pleasantly.

Looking to the patient and talking loudly into her ear, "Does it hurt when you pee?" I asked.

"WHAT?" the patient hollered at me.

"DOES. IT. HURT. WHEN. YOU. PEE?" I screamed into her ear loud enough that I was sure everyone in the emergency room could hear me.

"No," she said at a normal level.

"Oh, here is her hearing aid," the daughter said as she dug the hearing aids from her oversized purse.

Those would have been helpful at the beginning of this exchange, but I soon realized it was probably not done sooner because the daughter didn't want her mother to actually hear us talking about her. As the daughter continued to tell me about her mom, it was clear that she'd been talking to Dr. Google and not her family physician. Her mother clearly had dementia and it had progressed, but the daughter believed that it was just a urinary tract infection because she was living in denial. Plain and simple.

"Your mom will need to pee in this cup. Here are some wipes. There are directions in the bathroom. If you have any problems assisting her, please let us know," I said pleasantly while I screamed profanities in my head.

"I can't help her," the daughter instantly stammered as I headed for the door.

"Who helps her at home?"

"Well, I do," the daughter said.

"So why can't you help her here?"

"Isn't that your job?" she said looking confused.

"Ma'am, with all due respect, my job is to assess your mother's condition, assist the physician in finding and potentially treating your mother's condition, and then giving you information to continue that treatment at home. Nowhere in my job description does it say I need to clean your mother's crotch and help her get a urine sample. That, I'm afraid, is your job."

The daughter's mouth dropped to the floor and I continued out the door, confident I'd be fired once she complained to my supervisor. Until then, I was just going to just continue on with my day. Once I was back in the hallway, Sam was standing at my computer with *his* mouth hanging wide open.

"What the hell was that?" he asked, shocked.

"What?" I played innocent.

"Did you really just say that to a family member?"

"Yes, I did."

"Wow. I'm jealous," he said with a sinister smile.

"I know," I said as I headed to the break room for more coffee.

That was the day I realized that I had a problem. Well, maybe. Everyone told me I was not quite myself, but I was completely oblivious to it. It's not like it was necessarily a problem for *me*, but *I* was a problem for others. I denied the existence of anything being wrong for so long that once I did start to notice the problem, I didn't care that I had one.

I had become a new person. My personality had changed. Some days, I was the old me. Most days, I was a different version of me. As I contemplated *why* my personality had changed, I thought about all the possible reasons: family drama, nursing burnout, and possibly — admittedly the scariest option — menopause.

Then the day came that, one, I had to accept that there was a problem and, two, decide on a course of action. Each option had its own list of pros and cons, and I was left sitting in a room, alone, to decide which was the best. While all the options affected me, some of them affected others too.

I continually second guessed myself after I made the decision. Ironically, I wasn't one to second guess myself usually. I was confident in almost everything I did. As a nurse, I was used to facing high-pressure situations and rarely did I walk away wondering if I'd made the right choice. So why was I doing it now?

I'd spent the last twenty-one years working in the emergency room, ER, of our local hospital as a nurse. For as long as I could remember, I'd wanted to be an ER nurse. Growing up, I was fascinated with the human body and took all kinds of anatomy and physiology classes in high school. I also spent time job shadowing my aunt, a labor and delivery nurse. Confident I didn't want to deliver babies every day, I began working as a patient care associate, or PCA, in the ER instead.

Unfortunately, my dream for nursing had to wait until I could afford college or earn enough scholarship money. But when the time finally came, I applied to nursing school, studied hard, and proudly wrote those letters after my name, RN. And I was a damn good registered nurse.

I loved everything about the ER — patients, co-workers, the pace, and all the drama. It became my home away from home. Need your shift covered? Call me! If I wasn't at home sleeping, I was in that emergency room soaking it all up.

Of course, because I was always there, it wasn't crazy when I fell in love with orthopedic resident Dr. Parker Cordova. At first, he was just a dreamy newbie doctor I admired from afar. When he started his emergency medicine rotation, we worked side by side regularly. As the month came to an end, and he was set to head back to the operating room, our constant flirting turned into an offer for a first date.

I wanted nothing more than to go on a few dates with him, but after those dates were over, I wanted more. He was everything I'd imagined my husband would be — kind, attentive, funny, handsome, patient... Months later, we got married and over the years, I gave birth to three children. Everything was under control and my life was going smoothly. In fact, it was following the routine that I craved so much.

But a few months ago, things started to fall apart. I'm not sure where or when it started exactly, but between my husband, three teenagers, and my job, my life was pretty great. The people around me noticed I wasn't my usual self, but I felt fine, so I brushed them off. As time wore on, the changes in me became more and more obvious until shit really hit the fan. But I continued on even after noticing I had something going on. Despite feeling changes in my body and noticing my own personality becoming out of control, I tried to hide it or ignore it and just keep to my routine. Until I couldn't anymore.

As I sat in my car thinking about the options, my phone rang. I heard the voice on the other line and my mind went blank.

"Are you serious? Oh my God. I'll be right there!"

I hung up the phone and promptly forgot all about those options as I put my car in reverse.

Chapter 2

"New patient to room 11. New patient to room 11." I said over the pager as I escorted the patient from the triage area to room 11. "Please undress and put on this gown. It opens in the back. You may leave on your underwear, bra, and socks if you'd like. The nurse will be with you shortly," I said as I opened the curtain and stepped out.

"What's she here for?" Avalon asked as I passed her on my way back to triage.

"Abdominal pain," I said with a smile.

"I can't wait!" Avalon said with fake enthusiasm.

"That's why I gave her to you."

I returned to triage and called the next patient back and began my assessment as the patient care assistant, or PCA, began to take his vitals. The triage room was hardly bigger than a standard bathroom and in one corner contained a tiny desk with a computer, a few cupboards above the desk, and an office chair on wheels. The other side of the room held a scale, a chair for the patient, and a chair for whoever had accompanied them to the emergency room. It was painted a pale green color with beige tile on the floor that looked like vinyl with a coat of lacquer over it.

Avalon was my work bestie on the day shift. We'd been working together for so many years, I felt like we were more family than co-workers. She had younger kids than my three teenagers and her husband wasn't in the medical field, but we instantly clicked anyway.

"What brings you in today?" I asked in my best customer service voice.

"My neck hurts and it's causing my arm to go numb at times," the man said.

"How long has it been going on?" This was always my favorite question to ask.

"It's been off and on for the last month or so," he said as his hand rubbed at the back of his neck.

I entered the information into the assessment on the computer and in my head, I screamed at him. Why the hell are you coming to the emergency room on a Tuesday for something that's been going on for a month or so? Haven't you heard of a primary care doctor? However, I didn't say any of that and instead, continued to enter information and ask questions.

This had been the routine for so many years that it was second nature to keep my mouth shut and smile through the terrible screaming inside my head. I could have written a book on the misuse of emergency rooms, but it would go unread because there were thousands of articles out there saying the exact same stuff. Our emergency room wasn't any different from the thousands of emergency rooms across the country.

"Alright, please have a seat in the waiting room, and we'll get you back to a room as soon as we can," I said politely as I opened the door for him.

"Kate, what room did the ankle fracture go to?" Nora asked as she peeked into the triage room.

"Um... Room 6."

"Awesome. Thank you."

There weren't any other patients in the waiting room, so now it was my turn to wait. Wait for an open room or wait for a new patient. Triage wasn't always the most exciting assignment, but it was an important one. As one of the first faces many patients interact with, it was me that decided who needed treatment and how fast. It was me who prioritized the order the patients were seen in. I hated this assignment.

"Kate, are you ready for lunch?" Adel asked as she came into my little triage room.

"Finally!" I wasted no time logging out of the computer, giving her a quick update on who was in the waiting room, and headed to the break room.

I sat down at the table in our overcrowded break room with three other staff members and opened my lunchbox. A peanut butter and jelly sandwich, a container of applesauce, and a juice box. Shit. I'd packed my daughter's lunch in my lunchbox. She was probably sitting in the middle school cafeteria dining on last night's leftover lasagna, cherry yogurt, and my energy drink. Lucky kid.

"Kate, how's Carter's baseball team doing?" Avalon asked as she sat down next to me with a steaming plate of chicken dumplings.

Avalon hadn't washed her hands before she began to eat. As a self-proclaimed germaphobe, I couldn't stop picturing the nasty little bugs she could potentially be eating. Since Avalon was one of my closest friends at work, I also couldn't resist reminding her of this.

"Avalon, did you wash your hands?" She rolled her eyes.

"No, no I didn't," she said as she got up, moved to the sink in the corner, and began washing her hands.

"Thank you," I said as I watched her scrub between her fingers with pleasure. "Yes, Carter's team is doing fabulous."

"You never cease to amaze me, Kate. But I still love you," she said with a laugh.

"I know you do," I said confidently.

"What exactly are you eating for lunch?" she asked as she returned to her seat and eyed my lunch.

"Don't ask. Kamdyn is probably enjoying my lasagna and energy drink."

"You packed the wrong lunches?" Avalon asked with a laugh.

"Apparently. Doesn't this juice box suit me well?"

Kamdyn, my thirteen-year-old daughter, was in eighth grade at Franklin Middle School. She was my youngest, still sweet, and loved books. Her long brown hair usually went in a ponytail at the base of her neck. I hated that she was so quiet. I couldn't quite tell what she was thinking or feeling anymore, and that thought scared the hell out of me.

Finished with lunch, I headed back to the triage area for the second round of torture. Adel had helped keep everything running smoothly, but there were a few new patients waiting to be triaged and a few that were waiting for rooms. It was just another day in the ER, I thought to myself as I grabbed the next chart.

"Reginald?" I called into the waiting room for the next patient.

An overweight man appeared before me, breathless. I led him to the chair in the triage room, sanitized my hands, and began to take his vitals as I asked him what he was here for. I fought the urge to roll my eyes because I already knew why he was here, but I was forced to ask the question regardless.

"I was getting ready to eat lunch and checked my blood sugar but the thing said it was too high. The doctor said I had to come here," he said calmly.

"Did you eat before you came?" I asked, even though I already knew this answer also.

"Yeah, 'cause you guys never feed me when I come," he said with a frown.

"Now Reggie, you know why that is," I said with a motherly tone.

Reginald, or Reggie as he was called, was what we called a frequent flier. He came in about every other week for elevated blood sugars. It never mattered what we said to him, he wouldn't listen. As much as I wanted to give him sympathy, if he couldn't take care of himself, why did I have to?

Finished with his intake, I told him to have a seat in the waiting room, and we'd get him back to see the doctor as soon as we could. Then again, he knew the routine. Before I called the next patient back, I went to find Avalon.

"Hey, wanna do a pool on how high Reggie's blood sugar will be today?" I asked enthusiastically.

"He's back?" Avalon asked.

"Yep."

"I'll say 880."

"I got 798," Adel threw out her guess from the next chair over.

Dr. Tempest turned from her computer and added her guess of 1001. All of those blood sugar levels would mean unconsciousness for the average person, but not Reggie. His body was well acquainted with elevated blood sugars. I often wondered what he would feel like if his blood sugar was at a normal level, but realized that probably didn't happen too often.

Satisfied, I headed back to triage. I called the next patient back, a young teenage girl complaining of abdominal pain. Maybe I was becoming burnt out or else my "give a damn" was busted because I was just irritated and I hadn't even met her yet. I painted on a pleasant face and began the routine.

"How can I help you?" I asked sweetly.

"I think I'm pregnant," she said just above a whisper.

"How old are you?"

"Fourteen."

I fought the urge to roll my eyes as she said it and instead, began taking her vital signs and completing my quick assessment. In my mind, fourteen year olds were still children. They should be playing with dolls, not another person's genitals.

"Where are your parents?"

"My mom is at work and my dad is at home sleeping. He works the night shift," she said as if showing up to an emergency room in the early afternoon without parents was perfectly normal.

"I see. Do they know you're here?"

"No. I had a friend drop me off."

"Ahh. Why do you think you're pregnant?"

"Um," she said hesitantly and I eagerly awaited her explanation.

"It's okay. You can tell me," I encouraged with a friendly tone.

"Will you tell my parents?"

I thought about Kamdyn when she asked this. If this was *my* child in the emergency room thinking she was pregnant, would I want to know? Of course, I would, but this girl wasn't my child. The law said she was not old enough to consent to sexual intercourse yet she was old enough to be seen for sexual health issues without parental consent. I hated when laws and ethics were gray zones.

"Unfortunately, I cannot guarantee no one will tell your parents, but at this point, we don't have to," I said sympathetically.

She thought for a few moments and then I saw the tears well up in her eyes. I handed her a tissue and reassured her that we would figure everything out. In my mind, I thought of

16

how I'd want one of my fellow nurses treating Kamdyn and my compassion began to overwhelm me. Sometimes it was hard not to envision your own family in front of you. The irritation I had been feeling melted away.

"I think I'm pregnant because I haven't had a period in a while and I feel sick to my stomach most days," she finally said.

"Have you taken a pregnancy test?"

"No, I don't have any money for that. I'm too afraid to tell my parents what happened, so I can't ask them for money either."

"Are you having sex regularly?"

While I knew that I was supposed to just triage this patient and move on, something about her punched me right in the gut. Over the years, I'd learned that when your gut tells you something, you need to listen. I glanced at my computer and saw that someone else had grabbed Reggie from the waiting room and only one other patient was waiting.

"No. It's only happened a few times."

"A boyfriend?" I asked curiously.

"No. My uncle," she said so quiet that I could barely make out her words.

Had she just told me that her uncle had sex with her? And not once, but a few times? I needed to be absolutely sure of what she'd just said because that gray zone had just turned a solid color. If I heard correctly, I was mandated to report this. And morally, I didn't need a law telling me I had to help this girl. When you hear something like this, you help whether the law says to or not.

"I want to make sure I heard you correctly. Did you say your uncle?"

"Yeah."

"Can you tell me what happened?" I asked with a sense of alarm and I tried to keep my voice soft and compassionate, masking the surge of adrenalin I felt.

"I'm afraid to." I noticed her hands began to shake.

"Okay. I understand that it can be extremely hard to talk about it. You don't have to talk to me if you don't want to. We can get you back to see the doctor and find out what is going on with your tummy," I said as I headed towards the door. Then I added, "And whether you're pregnant or not."

"Wait," she said, stopping me. "I'm so scared that he's going to hurt me. Either he'll keep doing it or he'll hurt me. I'm scared my parents will be mad at me, but I can't take it anymore," she said with urgency.

Her wall came crashing down and she began to cry. I quietly requested Adel to come to triage and the social worker to meet me in room 10. This was serious and if she felt comfortable confiding in me, then I was going to be the one to listen. I was going to take care of her just like I would want someone to take care of my own fourteen-year old.

"Can we go to another room to talk?" I asked.

"Okay," she said as she stood up, straightened her back, and followed me to room 10.

By the time I had her truth uncovered and things settled, it was time to go home. Mentally, I was exhausted. This wasn't a new feeling though. I'd been feeling more and more mentally drained over the last few months, more than I ever had. Maybe I was just getting old? I might only be forty-six, but I certainly wasn't as spry as I'd been at twenty-six or even thirty-six.

After all the years of working twelve-hour shifts, I'd switched to eight-hour shifts once we'd paid off Parker's medical school loans. Even though I wasn't yet fifty, I didn't have to spend so many hours working and that was perfectly fine with me. I had plenty of things to keep me busy — like driving my children from activity to activity or getting cozy with a good book.

The moment I got home, I carefully hung my keys on the appropriate hook, took my shoes off, hung my purse on the kitchen chair, and hurried off to my bedroom to change my clothes. This had been my routine for years. I did my best not to deviate from it. Once my clothes were changed, I returned to the kitchen to check the family calendar hanging on the side of the refrigerator.

Our home was a beautiful, one-story home just on the outskirts of town. Six bedrooms, four full bathrooms, four car garage, and one large pool was the description that caught my eye four years ago when we were looking for a new home. Upon seeing it, I immediately fell in love with the oak library shelves, the gourmet kitchen, the sunroom, and walkout basement. It was an easy sell from that point forward.

Our three children, Kendall, Carter, and Kamdyn would all have their own space, and we would still have a room for guests. The walkout basement was a perfect space for teenagers to escape from their parents and that library was calling my name for the times I needed to escape from the teenagers.

Kendall, our oldest, had been quick to move into an apartment on campus as soon as the summer after high school graduation had ended. We rarely saw her anymore. I assumed this was normal and that she was off having the time of her life while getting the degree she always talked about.

Carter, our middle child, was my adventurous child. Involved in any sport he could get his hands on, it seemed he was always on the go, and he never stopped. When he turned sixteen this past year, it was like a light switch had flipped and my sweet boy turned into a girl craving bad boy. He was the child giving me headaches and making me dread phone calls from the school.

Kamdyn was my baby girl. She had been a welcome surprise. Probably because her brother and sister were so loud and never let her speak, she was also my quiet child. She would always be my baby girl, but the older she got, the less she wanted to hang out with me and the more she wanted to hang out in her bedroom reading. She was the spitting image of me at that age.

The calendar on the refrigerator showed that Kamdyn had no activities planned, but Carter needed a ride home from baseball practice at five. With about thirty minutes until Kamdyn's bus would arrive at the end of the driveway, I threw myself onto the couch to catch a quick nap.

My phone woke me up from a deep sleep some time later. What time was it? Glancing at my watch, I saw it was 05:30 p.m. Where was Kamdyn? Carter? Quickly, I hit the button to accept the call.

"Mom? Where are you?" Carter's voice shouted at me.

"I'm at home. Where are you?" I squeaked in panic.

"Why are you at home? You're supposed to be here at the school picking me up from practice!" He growled.

"Dammit," I said as I rushed toward the door and began putting my shoes on, all the panic gone and replaced with another feeling that I didn't have time to label.

"Are you coming to get me, or do I need to ride home with Jayden," he asked, sighing heavily into the phone. "His mom has been waiting with us just in case."

"Calm down. I just fell asleep on the couch is all. I'm on my way." I ended the call, grabbed my keys, and headed for my car.

I quickly located Kamdyn in her room reading and informed her I'd be right back. Ten minutes later, when I arrived at the practice field, Carter chose to sit in the backseat rather than next to me in the front. I'd learned life was just going to be this way for a while and drove home in silence. I didn't bother asking questions. I noticed his earbuds were in his ears anyway. He was mad at me, but I'd come to expect it.

Chapter 3

Safely home, I hung my keys back on their designated hook and removed my shoes. Carter bolted for the basement without saying a word the moment his shoes were neatly placed on the shoe rack. As I stood in the kitchen debating what to make for dinner, I realized how lonely being a parent to teenagers really was.

By the time Parker finally got home, I was in bed reading a new novel I'd picked up last week at the local bookstore. He climbed into bed without a word, kissed me on the forehead, and rolled over to sleep. Between some teaching at the university and working his shifts at the hospital, he didn't have much free time. I had known this would be this way when we met and I accepted it when I accepted the engagement ring a year later.

I closed my book, shut off my lamp, and nestled closer to him. I felt him sigh heavily. This was a typical day in our lives. I often asked myself if I'd want it another way, but the answer was always "no". I was okay with it. I was comfortable with it. It was safe and I loved the routine it provided.

The first few years of marriage had been hectic. We were both in school and knew that once he finished residency, we didn't know where we would be moving to. Once we were finally settled and the kids had come along, life became a routine. I loved Parker more than anything and I knew I couldn't live without him, but we rarely did things just the two of us anymore. Would someone say we'd drifted apart? I didn't think so — I thought things were great the way they were!

The next morning when my alarm went off, Parker was already in the shower. Kamdyn and Carter were still fast asleep. Kendall was across town in her own apartment enjoying her freshman year at college. I climbed into the shower with Parker, which he happily accepted. It wasn't something I regularly did, in fact, we didn't regularly have sex at all. We had become the old married couple my friends always referred to and that I swore we never would be.

"In the mood for a quickie?" he asked with a boyish smile and surprise.

"Would I have gotten in the shower with you if I wasn't?" I asked, returning the smile.

It *had* been awhile since I'd been intimate with Parker. It wasn't that I didn't *want* to, I just didn't have the same drive I used to. I don't know if it was my age or just being married for so long, but between that and his lack of time, we just didn't have sex as often as we probably should. Yep, we were definitely the old married couple.

When we first met, you could find us sneaking off to my tiny apartment for sex all the time or stealing five quick minutes in the call room at the hospital. Once we married, it didn't stop. Honestly, I was surprised we didn't have more kids than we do. In fact, I was surprised we didn't have them sooner!

Parker, at six feet three inches, was very physically fit. His hair was kept cut short, and he shaved practically every day. While he barely had time to sleep some days, he made a point to visit the gym at least twice a week. The operating room nursing staff had once told me that when he was waiting for his partner or for something to set, you might find him doing toe lifts or squats. I laughed when I pictured this in my head, but he was always trying to make the most of every second of the day.

I, on the other hand, ate like crap. As an emotional eater, I had packed on about twenty pounds more than I'd have liked over the last few years and exercised less. My excuse was it was leftover baby weight, but the reality was that that ship had sailed many moons ago. I thought standing and running in the emergency room for hours on end would be enough, but clearly it wasn't. My stomach had rounded a bit and my thighs were a little thicker. Of course, it never stopped Parker from trying to get a peek at me naked or making comments about how beautiful and sexy I was.

After our shower, we dressed and Parker headed to work while I headed to the kitchen to make lunches for everyone. Then, I woke the kids, forced them to eat some breakfast, and corralled them to the bus before heading to work myself. I enjoyed driving the same scenic way every day, parking in almost the exact same spot, and preparing myself for the day in the same way.

As I looked at the assignment board posted in the break room, I was relieved to see I wasn't working triage again. I was assigned to our "purple" team. Nothing fancy, and that was fine by me. Our emergency room had a total of forty rooms and was divided into teams of four patients. Whoever designed the ER picked ten different colors that were used to define each team and everyone took a turn working triage.

The big assignment board hung in the break room and basically told each nurse and patient care associate (PCA for short) which team they would be working on and who their doctor would be. Because all the rooms were set up the same way, with the exception of the ones specialized for certain things, it really didn't matter to me which team I was placed on.

The first step in my morning prep was to log into my computer and check my assigned patients. Well, the real first step was actually to drink a cup of coffee and check in with my work family, but if someone asked, it was to check the computer and my assigned patients. I wanted to get a feel for their conditions, needs, and status. Then, I'd drink coffee to mentally prepare for the craziness that I knew would follow. Sometimes it would actually be a second cup, but that's besides the point.

It was nice to see that I had zero patients to start my day. I sipped my coffee a little slower and chatted with Adel and Avalon, who's teams were on either side of mine. Adel's pale skin and English accent was a stark contrast to Avalon's dark skin and southern accent. I loved working with them both and knew that it would be a good day with the two of them next to me.

When my first patient was escorted to room 6, I finished my coffee and headed in to greet him. Before me lay a teenage boy my son's age with one ankle twice the size of the other one. He was dressed in soccer apparel and his shin protector was still on his good ankle. His face was contorted as he attempted to brush off the pain. His mother stood off to the side, glued to her cell phone. She did not look up when I walked in.

"Whoa, your ankle isn't looking too hot," I said as I walked in.

"Nope. But I scored the winning goal," he said proudly.

"Always makes it worth it, doesn't it?"

"Oh yeah. You should have seen the girls in the stands..." he trailed off.

"Oh, I bet! Can you move your toes at all?"

"I mean, I can, but it hurts pretty bad," he said, moving his toes and wincing in pain.

"Okay, that's good."

I asked a few more questions and finished up my charting before leaving his room just as another patient was brought to room 7 next door. From the door, I could see that the boy sitting on the bed had a broken arm. Now, I'm definitely not a doctor, but sometimes it's perfectly clear. The thing that struck me as odd, was that he was also wearing a soccer uniform. Had they been playing against each other?

"Must have been a bad day for soccer," I said nonchalantly to the mother hovering over her son.

"Oh yes! The other kid had a pretty messed up ankle," she replied.

So they *had* been playing against each other. It must have been a rather intense game of soccer, I thought. I assessed the kids arm, entered in my charting, and headed for the door. Curiosity stopped me.

"How did you end up breaking your arm?" I asked.

"I dove for the ball just as the kid from the other team kicked it. I was too late, and he ended up kicking my arm."

"Damn," I muttered as I left.

Tyrell, the nurse working triage that day, was known for always sending the ortho patients to my team. His thought was that since I married an orthopedic surgeon, I must enjoy orthopedics. He was wrong, but I never cared to fight him about it. There was always the chance that I'd get to run into my hubby and that would make the day that much better. The kid with the broken arm would most likely need an ortho consult so I had that to look forward to.

I headed for the equipment room and gathered the supplies for two IVs and headed back to my station. I went back into room 7. The boy saw the supplies in my hand, and I was pretty sure that's when he began to sweat.

"What are you going to do?" he asked nervously.

"Start an IV."

"Is it going to hurt?"

"Not compared to your arm."

"Wait. We haven't even seen the doctor yet. Can you really do that?" his mother asked quickly.

"Yes, I really can. Your son's arm is clearly broken, and he will need an IV. Rather than waste time after he's seen the doctor, I'm going to start this now, if that's okay with you." I returned to prepping my supplies.

The mother shrunk back to the other side of the room and watched. He turned his head away as I applied the tourniquet to his good arm. He flinched and pulled his hand from me just as I applied the cleaner.

"No!" he said reflexively.

"No? We can do this the easy way or the hard way," I said with irritation.

"He said no," the mother says feebly from behind him, clearly trying to assert some control but knowing that it would be useless.

"Okay, you'll dive towards a ball being kicked by a grown man but won't let me stick you with a teeny needle to give you pain meds. Got it." I got up, set the stuff on the counter, and left.

I returned to room 6 and prayed I'd have a better outcome at starting an IV with this kid than the last. He quickly sat himself up and wiped away some tears when I entered, but his mother remained glued to her cell phone, completely oblivious to her son crying in pain next to her.

"I'm going to start an IV so I can get you some pain medicine, okay?" I said quietly to him.

"Whatever you have to do," he said through obvious pain.

I set up my supplies, and he allowed me to start the IV without so much as a peep. The mother briefly looked up, saw what I was doing, and returned to her phone. I wanted to smack the phone out of her hands, but maintained my self-control. The boy actually thanked me once I had the IV secured to his hand.

"Is that your mom?" I asked quietly.

"Yeah," he said shrugging his shoulders.

Something came over me just then and I ran with it. "Excuse me, ma'am."

She looked up at me, irritated to be disrupted from whatever she was doing that was *so* important. The look she gave me only made me more irritated. I couldn't imagine completely ignoring my kid the way she was her's.

"You must be super important," I said, nodding in the direction of her phone. "What do you do for work?"

"Huh?" she asked, confused.

"You're so important that you can't even drop the damn phone long enough to pay attention to your son who has broken his ankle and is crying in pain. I've never met someone as self-important as you. Can I get your autograph?" I asked with a sweet, fake smile on my face.

"Excuse me?" she asked now that I had her full attention.

I continued to stare at her waiting for answers to my questions, knowing they were never coming. The boy's hand went to his mouth to hide the giggle he was suppressing.

"I'll see you in a bit, bud," I said to the boy as I left, watching the smile on his face.

I sat down at the pod of computers across from my rooms. Avalon was already there charting on her patients and looked up when I sat down. I filled her in on my exchange with the mother and when I saw Dr. Little heading into room 6, I knew the pace would pick up now that the doctor was seeing my patients.

Dr. Ron Little was completely opposite of his name. At six feet five inches, he was intimidating. He would chew up that mother and spit her out if she didn't pay attention to him. That was one thing I knew about him, he loved pediatric patients and didn't appreciate parents that weren't paying attention. I couldn't decide if I should go into the room and witness it first hand or hang back. Hanging back won.

I heard the volume rise from the room and sat back with an evil smile. I decided now might be a good time to make a second attempt at poking room 7. Upon opening the curtain, I saw his mother combing hair out of his face and giving him a spit shine. I cringed.

"Are you ready for that IV yet?" I asked patiently.

"I guess," he said, his resolve weakened as the pain wore him down.

I was finally getting somewhere when my pager alerted me to a new patient in room 8. The moment the needle touched the boy's skin, my pager came to life again and informed me that the patient in room 8 was already hitting the call light. I rolled my eyes instinctively but continued on with my work.

With the IV securely in his arm, I thanked the kid and headed to meet the pain in the ass in room 8. I wasn't sure what to expect, but I hadn't expected to see a grown man fully clothed sitting on the stretcher. He immediately informed me he wasn't going to be wearing a patient gown, and he only wanted to see Dr. Little.

"I'm sorry to disappoint you, but that isn't how this works."

"I'm a doctor here and fully aware of how all this works," he mocked rudely. "I don't need the gown as I'm just here for a sore throat."

"Well, doctor or not, you're just another patient while you're here. You need to wear the gown or none of the doctors will see you and you'll end up seeing whichever doctor grabs your chart first," I said.

I tried hard to keep my eyes from rolling or my head from moving side to side as I said it. He wasn't going to back down, but neither was I. I'd been doing this way too long to let a doctor intimidate me. The rules were the rules and today, I didn't feel like bending them for someone who had zero respect for the job I did.

"Whatever. I'm going to just send Dr. Little a text," he said as he pulled his phone out.

"Okay. I'll let him know there is a pompous ass in room 8," I said as I walked out of the room.

Kate — 1, Pompous ass — 0. His face turned a deep shade of red and I knew I'd hear about it later, but I didn't care. As a doctor, he should know that acting like that to the nurses that are there to assist you is absolutely the *wrong* move.

I saw Dr. Little charting at the bank of computers reserved for physicians only — insert eye roll — and reported on the new patient in room 8. I'd known Dr. Little a long time, and I knew he didn't play favorites. After I finished telling him about the encounter, he rolled his eyes and told me he'd already gotten the text message. He'd replied that a patient gown was required, and he couldn't guarantee to be seen by anyone, regardless of being a doctor. I couldn't contain my giggle as I walked back to my own computer to check on orders for my other two patients.

I managed to survive, keeping my attitude in check until lunchtime. For the most part, I was pretty easy going and had no problems keeping my thoughts to myself. Parker used to laugh at me because he thought it was funny that someone who loved routine the way I did, enjoyed working in an environment completely void of any routine. However, the lack of routine at work seemed to always be okay and I always felt in control of my surroundings. And myself.

I got a page that the unit supervisor needed to see me in her office. AnneMarie had worked in the emergency room for decades, working her way up from the bottom, and was now running the show. Being called to her office was equal to being called to the principal's office. Avalon just laughed as she continued on towards the break room without me.

"You asked to see me?" I said as I appeared in her doorway.

"Yes. Dr. Tibiani contacted me regarding your demeanor while he was a patient in our ER."

"Really? He's *still* a patient in our ER," I noted.

"Well, he was unenthused with your attitude. I don't know what's going on with you, but please try to be nice," she suggested.

"I was being nice. I had to remind him of the rules and our procedures, and he didn't like it," I argued.

"I know. Please find a nicer way to say it next time, I suppose."

"Okay, be nice. Check. Anything else?"

"Uh... no... that's it."

Wow. Can you say ego? Dr. Tibiani really thought his shit didn't stink, didn't he? I wish I could say I was surprised, but I wasn't. What aggravated me more was that AnneMarie had to call me into her office because Dr. Tibiani thought his medical degree warranted special attention. He must have forgotten that emergency rooms treat patients based on the severity of medical needs and not based on anything else. The fact he was only here because he was too busy to see his primary physician made it all the more irritating.

"Wait! Actually, there is something else I wanted to talk to you about," she said just as I turned to leave.

"Yeah?"

"I'm not sure if you heard or not, but Tina on night shift turned in her two-week notice. She's headed to the ICU. Her preceptor position will be open. I know we've talked about you moving to a preceptor position in the past and I wanted to see if you're still interested."

"Really?"

"Yeah. Of course, it's night shift and it's full time."

"I worked my butt off to get to day shift and now you want me to return to the dark side?" I asked with a laugh.

"Well, kinda. It's the preceptor position. Not exactly floor nursing. You'd be perfect for the job. Just think about it and let me know in the next week or so, okay?"

"Will do. I'll let you know when I get back from vacation."

I caught up with Avalon in the break room. In a hushed tone I told her about my conversation with AnneMarie. She was both excited for me and disappointed — she wanted me to jump at the opportunity, but would miss having me on day shift with her. I wasn't sure I wanted to go back to night shift let alone go back to full time status. I would really have to think about it.

Chapter 4

After my uneventful lunch, I returned to the purple team to find that my ankle injury was scheduled to be whisked off to surgery within the hour and my broken arm was going to be getting conscious sedation and a visit from the ortho tech.

I looked around and eyed Parker talking to the other doctors and looking at the x-rays. He had been dressed in khakis and a collared shirt when he'd left that morning, but now he was wearing blue surgical scrubs and his white lab coat. His short hair with flecks of gray in it. He was drop dead gorgeous and I felt so lucky that he was mine. I made my way over to them and began looking at the x-rays over his shoulder.

"Wow, Dr. Cordova, that looks like it'll be a real challenge to fix," I said with a smile as I looked at the boy's shattered ankle on the screen.

"Might take me a bit to get it back into one piece, but as you know, I'm top-notch and will make it perfect," he said returning the smile.

"Is that so? You seem awfully confident," I said with a wink.

"I'm confident about a lot of things," he replied and flashed a winning smile.

While in the emergency room, we tried to keep things professional, but something about his demeanor today was pushing my professionalism to its limit. The most you'd usually get from us was smiles and sassy comments. No PDA for us. I also called him Dr. Cordova when we were in the hospital. We'd been doing it so long, it was second nature. Since he had been Dr. Cordova when we met, it wasn't difficult. Once in a while, I'd accidentally call him Dr. Cordova at home and the kids would laugh at me. Honestly, sometimes I did it on purpose.

"That's why you make the big bucks." Everyone laughed.

I headed back to the bank of computers where Adel was charting. Avalon emerged from one of her rooms and asked for help. I gladly offered my services and blindly followed her. However, the moment I got into the room I was re-thinking my decision.

The help she needed was holding down a child while she inserted an IV. The one thing I hated more than anything was having to start IVs on children. I could tolerate the screams of the child, but their mothers always seemed to be helicopter moms, the ones that watched closely over my shoulder and made me nervous. I understood it, of course, but it didn't make me enjoy it.

I sat down and placed the child on my lap. With my arms around her in a bear hug and my legs securing hers, she was unable to move her body. Her little dehydrated veins were incredibly difficult to find, and she screamed as if the world were ending, even though Avalon hadn't even poked her yet. In a desperate attempt to gain freedom, just as the needle punctured her skin, she reared her head back, straight into my face. I immediately screamed but did not let my grip lessen. My face throbbed in pain, but within moments, Avalon announced that she had "gotten it" and was securing the site.

The child's mother apologized profusely, but my face was already bruising and sore. I could only imagine what was going through the child's head. She didn't feel good and now strangers were holding her down and coming at her with needles. Poor baby!

I released my grip once Avalon had everything secure and covered, but the girl continued to cry. When she would start to calm down and whimper, she would look at the white gauze wrap on her arm and begin to cry all over again. Between apologies to me, the mother tried to calm her frightened daughter. I understood. My kids had been in this type of situation before. I'd been in her shoes. And I'd worked with a lot of kids and their mother's over the years.

I didn't have a chance to breathe since I was paged for the ortho tech arriving, a new patient being placed in one of my rooms, and the patient transport team arriving to take the broken ankle to the operating room. I felt like the room was spinning. Why did it seem like everything always happened at once?

As a seasoned ER nurse, this felt like just another day though and I quickly prioritized. By the time three o'clock rolled around, I was exhausted and ready for a nap. I had never been one to nap, but lately, it was routine to take a brief nap after work. I quickly reported off on my patients and headed for home.

Arriving home, I placed my keys on their hook, removed my shoes, and changed my clothes. Then, I went straight to the refrigerator calendar and verified that no one needed to be picked up anywhere. I wouldn't make that mistake again.

I decided that rather than nap I would run on the treadmill for a bit before the kids got home. Maybe that would give me some energy. If nothing else, it was a better use of my time than taking a nap. I changed into my running shorts, sports bra, and a racerback tank. I grabbed a bottle of water from the refrigerator and made my way downstairs to the treadmill.

I'd turned one of the spare rooms in the basement into my own personal gym. In the room, I had my treadmill and some weights, a few mirrors hung on the walls, and a television positioned along another wall.

Earbuds in, I turned up the speed and began to run at a slow jog while listening to my book. My legs burned and it felt good. Why didn't I do this more often? After some time running, I felt I was being watched. Instinctively, I glanced at the door and saw Kamdyn standing there. Startled, I tripped and the treadmill sent me flying into the wall.

I saw it all in slow motion as it was happening. Tripping over my own two feet, trying to catch myself but failing miserably, and then feeling the belt sweep my feet from under me. Landing with a thud on the belt, its continued movement at an accelerated speed sending me flying into the wall behind the treadmill and leaving me crumpled on the floor. How I wished it had been recorded — the treadmill showing me who was the boss and tossing me like a rag doll.

I laid there laughing as Kamdyn rushed to my side.

"Are you okay? Why are you laughing?" Kamdyn said.

"I'm not sure. You scared me." I clutched at my chest for dramatics.

"I didn't mean to." She paused before continuing, " Do you remember what today is?" she asked with a serious face.

"Uh... Wednesday?" I asked, completely clueless.

"Yeah... And..."

"And... I have no idea, Kamdyn. What is today?" I said, no longer laughing.

"It was my cupcake day at school!" she said angrily.

"Shit!"

"Yeah. You totally forgot to bring cupcakes for me," she said as she stared at me.

"Sure did," I said as I began to laugh again.

"*Why* are you laughing?" she demanded.

"I don't know."

"Well, I don't think it's very funny."

"I'm sorry," I said as I tried to stop laughing. "Can you help me up?"

"No, you should lay there and think about what you've done," she said sarcastically and then turned to leave. "Or what you *didn't* do, I should say!"

Rather than get up, I laid back down and let all the laughter stream out of me until my abdominal muscles hurt. Of course, when the laughter finally stopped, all of that exhaustion from earlier caught up to me and I had no desire to get up, so I didn't. I happily laid on the floor next to the wall, staring at the ceiling until I fell into a light sleep.

"Kate?" Parker asked as he stood in the door a while later.

"Yeah?"

"What are you doing?" He cocked his head to the side so he could see from the same angle as I was looking.

"Kamdyn asked me the same thing and I still don't know. What I *do* know is that I was running on the treadmill when Kamdyn startled me, I tripped, I was thrown off the damn thing, and then I couldn't stop laughing. And when I did, I was too tired to get up, so I didn't," I said in one really long run-on sentence.

"How long have you been laying there?" he asked.

"Well, what time is it?"

"Almost 06:30 p.m.," he said as he glanced at his watch.

"Is it? Wow. I've been down here since I got home from work," I said, still lying on the ground.

"Well, how about I help you up, and we make some dinner?" he said as he came beside me and offered his hand.

"I really think you should lay down here sometime. Quite comfortable," I said sarcastically.

"I appreciate the offer, but I think I'll pass."

"Suit yourself," I teased.

"I have to admit, you looked gorgeous today in your scrubs," he said as he gently brushed my cheek.

"What should we make for dinner?" I asked, ignoring his complement.

"Why do you always do that?" he asked, frustrated.

"Do what?"

"Refused to take my compliments?"

"I don't know."

I grabbed his hand and allowed him to help me to my feet. I asked about his day in surgery and if he'd successfully put my patient back together as we walked up the stairs. He mumbled something cocky about being the best at putting people back together, and we headed for the kitchen.

As I began to browse through the cupboards, I noticed they were pretty light on the groceries. Parker looked through the refrigerator and freezer and came up empty-handed as well. I tried to think back to the last time I'd gone grocery shopping, but couldn't remember.

"Uh, babe? We don't have anything to make dinner with," he said, looking confused.

For the length of our entire marriage, I had been known as the most organized wife. Our bills were always paid ahead of time, the kids permission slips returned on time, appointments scheduled when they were supposed to be, and groceries shopped for every two weeks like clock work. But clearly I had missed a step in my routine as I couldn't remember going grocery shopping, and we didn't have much food in the house.

"Pizza?" I asked as I picked my phone up off the counter.

"I guess so," he said as he shook his head.

"Did someone say pizza?" Carter asked as he skated into the kitchen.

"Yep, what would you like on it?" I asked.

"Anchovies," he said as I prayed he was only kidding.

He went to the cupboard, grumbled about how there was never any food in the house, and then went back to his room.

"Teenagers," Parker said, shaking his head.

"Yep. Where did we go wrong?" I asked, looking at Parker.

He pulled me into him and said, "I don't think we went wrong anywhere. It's always felt perfectly right to me."

I lightly pushed him away and giggled, "Oh stop it."

"See! You did it again!" he said.

"I don't even realize I'm doing it."

The pizza arrived forty-five minutes later and the entire family scarfed it down in nearly ten. As I tossed the empty pizza boxes into the trash can in the garage, I heard a muffled conversation from somewhere nearby and strained my ears to hear it.

I put on my slippers that were right inside the door and moved around the garage, my ears perked up listening carefully. I stopped and tried to decipher any of the words, the voice, any clue that would help me figure it out. I got nothing. I opened the side door that lead to the back yard but didn't see or hear anything out there either.

Unsuccessful, I gave up and went back inside. I plopped down on the couch next to Kamdyn and together we watched our favorite show before calling it a night and heading to bed. I was lying quietly in the dark trying to sleep when I heard Parker sneak into the room. He played on his phone for a bit before shutting it off and going to bed.

The alarm sounded far too early the next morning and when I glanced over at the other side of the bed, Parker was already gone. I groaned and debated whether to get up or not, but knew that not going to work just wasn't my style, so I dragged myself out of bed and into the shower. Once I had the kids on the bus, I grabbed my keys from their hook, and I was off to work whether I liked it or not.

As I sat at the bank of computers sipping my coffee, I saw Tyrell bring my next patient in and I practically spit my coffee right back out. This poor girl had a sex toy stuck to her nose ring. Not just the cute stud in the side of her nose, the type of ring that goes right through her septum and forms a hoop like a bull. I'd seen a lot in my career, but this was definitely memorable.

When I went in the room, I didn't ask why or how. I focused on just maintaining a straight face and being professional. It didn't matter though because she had absolutely zero shame in the fact that a sex toy was attached to her nose. The man, or woman, she had been using this sex toy with was nowhere to be found. I'm guessing he or she was too mortified to be seen in public.

While I was avoiding the question about how this all came to be, she saw the elephant in the room and began explaining how it happened without ever having been asked. The part I found even more shocking was that this wasn't her first visit to the ER with a sex toy mishap. Whatever had happened three months ago was worse, in her opinion.

Finally, I broke and asked her, "But why?" and she laughed.

It had been the wrong question to ask because she began launching into an entire story about erotic feelings before I held up my hand and cut her off. Some things were just beyond my comprehension and some things I just didn't want to know. I finished what I needed to do with her and followed my escape plan flawlessly. Within no time I was back at the computer finishing my coffee.

"Did you see her?" I asked Avalon as she watched me chug cold coffee.

"How could you miss her?" she asked, a smile spread across her face.

"I can't wait for Dr. Farmer to see her," I snorted.

Dr. Arin Farmer was an absolute pain in the butt. From the moment he'd accepted the position after he finished his residency, he felt high and mighty. Almost like he no longer needed a nurse to help him. You would never find him smiling or talking with the nursing staff. He was too good for us. No one wanted to work with him, and therefore, I was the one who usually ended up drawing the short stick. Because I was married to a doctor, he tolerated me best, which was pathetic.

"Ha! His stone-cold face will probably crack when he has to inspect it and figure out how to detach it. Tyrell is a genius for assigning her to a room Dr. Farmer is assigned to," Avalon said.

"Amen!"

Before I had a chance to watch the show, an ambulance arrived to the next room with a patient struggling to breathe. Wasting no time, I followed them into the room, and we got the patient settled on our stretcher and an oxygen mask on. The paramedic reported he had been in the bathroom when the shortness of breath began and his wife had called 911.

I contacted respiratory therapy and began a quick assessment. My priority was to get him breathing better because his gasps for air getting shallower and shallower. Respiratory therapy arrived quickly along with Dr. Farmer and over the course of the next ten minutes, we worked to get him stabilized.

I was finally able to go retrieve his wife from the waiting room when I quickly realized she might actually have been the one to set off the asthma attack in the first place. Her floral perfume was applied so thick, even I choked on the surrounding air. There was no way she would be able to be in a confined space with him in his current condition so just gave her an update and told her we would bring her back when we could.

"Wow, you stink," Avalon said when I returned from the waiting room.

"Gee thanks. That's Mr. I-can't-breathe's wife's perfume."

"Shit, that's bad. Now it makes sense."

"Yeah, I know what he's getting her for Christmas this year," I said with a laugh.

"Has Dr. Farmer gone in to see the sex toy queen yet?" I asked as I sat down to chart at the computer.

"I think he's about to," she said as I followed her gaze to the bank of physician computers where Dr. Farmer was picking up his stethoscope and heading our direction.

"Ooo, ladies and gentlemen, the show is about to start," I said as I picked up a pen from the keyboard and pretended it was a microphone.

Avalon and I sat quietly at our computers, pretending to chart, as we listened desperately for any reaction from the room as Dr. Farmer entered. We were disappointed that we heard and saw absolutely nothing. But when Dr. Farmer emerged from the room, he requested my assistance and I couldn't help but become excited.

"Hold this," Dr. Farmer demanded once I'd put on gloves.

He began to work with pliers and tweezers, trying to work the toy free from the ring. After nearly five minutes of jerking, tugging, and bending, she was free. She immediately jumped off the stretcher and launched herself into Dr. Farmer's arms for a hug. He had been completely unprepared and together they landed on the floor, patient on top of physician.

I should have rushed to his assistance, but I couldn't. I was glued to my spot, laughing. If looks could kill, I'd have been dead because I could see that Dr. Farmer did *not* find this funny. The patient quickly removed herself from Dr. Farmer, apologizing as she did, and returned to the stretcher. Dr. Farmer said nothing as he stood up and walked straight out the door. The moment he was gone, the patient and I began laughing again.

"What the hell happened in there?" Nora asked when I finally came back to the computers.

"What do you mean?" I said, still smiling.

"Dr. Farmer is *pissed*. Even that might be an understatement," Avalon said.

"Well, besides having to try to free a sex toy from a woman's nose ring, she attempted to give him a hug as a thank you gift, and they tumbled over. She landed on top," I said as we all began laughing.

"I would have died to seen that!" Nora said quietly through her laughter.

"It was worth whatever punishment comes my way!"

"Uh oh, looks like you have another patient," Nora said as she looked at Tyrell bringing an elderly gentleman to my empty room.

"It was fun while it lasted," I said as I followed them.

It turned out that the old man was having chest pain. I went to get supplies for an IV and asked my PCA to run an EKG. I didn't need a doctor's order since it was our protocol when someone comes into the ER complaining of chest pain. The PCA was in the room first and quickly got the EKG. I went in to start the IV while another nurse was taking a health history, and I had the PCA take the EKG print out to Dr. Farmer for official interpretation.

Just as I finished securing the IV, Dr. Farmer stuck his head in and asked if he could speak with me quick. I politely excused myself and stepped out. Dr. Farmer stood just outside the door, his face as red as a ripened tomato.

"What the hell is this?" he said.

"Uh... an EKG?"

"I know that. Why do I have an EKG when I haven't even evaluated the patient?" he said as he waved the paper in my face.

"The patient is having chest pain. Protocol is an EKG," I replied.

"Not on my patients," he said as he threw the paper at me and stepped into the patient's room.

Confused, I picked up the paper from the floor and looked at it. The patient was having a heart attack. Was Dr. Farmer being serious or just being an ass? Either way, I didn't feel bad about getting the EKG or starting the IV. I took a deep breath and re-entered the room to finish the work I'd started.

Ten minutes later, the patient was off to x-ray and I had time to check on my respiratory patient. By this point, he was breathing easier but I had yet to re-introduce his wife back into his presence. Hesitantly, I went to get her from the waiting room, and she gladly followed me back to his room.

Stepping into the room, I watched his breathing change from calm and even breaths to short and forceful breaths. His lips became more pale and I noticed his eyes widen as he began to struggle to breathe again.

Another page to respiratory therapy and another breathing treatment later and his respiratory rate had slowed back down. However, now he complained of chest heaviness and feeling his heart doing funny things — his words. I didn't dare get the

EKG before Dr. Farmer was alerted this time, so I casually walked over to him and told him of the patient's new symptoms.

"Where's the EKG?" he demanded.

"You haven't ordered one yet," I said with a smirk.

"I shouldn't have to. He has chest pain."

"Oh come'on. Grow the fuck up!" I said as I walked away feeling frustrated and angry.

Was he trying to punish me for laughing at him earlier? In all the years I'd worked in the emergency room, I'd never worked with such a difficult doctor. My frustration was at an all-time high and I hadn't ruled out screaming. I'd also gained an immense amount of knowledge over the years — what needed to be done, what would be ordered, and how to handle situations. I might not have gone to medical school, but I had real-world experience. Having chest pain wasn't a new concept to me and I certainly knew what needed to be done right away.

Dr. Farmer's attitude was insulting. And I wouldn't let his personal vendetta against me jeopardize patient care.

Before I could get in the room to do the EKG though, the wife rushed out of the room, eyes wide like she'd seen a ghost, screaming that he wasn't breathing anymore. I flew into action, all frustration with Dr. Farmer erased from my mind.

I rushed to the patient and began trying to wake him. Several other nurses arrived to the room as I began to feel for a pulse and check for breathing. None. Shit.

"Code blue!" I called out of the room.

Chapter 5

Someone handed me a flat board and I slid it under the patient as another nurse rolled him to one side. Then, without discussion or thinking, I ripped open his shirt and sent buttons flying around the room, hearing pinging noises as they landed on the floor. As I folded my hands together and placed them on his chest to begin compressions, Dr. Farmer entered the room. I glared at him and began compressions.

Another nurse tilted his head back to open his airway as I counted out compressions. Suddenly, liquid flew from the patient's mouth and landed on my face. I flinched, but kept on compressing and counting, my hands sliding in the liquid that had landed on his chest.

"Airway is clear!" the other nurse shouted as she applied a mask with a bag attached and began giving breaths.

In hindsight, it was funny. In the moment, none of it mattered. Someone appeared with paper towel and dried up the liquid around me while I continued to pump. Before the defibrillator pads could be applied and a rhythm analyzed, the patient coughed and sputtered to life.

"Hey there. Welcome back!" I said with a smile to the patient.

Dr. Farmer nodded and moved toward the patient as I stepped away and began trying to catch my breath. Once he completed his own assessment, he looked at me and demanded I get an EKG before he stormed out of the room. I wanted to scream back at him, but didn't have the breath to do so. I felt the rage boiling inside me and continued reminding myself to stay calm. I couldn't let him get to me.

It took a while, but once things had settled down, I practically sprinted to lunch. I needed fresh air. I needed a chance to release the built-up energy buzzing in my body and to come down from the adrenalin high I was riding. Saving a life is spectacular, but also exhausting. Physically, and mentally. The actual chemical changes in the body during an emergency situation produces one of my favorite highs, but ultimately leads to me feeling drained afterwards. It's a vicious cycle because once I recover and regain my energy, I'm off chasing that high all over again. I'd been doing it for so long that I stopped realizing I was even doing it.

As I usually did after an adrenaline high, I found a quiet corner along a random hallway and sat down on the floor. I placed my head in my hands and just focused on my breathing. Within ten minutes or so, I was feeling significantly better and returned to the break room to scarf down some food and get back on the floor. When I thought about returning to Dr. Farmer, I reminded myself that I only had a few more hours and gave myself another pep talk.

I quickly used the bathroom and then returned to the floor to check in on my patients. First though, I wasn't going to continue working with Dr. Farmer the way things were going. The stick needed to be removed from his ass and I didn't have a problem being the one to do it.

I found him at his computer looking over x-rays. I took a nice, slow breath and prepared for a battle. I felt a bit of adrenaline return to me. I wouldn't be bullied by him. We were supposed to be a team.

"Arin, can I talk to you for a minute?" I said calmly.

"Excuse me?" he snarled as he turned around.

"Can I talk to you for a minute?" I repeated.

"Don't ever call me Arin. It's Dr. Farmer to you. What do you want?" he hissed.

"I want to remove the stick from your ass," I said without flinching.

Dr. Little sat on his chair drinking coffee until the words left my mouth, at which time he practically spit the entire gulp all over his computer. Adel had been walking by and I saw her eyes grow to the size of full moons, and she froze in horror. Dr. Tempest was walking back to her computer and heard me say it, stopping mid-step, her brain processed what I'd just said. And then she began to clap.

Other staff members who had witnessed me say that one sentence were initially shocked. When Dr. Tempest began clapping, they stood and clapped as well. Time stood still as I stood in front of Dr. Farmer and waited for some type of response from him. I didn't move a muscle. The wait was agonizing, but I wasn't going to let his silence break me down. I wasn't going to back down and begin apologizing.

I watched as he looked around and saw just how many people had heard the interaction and how many were now standing and clapping. That is until AnneMarie appeared at the desk. Her eyes were narrow and her lips tight. She did not appear happy.

"What the hell is going on? Everyone, back to work. Back to work, now," she said firmly.

I still didn't move. I was determined to remove the stick from his ass. No one was going to treat me that way and I knew that I was standing for everyone else as well. AnneMarie looked from Dr. Farmer to me and back again.

"Well?" she said, still waiting for her answer.

"What the hell is your problem?" Dr. Farmer finally said angrily at me.

"Let's take this somewhere private," AnneMarie suggested quietly.

"Everyone in this ER is sick of being treated like shit on your shoe. I usually can tolerate your bullshit, but not today. You pushed me over the edge with that EKG stunt that could have cost someone their life just for the sake of your own fucking ego," I snapped.

"Kate!" AnneMarie hissed.

"No, let her finish AnneMarie," Dr. Little said, supporting my outburst.

"Can't we take this somewhere else?" AnneMarie insisted again.

"Sure," Dr. Farmer said.

I still hadn't moved. I continued to stand tall with my shoulders back, and my eyes narrowed and staring straight at Dr. Farmer. Eventually, he just shrugged his shoulders and walked towards AnneMarie's office. I stood there debating if I wanted to go there or just resume my patient care.

Everyone waited and watched as I made my decision, but I felt that our patient care would only improve if I got the stick out of his ass, so I followed. AnneMarie closed the door behind us and I saw Dr. Farmer's face was bright red, and he was trembling.

"Thank you. Now let's work this out. Kate, what has gotten into you?" AnneMarie asked.

"I can't work like that, Arin. I can't have you being pissed I followed protocol and got an EKG on someone with chest pain before you ordered it and then turn around and be pissed I didn't get one for the same situation on someone else. He could have died while you were busy riding your high horse," I snapped. "I've been at this long enough that I'm not an idiot. No one wants to work with you because you treat the nurses like shit. I'm just over it. Not gonna happen when it potentially affects someone's life."

"Is that all?" Dr. Farmer said finally.

"Yeah, I think that sums it up."

"Good, can we get back to work?" he said.

"You don't have anything to say?" I asked in surprise.

"Nope, not going to stoop to your level," he said as he stood and left the office.

"Why did he bother coming in here if he didn't really want to address it?" I asked AnneMarie with frustration.

"Honestly?" she asked with a smirk. "He was hoping I'd chew you a new one for talking to him like that and knew it would be more likely if you were in a private office."

"What an arrogant ass," I said with a sigh.

"Always has been and most likely always will be," AnneMarie said.

"Now what? I am stuck working with him?" I asked.

"No, I'm going to pull Adel and put her on your patients and send you to your favorite assignment, triage," she said laughing.

"Right now, I'll gladly take triage," I said with a smile.

I quickly gave Adel report and took up post in triage. Nearly every five minutes I had another nurse at the door giving me a thumbs up, and I was proud I'd finally had the courage to stick up for myself. To stick up for all of us, really.

I glanced at the list of waiting patients and saw that three of them were waiting to be seen because their throats hurt, two probably had sprained ankles, and one had an infected tooth. I just shook my head and looked at the open rooms available and began to escort them back as I was able.

Just as I jumped from my chair and headed to the waiting room to call the last patient back, the automatic doors opened and a woman came in screaming about her husband in the car.

I did a quick assessment of the woman but found all limbs intact and no signs of blood anywhere. I was finally able to understand what she was screaming for when a man walked in behind her holding a bloody towel around his arm.

I dropped the papers I was holding and rushed to him as the PCA working with me handed me a pair of gloves. I removed the towel carefully and saw a deep gash down to the bone as well as clear trough in the bone. I wrapped the towel back around his arm and began asking questions as the PCA helped him into a wheelchair, and we wheeled him to the empty room.

"Can you calmly tell me what happened?" I asked as I pushed the wheelchair.

"Yeah, I was cutting up a tree with my neighbor when my wife yelled at me, and we both turned around and his chainsaw got into a fight with my arm. The chainsaw won, by the way," he said with a little laugh.

"Shut up, Tim!" the wife said as she smacked playfully at his good arm.

"What? It's the truth," he said, giving her a look.

"Do you have any allergies?" I asked, trying to steer the conversation back.

"Nope."

"Take any mediation?"

"Just something called a statin or something for blood pressure, but I'm thinking it's not a problem right now," he said, and he instinctively flinched as if expecting his wife to swat him again.

"Okay, well, there's going to be a lot of things happening really quick so just hang in there and ask questions if you need to, okay?" I said as I helped him onto the stretcher in the room.

Dr. Little peeled back the towel and saw the damage to the arm. He looked right at me and directed me to get the IV in the good arm as quickly as possible and get fluids hanging. Then, he excused himself and left the room. When Avalon entered the room, we began working to get his IV in, but my first attempt failed. Avalon made her own attempt but was unable to get it as well.

We only had one arm to work with, and we were running out of viable veins, but we had one secret weapon up our sleeves. Tyrell was working and he was the "King of IVs". He could get an IV started on a neonate with his eyes closed in the dark. And as predicted, it only took him one try to get IV access in the good arm.

I returned to triage and assisted the patient I had started to take back, into an empty room on the other side of the ER. I glanced at the clock and I wished it was moving faster, but it wasn't. I sat on my stool and glanced at the waiting patients and the status of the rooms, but no one was going anywhere. I closed my eyes for a brief moment but must have fallen asleep because my head hit the door of the cabinet above the desk. It hurt and I quickly glanced in the mirror and saw a nice big red mark. Great.

Just as I started to rub at the red mark, the receptionist at the front desk called for me to come to the front. I took one last glance at my forehead and made my way to the front of the triage area.

A younger man was slumped over in a wheelchair, barely conscious and barely breathing. In fact, I might have thought he was just sleeping except for the moist rattling noise coming from his throat when he *did* take a breath. As I moved around to the front of his chair, I saw that his fingers were blue and his skin was the color of ashes.

I looked at the woman who was standing by his wheelchair and asked, "Did you bring him in?"

The woman wore expensive jewelry, carried a Dolce & Gabbana purse, and was dressed in a sparkling black evening gown. The man, maybe her husband, was dressed in a black tuxedo complete with a bow tie. Based on their attire, it was pretty obvious they had come in together, but I'd learned never to assume in my line of work.

"Yeah. We were at a ball when he started acting really weird. And then he just slumped over. I brought him right here," she replied.

Not wanting to waste precious time, I leapt into action and immediately wheeled him back to an empty trauma room where Avalon and Dr. Little quickly began to attend to him.

"Did he take anything tonight?" Dr. Little asked the woman.

"Not that I know of. He drank about three glasses of champagne but that's it," she said with a serious look.

"Okay, no street drugs?" Avalon asked bluntly.

"Of course not!" the woman replied, offended.

"If there is any chance this is an overdose, we need to know now. Otherwise, we will waste time looking for the cause, and we might miss our chance to save him," I explained as I looked straight into her eyes.

"Okay, okay," she relented. "He was super nervous about a small presentation he had to give at the ball, so he got some white powder stuff from a college kid who told him it would help keep him calm! It was only about five minutes later when this started!" the woman said as worry crossed her face.

Avalon, Dr. Little, and I all tried to mask the look of irritation on our faces. Avalon grabbed the Narcan and began to administer it. It was becoming quite common to have overdoses and it didn't matter what they were wearing. However, one thing I noticed was that the better dressed the patient was, the harder it was to admit to their drug use. I knew Avalon could handle it with Dr. Little at this point and I headed back to triage.

I heard arguing before I got to the desk and saw a tall, buff man holding a cloth to his abdomen and his shorter, skinnier friend arguing with the receptionist about when he would be seen.

"Can I help you?" I asked, trying to defuse the situation.

"Yeah, my friend got in a fight and needs to be seen right now," he said as he pointed to the friend's abdomen.

"Okay, come in this room and I'll take a look."

"No! He needs a doctor," the friend said loudly.

"Sir, I have to see your friend first, and we will go from there."

"Bitch, listen to me. I know what I'm talking about. My momma a nurse, and she said he need a doctor like right now," he yelled.

"Whoa. I'm here to help you, but you're wasting time arguing with me," I said as I moved around the desk and began guiding the patient towards the triage room.

A small trail of blood was trickling behind him on the floor and I noticed that with every step, he began to lean on me more. The friend followed closely behind, continuing to tell me how to do my job the entire way. I tried to keep my cool while I took his vital signs, but with every word from his mouth, I was losing it.

"Shut up! I can't concentrate with you running your mouth like that," I finally said as I turned to give him a dirty look.

I then returned to the patient, who was now going pale and moaning faintly. I had the PCA take the friend back to the waiting room, and he did it without a fight. Then, I quickly pushed the wheelchair to the back and straight into a trauma room as I called for more help.

The patient hadn't just gotten into a fight as the friend had implied. He had been stabbed in the abdomen with a double bladed knife. The cut was approximately ten inches long and was jagged. When I had finally been able to look at the wound, I had realized that this knife had not only cut into layers of skin, but down through muscle. This wasn't just an easy laceration repair.

With the trauma team now in the room, I headed back towards triage. As if nothing had happened, I called the next patient back and began to triage again. Sure, I had a few drops of blood on my shoes, but they were rubber and it would clean off easily.

Chapter 6

The kids were on the home stretch of the school year, and I was looking forward to our annual spring break vacation in a few days. I had five lists going — one for each member of the family — and felt completely scatterbrained despite them. Parker and I had decided to include Kendall despite the fact she was now a college student. We both felt that if she wanted to continue being included, we should continue making new memories as a family while we still could.

The Cordova crew would be headed to Miami this year to board a cruise for spring break. Usually, I would spend months browsing travel sites to find fun things for the family to do. This year, I didn't have to do any of that and it was, honestly, quite a relief. My mind just hadn't been the same in the last few months, and I was glad that this year we would finally have a relaxing vacation.

Kamdyn had always wanted to do different things that Kendall had deemed "too young for her". It had created controversy over the last few trips. This year, there would be something for everyone.

I had pulled the suitcases from the attic and placed them in everyone's bedroom. Taped to the top of each suitcase, was a list of items that I expected to be packed. I had been mocked for being an over planner before, but this year I felt it was necessary more than ever.

"Kate, have you seen my shark swim trunks anywhere?" Parker asked as he dug through his closet.

"No, I haven't."

Packing for a vacation with Parker was always an endless stream of "do you know where my insert-item-here type" questions. I could barely keep track of my own things, let alone those for a grown man! Maybe if he did laundry once in awhile he ould know where his things were, but that was a topic for a different day.

By the time the day arrived, I was exhausted. I had a merciless pain behind my eyes. I was absolutely, 100%, without a doubt, ready for vacation. When everyone was piled into the car, we headed to the airport three different times before having to turn back because someone had forgotten something. Then, we ended up stopping twice for bathroom breaks and snacks. By the time we arrived at the airport, my patience had worn thin and the pain behind my eyes was worse.

I was relieved that I managed to get everyone through security, on the plane, through a flight, and out of Miami International without incident. Once settled into the hotel for the night, I was mentally and physically drained. With two rooms booked and a door between us, I felt comfortable falling asleep that night, but I was too exhausted to sleep.

The next morning, I wanted to pull my hair out. Not only was my routine disrupted, my children were being little shits. Don't get me wrong, I loved them dearly. However, when they lacked sleep, they turned into teenage monsters. Someone was always whining, they were picking fights with each other, and doing things to intentionally irritate their siblings.

Despite the lack of sleep, my beautiful family boarded the big ship and set sail on the Caribbean Sea. I stood on the deck of our cabin and tasted the salty air as it breezed past me. No clouds in the sky and perfectly blue water. I closed my eyes and inhaled deeply, savoring the moment. As I exhaled, I tried to imagine all the stress leaving my body.

I wasted no more time and changed into my bathing suit and forced Parker to join me by the pool. I pulled his lounge chair close and laid out towels for each of us. Then, I grabbed my book and let the warm sun soak into my skin. This was Heaven, or as close to it as I could imagine.

With no phones or internet, the kids were already annoyed with the idea of being away from their friends, but Kamdyn had signed up for some classes while Carter and Kendall joined us by the pool. Of course, they wouldn't lounge near us because that would "cramp their style".

"This is nice, Kate," Parker said as we laid out.

"Yes it is. Remind me why we haven't moved south."

"I'm wondering that myself," he said with a smirk.

I knew exactly why we hadn't moved south. He had been offered a sweet gig at the university to teach and was then able to maintain a practice at the nearby hospital. Despite wishing for better weather, our jobs were pretty nice. Luckily, we could always have the luxury to traveling somewhere warm when time allowed. Soon, our kids would all be out of the house, and we could do this more often.

"When is the last time we did anything alone?" I asked rhetorically.

"The day before Kendall was born?" he joked.

"What do you want to do this week?" I asked as I perched myself up on my elbows to get a look at the pool in front of me.

"Gamble, eat, soak up the sun, *sleep*, and make crazy passionate love to my beautiful wife," Parker said as he jabbed playfully at my thigh.

"Is that so? Good luck," I tease as I shot him a look.

"Really?" he said, sitting straight up, his body tense.

Parker reached over and tried to hold my hand, which made reading a book near impossible. I shook it off and explained I wouldn't be able to read a book and hold his hand. I knew it was the wrong thing to say and do, but I couldn't stop myself. He was angry at my rejection. He kept watching me for a minute, disappointed that I had been so cold, but used to it, I supposed.

"I'm just gonna go take a nap. Wake me up for lunch," he said as he sulked off towards our cabin.

With his sleep cycle completely thrown off from his crazy work schedule, it was pretty typical for Parker to spend the first few days of any vacation sleeping on and off. I looked forward to the chance to read and soak up the sunshine anyway, so I didn't bother to chase after him.

I was disappointed when I finished my book, but glanced at my watch and realized it was already almost 03:00 p.m. I'd completely forgotten about eating lunch and tried to remember what time Kamdyn's class ended. While I was okay sending my eighteen and sixteen year olds off without supervision, fourteen was still a little too young for my comfort. I didn't trust the sickos roaming the planet these days. I grabbed my book and headed back to the cabin where I found Parker still fast asleep.

"Parker, wake up," I said sweetly into his ear.

He groaned and opened his eyes. He smiled though when he caught sight of me and then slowly sat up on his elbows. He reached for me and I let him pull me into him. It had been awhile since Parker and I had really had intimacy beyond occasional, convenient sex. Feeling his arms around me felt good and I felt myself relax.

"Are you ready for lunch?" I asked as he finally appeared awake.

"Uh yeah. Thank you for letting me sleep. I really needed that."

I changed into a flowered sundress and slipped on my flip-flops. We made our way to the first buffet we found and quickly found empty seats. There were three different themed spreads spaced out across the room. Looking around, I saw young, attractive singles scattered throughout, but no other couples. My stomach growled telling me that it didn't care *who* was in the room. Parker and I headed in different directions.

My carb addicted ass headed straight for the Italian display. As I helped myself to spaghetti noodles, an incredibly attractive man approached my right and began helping himself to the bowtie noodles. His brown hair was swept to the side and held in place with gel. His blue eyes reminded me of the ocean outside. And his biceps bulged through his size-too-small collared teal shirt.

"Hello," he said with a British accent.

Nervous, I looked around to see if he was talking to me or if there was someone else near us. Seeing no one, I started to freak out inside. Sure, I had patients hit on me all the time, but it had been a very long time since someone else had been hitting on me. Maybe I was overreacting and he was just being friendly. Where had all this self-confidence come from that made me assume he was attracted to me?

"Hi," I said as I moved to the sauce selection and began drizzling the pasta with marinara.

"I'm sorry to interrupt, and this may be a bit forward, but are you spaghetti?" he said with the sexy British accent and added a smile that showcased sweet dimples.

"Excuse me?" I asked, confused.

"Are you spaghetti?" he paused for dramatic effect as I continued to look clueless. "Because I want you to meet my balls," he finished as he began to laugh.

60

I'm not sure if I was as shocked as I was humored, but I began to laugh. He *was* trying to hit on me, but this was the worst pick up line I'd ever heard. And that's saying a lot since I've heard plenty of awful pick up lines working in the emergency room for over twenty years!

"Wow, that was bad," I said through my laughter.

Then, I snorted. What the hell was getting into me? Too much fresh air? Why did I feel so alive having someone hit on me? Parker tried cheesy pick up lines with me all the time and I always brushed them off. But now, from someone else, I felt alive inside. My shock turned to confusion. Confusion with my own feelings that is.

"I know, but it worked, didn't it?" His lips turned upwards like a teenage boy hitting on the prom queen.

"I suppose it did get my attention," I admitted.

I glanced around the room to see if Parker was watching me, but he was engrossed in eating and reading something on the table. I knew I needed to get back to my husband, but I also didn't want to leave this gorgeous man. I was so conflicted and I knew that I shouldn't have been. Was it the distance between Parker and I lately or was it something else?

"I need to get back and eat my spaghetti," I finally said.

"Yeah, my balls are getting cold," he said as he poked one of the meatballs on his plate. "Meet me at nine o'clock at the Lookout Club," he said as he turned and walked away.

My mind raced as I walked to the table where Parker was waiting for me. First, what the hell was I doing? Second, why the hell was I even thinking about this? Third, who the hell have I become? I've been married for over twenty years and the thought of another man has never crossed my mind, but now, it's all that's on my mind.

"Who was that?" Parker asked as I set my plate down.

"I don't know. Some British guy talking about spaghetti."

It wasn't a lie. It was a half-truth. But I pushed the British man and his spaghetti talk from my mind and tried to focus on Parker. I tried to focus on the topics he brought up, the things he said, the way he looked at me, and the way I felt toward him. Maybe I had been missing the obvious things all along as they had become familiar.

I noticed that his eyes lit up when he talked about our family. His cheeks flushed when our hands touched. He laughed when I told jokes or teased him. He rested his foot near mine under the table. He paid attention to what I was doing and seemed to notice what I was feeling.

How had I missed all these things? Why had I stopped paying attention to the way Parker told me he loves me in our daily lives? Why had I started to ignore the subtle, non-verbal cues? And suddenly, I felt ashamed and tears glossed over my eyes.

"What's wrong?" he asked, sensing a shift in my emotions.

"Nothing is wrong. Absolutely nothing is wrong," I admitted.

"No, just tell me," he begged.

"Honestly, nothing is wrong. I just... I just love you, Parker."

He watched me for a brief moment before pushing his chair away from the table, standing up, and reaching for my hands. He pulled me up and hugged me. Then, he placed a hand on each side of my face and kissed me deeply and passionately. My stomach came alive with the butterflies that I thought were long gone.

When the moment was over, we finished our lunch. Then, we left our plates and went for a walk, holding hands, talking like teenagers, and taking in the breathtaking sights. I couldn't remember the last time we'd been able to do something like this together, just the two of us, and I was soaking up every minute of it. While I might not ever admit it, our marriage had become so routine, I might have forgotten these small things. The intimacy in non-sexual ways that helped keep the spark between us. Or even just the friendship.

When five o'clock hit, we were both present to meet Kamdyn at the end of her class and take her down to the pool. By seven o'clock, the entire family was sitting down for dinner and finally enjoying conversation without electronic devices distracting one of us.

As the night came to an end, the kids went to their cabin while Parker and I returned to ours. I sat on our balcony drinking a glass of wine when Parker came out wearing nothing but boxer shorts and I felt his hands begin to rub my shoulders. I felt the muscles relax and any tension I had disappeared. Unexpectedly, I also felt a passionate heat begin to rise inside me and it confirmed there was still plenty of attraction left between us. I grabbed his hand and he led me back inside.

In the morning, I found myself tangled around Parker, and completely naked. The last time that had happened, I was probably in my twenties. The sun shining in through the sliding glass door highlighted Parker's cheekbones and blond hair. He caught me looking at him when he suddenly opened his eyes.

"I thought someone was watching me," he said with a smile.

"Hmm... Who could it have been?" I asked playfully.

"I don't know. Thought maybe it was that woman from last night or something," he said before leaning over and kissing my neck.

The moment was rudely interrupted by pounding on our door and demands for Mom and Dad to appear. I groaned as I rolled over and began dressing. Parker threw on a pair of basketball shorts that made me want to jump over the bed and tackle him, but I maintained some self-control.

"What were you guys doing?" Carter said with disgust.

"What do you mean?" Parker asked with innocence.

"It took you long enough to answer the door. Were you having sex or something?" Kendall asked even though she didn't really want the answer.

"Ewww," Kamdyn said at the thought of it.

"Kendall!" Carter scolded his sister as the vision crossed his mind.

"No! We weren't having sex. We were sleeping," Parker said louder than I'd have liked.

"I don't believe that. You two haven't slept past eight in years," Kendall said with an eye roll.

"I don't really care if you believe me or not, thank you very much."

The three kids pushed their way into the room and sat on the available seating and began to pepper us with questions about the plans for the day. I felt a slight pounding behind my eyes and gladly put on a pair of sunglasses. I pulled out my mom card and began to ask too many questions in return and within minutes, the kids had retreated to their own room, and we were alone once more.

"What *are* our plans for the day?" I asked as I searched for the itinerary.

I finally found the itinerary under the bed, along with my underwear from the night before. I was momentarily embarrassed when I pulled them out and felt like I'd been caught doing something I shouldn't have been. I had to remind myself I was a married woman and had sex with my husband. Was I really that out of practice? What had our marriage become?

Over the following few days, the entire family was busy sight seeing at the port stops, enjoying onboard entertainment, and eating at every chance we got. It was nice to spend time with Parker and have the romantic spark again that we used to have, like holding hands when we walked. We were just thankful that everyone was getting along and everything was going better than we had hoped for. Admittedly, it was the best family vacation we'd ever had.

As the week came to an end, I was sad to leave this enjoyable lifestyle behind and return to reality. Usually, I enjoyed getting back to the routines I loved so much, but this time, everything just felt different. I craved the spontaneity and the constant change. The only thing I didn't like was how uncertain of myself I had become. I just felt different and I wasn't able to figure out why. Was it that I'd rediscovered the spark with my husband? I didn't have the answers, but I was perfectly okay with the way things were going.

Before catching our plane home, Parker and I stopped at the airport bar to get the kids some food and drinks for ourselves. Once I'd finished a quick glass of red wine, I was finally ready to take flight. I got everyone settled in their seats and the plane took off. As soon as we hit cruising altitude, I felt Parker's shoulder lightly bump into mine and electric sparks jolted through my body. I looked over at Parker and felt a surge of warmth in my body.

I don't know what, but something took control of me. Those butterflies had returned to my stomach and suddenly I was a hot and horny teenager. The change was sudden and strong. It felt as if my choices were to act out whatever was asked of me or face pending doom. The sudden desire for my husband wiped out all sense of maturity and dignity. I needed him, and I needed him now.

"Hey," I whispered to Parker.

"Hey," he replied with a raised eyebrow.

"Wanna meet me in the bathroom?" I said as I placed my hand on his thigh.

Carter, who was sitting on the other side of Parker, was busy watching an in-flight movie. Kamydn and Kendall were sitting across the aisle and both were reading books. They wouldn't notice if we disappeared for a little bit, would they?

"Are you serious?" he said with both interest and skepticism.

"Uh, yeah."

"Who are you?" he asked.

Rather than answer, I stood up and stepped over both him and Carter and headed for the back of the plane. I didn't look back and hoped he would follow. If not, I guess it would be lonely in the bathroom. With no line, I slid into the stall, closed the door, and tried to patiently wait.

I didn't exactly know how this was supposed to go, but I was willing to try. I'd never wanted to join the mile high club. I'd been the girl trying to figure out how people logistically managed to knock boots in a room barely big enough for one person. I also liked to follow rules. I know there is no official rule about sex in an airplane bathroom, but I wasn't the type of person to break the unspoken rules of society either. But right then, something was different about me and it was something I wanted, or needed, to try.

I continued to sit on the lid of the toilet and wait. About two minutes after I'd sat down though, a familiar rhythmic knock on the door told me that Parker had made up his mind and had followed me. As I let him in, I quickly wondered what

66

would happen if we were caught. I'm sure our kids would be mortified, but I doubted we'd be arrested or anything.

I smiled and began to passionately kiss Parker as he fumbled with his belt. He dropped them just enough that I could see he was already hard. With his back to the door, I bent over and put my mouth around his erection and sucked while my tongue flicked against his tip. I heard a quiet moan escape from his mouth as he reached his hands towards the walls to help hold himself up.

I couldn't recall the last time I'd done this. In the last few years, we had generally just had sex and gone to sleep — almost more like a routine than for fun. I'm sure that the pure surprise of this act was turning Parker on more than the act itself. I felt his erection stiffen harder and his legs trembled just as the plane hit turbulence. Unintentionally, the jolting action pushed his penis to the back of my throat and my upper teeth to dig into it. I began to gag while he screamed and jumped backwards, which knocked the door open, and we spilled out into the aisle way outside the door.

Parker struggled to pull up his pants and handle the intense pain I had caused while everyone in the back of the plane turned around to see what caused the commotion. Mortified, I attempted to quickly stand up as several younger gentlemen stood up and began to clap. My cheeks were as red as a stop sign and I realized the irony of it all. Parker and I took the walk-of-shame back to our seats and prayed that our children would never know what had happened.

"What the hell was *that*?" Kendall hissed from her seat as we made our way back.

"Hush," I scolded and hurried to take my seat.

"That was fucking embarrassing," Parker said into my ear.

"Tell me about it. How's your penis?" I asked sympathetically.

"I'm pretty sure it's still attached, but it hurts like a son-of-a-bitch."

"Yeah, I'm sorry about that. It was a bad idea."

"No, it was an amazing idea, just bad execution," he laughed.

"True."

"I appreciate the effort. I really do," he said as he gave me a kiss and I felt his hand rest on my thigh and squeeze.

The car ride home from the airport was silent. Parker and I held hands in the front seat as the kids ignored us with headphones on and playing with electronic devices. The vacation had been Heaven and I dreaded going back to work for the first time ever. I loved that Parker and I were able to just enjoy each other again.

It honestly felt like a new relationship or the fire had been rekindled. As I crawled into our bed that night, I snuggled a little closer to him. I felt his warm breath on my bare shoulder, his strong hand resting on my hip. This was exactly where I wanted to be.

But the next morning, I was drinking coffee in the emergency room and not on a boat floating in the Caribbean. If I closed my eyes, I could pretend to feel the breeze in my hair again, but when I opened them, I saw it was just from the night shift staff running out the door.

Chapter 7

Not only was I not excited to come back to work after our cruise, I was disappointed to see that I'd been scheduled to work triage again. Was it too late to turn around and call in? No, that wasn't me and I'd already started with my morning coffee. With a deep sign, I walked to the front of the emergency room and was updated by the night shift nurse.

With no patients in the waiting room, I was able to slowly drink my coffee and savor every drop. I'd added vanilla creamer and three sugars this morning and it felt like liquid gold as it rolled down my throat. I wished I could drink coffee all day long, but Parker had been a kill-joy when he reminded me of the problems I'd encounter if I did. Was I ancient enough that I had to worry about cardiac issues already? My body was failing me far too fast.

As if fate hated me, the moment I stood up to get myself a second cup of coffee, a new patient walked in and I was forced to sit back down and be pleasant again. I plastered on a fake smile and greeted the woman when she entered. She practically collapsed into the chair, and I began taking her vitals.

She had been out for a morning run, something I genuinely missed but refused to do so early in the morning, and had felt weak and dizzy. When she went home, she couldn't stop sweating and began to have shortness of breath. I quickly saw that her oxygen levels were borderline, and she was now wheezing, so she was promptly taken back to a room and respiratory therapy was paged. That was the end of my job and back to triage I stomped, but not without stopping for that second cup of coffee.

"So, how was it?" Avalon asked as she stuck her head into the triage room.

"Absolutely amazing!" I reported, unable to control the smile on my face.

"Yeah? Which part?" she said, almost surprised at my response.

"Well, let's see... There was the man who hit on me at the buffet, the glasses of wine on the balcony, the hot sex with my husband every night, the sights, the swimming... Take your pick," I said with a laugh.

"Hot sex with your husband? Every night?" she asked with one eyebrow raised.

"Oh yeah," I said with a bigger smile.

"Wait, weren't your kids on this trip with you?"

"Yeah, but we had our own cabin."

"Sex every nigh, eh? Well that was a long time coming, wasn't it?"

"That's what she said," I mocked in a manly voice, and we both laughed.

"Oh geez," she finally said, "You're gonna make me pee myself if I keep laughing like this."

"Sorry. Anything new while I was away?" I asked.

"Absolutely not. Come'on now, you know things don't really change around here."

"I know, but I still had to ask. Mandatory question, I suppose."

"Have you talked to AnneMarie about the preceptor job yet? Are you gonna leave me?" she asked with a whiny voice.

"Most likely, but I don't want to. I mean I do, but I don't," I said uneasily.

70

"I know what you mean."

"I could have stayed on that boat forever," I admitted dreamily.

"What has gotten into you? You were dreading this vacation. And sex with Parker *every* night? Who are you and what did you do with my best friend?" she accused with a laugh.

"I don't know! I just felt alive or something. I really don't know what's gotten into me. I just feel different, but I can't exactly explain it," I admitted.

"I'm just kidding with you. Don't have to be all serious and shit, do you?" she said.

"No, of course not. I just feel like everything was re-kindled or something. I can't explain it."

"Well, what happened exactly?" she asked with interest.

"It started after the guy hit on me at the buffet. I don't know, it like started a fire in me or something. I went back to Parker and I started looking at him. Like really looking at him. Did I miss the way we used to be? Hell yeah. We pretty much spent the week dating each other again and it was amazing, like it used to be."

"Oh Kate! That's a good thing, right?"

"Yeah, I just don't know if everything is going to go back to the way it's been or if it's going to stay like this. I don't know. I know I haven't exactly been flirty and stuff myself — like it isn't all his fault. Ugh, I don't know what I'm talking about. I'm rambling," I said with a sigh.

"I'm sure you'll figure it all out. You always do!" she encouraged with a little love tap on my arm.

"Get back to work!" I said with a laugh, but she listened and headed back to the department after blowing me a kiss.

My next patient was a quiet, young pregnant woman who wanted to be seen because she'd been unable to keep anything down for more than twenty-four hours and her obstetrician had no appointments available. She was wearing a skirt and bonnet and I guessed she was Mennonite. She looked at the floor as she spoke and was very polite.

"Do you know how far along you are?" I asked.

"I haven't had an ultrasound. My estimate is ten weeks," she said confidently.

"Are you nauseous or just vomiting?"

"I feel like I could puke all the time, but then I'll be near something and see it or smell it and without warning... well, I'll puke," she said hesitantly.

I grabbed some alcohol prep pads and asked her to smell them when she felt the most sick to her stomach. If looks could kill, I'd be dead. I had to coax and encourage her that it was a legitimate practice, but I wasn't sure if she would ever believe me. After I finished her assessment, I walked with her back to a room and gave her the talk about the gown and such and closed her door on my way out.

"Did you really give her alcohol prep pads to sniff?" Avalon asked as I walked past on my way back to triage.

"Uh, yeah, I did," I said with an eye roll.

"Are you crazy?"

"No, why? That's a legit thing!" I argued.

"Yeah okay," she said as she laughed and turned her attention back to her computer.

Crying could be heard from the front and I picked up my pace and headed out to the reception area. A young girl cried in her father's arms as he tried to complete the paperwork to check her in to be seen. I approached them and could see her arm was swollen, red, and she was clinging to it.

"What happened?" I asked the girl.

"I fell off the teeter totter!" she wailed in response.

"Oh no! Can I look at it?" She stopped crying for a moment but began to whimper. "Will you come with me to my special room, so I can see it?" She nodded.

In the triage room, I took her vitals, found out she was six years old, and was able to get a better look at her arm. While the skin remained completely intact, the gentlest touch caused her to cry out in pain. I smiled at the father.

"How are you doing?" I asked, trying to be friendly.

"I'm okay. I was at work when the school called and said she fell. I rushed right there and then right here. Is she gonna be okay?" he asked with a worried expression.

"I don't know. I'm not a doctor, I'm just a nurse."

I quickly helped her back to a room and turned my focus back to the patients waiting to be seen and a few new ones needing triage. One by one I called back the patients or helped others to rooms until the clock finally struck three, and I was bolting out the door to my car and safely on my way home.

When I got home, I hung my keys on their designated hook, removed my shoes, and headed to change my clothes. I was in the zone as I completed my routine tasks and the sound of my phone ringing made me jump.

"Hello?"

"Mom?"

"Kamdyn, what's wrong?" I asked frantically.

"I'm okay. I wasn't feeling good though and I ended up missing the bus. Can you come pick me up?" she asked quietly.

"Of course. Give me five minutes to change my clothes and I'll be there, k?"

I hurriedly threw on jeans and a shirt, socks and shoes, and grabbed my key back off the hook. In total, it took me ten minutes before I pulled into the pickup drive of the middle school and saw Kamdyn standing by the side of the building. Seeing me, she came running to the car and I saw she had been crying.

"What's going on?" I asked sympathetically once she was in the car and her seat belt fastened.

"Nothing," she mumbled.

"Whoa. You know that won't fly with me, baby girl. I can tell something is bothering you so fess up. Tell me what's going on," I urged, but it was like poking a sleeping bear.

Tears began to pour out of her eyes as she said, "I started my period today for the first time. I didn't know and I bled through my pants. I found out when Brett Murray, only the hottest boy in our class, pointed to the back of my pants and started laughing."

My heart shattered into a million pieces for her. It was a ritual most girls looked forward to, however disappointed they would eventually become once it finally was bestowed upon them. Kamdyn had been talking and asking questions about periods for the last year, since her best friend Lydia started hers. I had thought she was prepared, but I'd been dead wrong. Now, my baby girl was mortified, and hormonal.

I was more worried about her being hormonal than mortified. It would be so easy to say the wrong thing, even if that wasn't my intention. I had to plan my words ever so carefully. This was a big deal. Kendall had been easy, but Kamdyn wasn't Kendall. Kamdyn was sweet and sensitive. Starting your period with the best looking boy in class finding your wardrobe malfunction was the end of the world.

"Can you homeschool me?" Kamdyn asked with her lips still quivering and her eyes ready to pour out more tears.

"No, I can't. I know this is horrible, but it's really going to be okay," I said.

74

"No it's not. I can't go back ever again," she cried.

"Kamdyn, you can and you will. You're a beautiful, smart girl. Tomorrow, you're going to hold your head high, march into that school like you own it, and give that boy a piece of your mind!"

"I am?" she questioned.

"Oh yeah. And I have an idea!" I said with a glimmer in my eye.

Sitting in the middle school drive, I explained what I wanted her to do the following day at school. We talked about the possible outcomes and how she could handle those. Most importantly, I encouraged her to be a strong woman and not let some asshole teenage boy dictate how she feels about herself.

Maybe I was telling her this because I had spent my own middle school years re-playing these scenarios when I faced similar situations. Instead of standing tall, I'd allowed myself to become backed into a corner. I'd become an introvert. I found myself a bookworm who liked routines and was too scared to break rules. Basically, I was labeled a nerd.

Kamdyn could be labeled a nerd, that was perfectly fine. What I didn't want was thinking that she couldn't stand up for herself. My own teenage years were hell and I would do anything in my power to prevent my own flesh and blood from experiencing it. Middle school just sucked and it was such an awkward time in life.

Kamdyn's frown turned into a smile and I heard the excitement in her voice return. Honestly, I was prepared to receive a call from her principal in the morning and I'd gladly come into his office and explain. *His.* Oh yeah, that principal wouldn't stand a chance against this momma bear.

That evening, Kamdyn helped me make dinner and it felt like old times again. Kamdyn and I working in tandem, laughing and joking. My sweet baby girl adoring me, excited to get advice from me, and loving me. I didn't know what the future would bring, but I'd always tried to cherish these small moments in case they never existed again.

"Should we make cookies tonight?" Kamdyn asked when the casserole went into the oven.

"I don't think we have the right stuff for cookies. Can I take a rain-check?"

"Sure," she said, seemingly disappointed.

When we all sat down to eat, Parker innocently enough asked how everyone's day had gone. Carter just shrugged, talked about baseball practice, and rambled on like usual. Kamdyn and I just smiled at each other as Kamdyn said she'd had better days, but everything was alright.

I was just glad she was being kind, sweet, and social. Kendall had been easy when she started her first period mostly because she locked herself in her bedroom and only came out for meals and school. I like this teenager better, but knew that it could change at any moment.

As I crawled into bed next to Parker that night, I told him about the middle school boy who embarrassed our baby girl. I watched Parker go from relaxed and sleepy to stiff and wide awake. I repeated to him what I'd told Kamdyn to do about it the following day and Parker laughed.

"You think she'll do it?" he asked, still laughing at the thought.

"I'm not sure but I certainly hope so. I just wish I could be there to see the asshole's face when she does," I thought out loud.

"I bet you do," he said as he kissed me on the forehead, rolled over, and turned off the bedside lamp.

I woke up smiling the next morning, my head feeling clear. My smile continued as I woke up Kamdyn and Carter, and practically pushed them out the door for the bus. I winked at Kamdyn as she watched me from the window by her seat as the bus drove away. I decided to brew the coffee I'd been saving for a special occasion, poured it into my travel mug, removed my keys from their hook, and headed into work.

"You look happy today," Avalon mentioned when she walked into the break room to start the day.

"I am," I replied with a suspicious grin.

"Speak," she directed anxiously as she sat in the seat next to me. "Parker?"

"Nope. Kamdyn!"

I filled her in on Kamdyn's dramatic day. Her reaction mimicked mine until I told her what I'd told Kamdyn to do about it. At that point, she busted out laughing and everyone turned to look at us. We didn't care.

"I'm just waiting for a phone call that my precious baby girl has been suspended and I have to pick her up from school," I laughed.

"I can't believe you told her to do that! What are you gonna say to the school?" Avalon asked with curiosity.

"What am I gonna say to them? Ha! I'm going to tell them that if that little ass hat doesn't behave, then my daughter will continue to put him in his place. They have this zero tolerance stance on bullying and I fully expect them to use it. That ass hat *won't* be bullying my daughter for her body's natural function *ever* again," I said with a little cock of my head.

"Wow, Kate. Who are you?"

"What do you mean?"

"The Kate I know would have told her daughter to just let it roll off her shoulders, that she's better than that, and to ignore the person. I like this Kate. The Kate that doesn't take bullshit from anyone, even a little teenage hellian." Avalon held her fist in the air and I obliged, bumping our fists together in a new-age high-five.

Chapter 8

I took a long sip of my coffee, glanced at the clock, and went to the floor to get report from Daisy, one of the new nurse grads we'd hired in January. She was still excited about nursing, not quite yet jaded. I loved taking over her patients because usually they had been well taken care of and were usually in a pleasant mood when I walked in. It also meant most things were done and I could enjoy my first cup of coffee before the actual work started rolling in.

When I found Daisy, she was excited to report that I had zero patients to start out my day and it was welcome news to my ears. I knew the patients would come, they always did, but I would be able to enjoy a cup of coffee before they did. That always put me in a good mood.

I logged into the computer and saw that there were a total of two patients waiting in the waiting room and that was only because of shift change. I checked my phone, but it was still too early to be getting a call from the middle school, so I logged into my work email instead and began sifting through the screen full of hospital advertisements and junk newsletters.

"Good morning, Kate. Did you have an enjoyable vacation? Have you made a decision on the preceptor job yet?" AnneMarie said as she approached me.

After having discussions with Parker on vacation, we decided I *would* take the night shift preceptor job. I would miss everyone that I worked with on day shift, but I knew I'd see them all the time. I hadn't rushed to tell AnneMarie because I wanted to enjoy day shift for a few more days before I broke the bad news to them.

"Yeah," I said casually, as if it were no big deal.

"Yeah as in you made a decision or yeah you're taking the job?" she asked hopeful.

"Yeah, I'm taking the position." I took another long sip of my coffee so she couldn't see the giant smile across my face.

I'd been trying to get a management role for the last few years — working extra shifts, tackling extra projects, and volunteering for extracurriculars to show current management that I was the right woman for the job. It was *finally* my time to shine, and I was, admittedly, excited about it. AnneMarie obviously was as well because she hugged me right there at the computer.

My pager vibrated to alert me that I was getting one of the patients from the waiting room. AnneMarie let go and told me we'd talk later. I watched as Tyrell brought the patient from the waiting room to one of my open rooms with a pleased smile and finished the rest of my coffee, ready for the day ahead.

The patient was a sixty-two-year-old man complaining of heart palpitations. He was short of breath, dizzy, and feeling weak. The moment his butt was on the stretcher, the PCA was placing electrodes on his chest for the EKG, and I was attempting to start an IV. Before the EKG was completed, Dr. Tempest stuck her head in to see the results and without taking much time to analyze it, knew the cause of his problems.

"Have you ever seen a cardiologist before?" Dr. Tempest asked the patient.

"No."

"Well, I think we're going to see one today. You're currently experiencing something called atrial fibrillation," Dr. Tempest said before she went on to explain further.

Once we had the patient stabilized, it seemed like a good time to head to the break room for a second cup of coffee if you asked me. I looked inside the coffee pot and saw that no one had made a fresh pot that morning. I was instantly turned off seeing something floating in the pot. I was not to be deterred though and I went straight to the sink and began scrubbing the pot. Once the pot sparkled, I made a new one before I poured myself a cup and slowly headed back to the floor.

Deep in my gut, I felt that it was going to be a difficult day. Whenever my gut began talking, I listened. I swear it could tell the future. I settled into my cubby for the day and checked for new orders on my patient and with another drink of coffee, I headed to the medicine closet to gather the ordered medications.

It hadn't even been an hour into my shift when it happened. There had been a massive pileup on the freeway, and we would be getting car accident victims. The dispatcher had been unsure of the number of victims, but knew that it was more than five. With only four trauma bays, this meant a higher acuity patient in non-trauma rooms as well as potentially receiving a trauma patient. It was about to be very busy.

Didn't anyone know how to drive in the rain anymore? I had heard it was like a monsoon outside, but getting a multiple car pile up solidified this. It was like this when we got the first snow of the season or just snow in general.

My first patient received from the trauma was an elderly woman with neck pain. She was strapped to a backboard and yelled out for help every five minutes. Loudly. One thing I quickly noticed was the lack of a cervical collar around her neck. Who puts a car accident victim on a backboard but forgets to protect their neck? I rolled my eyes *and* shook my head.

"What the hell, guys?" I said as I looked at each of the two medics standing in front of me trying to give report.

"What?" Medic #1 said.

"What? What is she here for again?" I asked with irritation.

"MVA but you already knew that, so I'm confused," Medic #2 said.

"Yep. Notice anything missing?" I said as I motioned my hand over the woman as she continued to scream.

"Uh... no, not really," Medic #2 said with a confused look.

"How about a collar?" I practically screamed, referring to the protective brace that should have been around her neck. "You have an elderly patient who was in an MVA... A freakin' motor vehicle accident and her chief complaint is neck pain! Where the hell did you go to school at? Get the hell out of my ER," I said, finally becoming too frustrated to even argue or chastise them further.

Their eyes grew wide as they realized the error and scurried from the room like little mice. The poor woman could be paralyzed from an error like this, and I was angry. I had the PCA go straight to the supply closet and grab a collar and I applied it myself, all while rolling my eyes.

I had managed to ignore the patient's cries while I applied the neck collar and got her vital signs but just as I was assessing her head for injuries, she released a blood-curdling cry into my ear and I nearly jumped out of my scrubs.

"Holy shit! Shut the hell up and let me concentrate, would ya?" I snapped.

He had a way of letting boys get away with things by saying that "boys will be boys" and if the girls did the same thing, he'd practically throw the book at them. Carter and a classmate, Jasmine, had pulled a prank on their teacher one year by placing live frogs in her desk drawer. When Jasmine's mother and I arrived at the office to claim our children, Carter was excused with just one detention while Jasmine got five.

I had been too afraid to say anything about the injustice. I had seen the look on Jasmine's mother's face, but I was stunned into silence. It was unfair. They had participated in the same amount and should have received the same punishment. So I was prepared for the principal telling me Kamdyn couldn't stand up for herself.

"This is Kate."

"Uh, Mrs. Cordova?" a voice on the other end said.

"Yeah, this is she."

"Good. This is Mr. Fuller. I have your daughter Kamdyn here in the office with me. She's okay, but I'd like you to come in so we can talk in person regarding her behavior today," he said nervously.

"Of course, of course. I am getting out of work now and can head that way if that will work for you?" I asked, trying to mask the excitement from my voice.

"Uh, yeah that should be fine."

I hung up, flushed the toilet, and washed my hands. I was practically skipping down the hall when I saw Avalon.

"She did it!" I said gleefully.

"Huh? Who is *she* and what did *she* do?"

"Ugh... Kamdyn. Remember? I don't know yet!"

"You got the call?"

"Yep! I'll text you later when I have the details."

"Sounds good."

I shifted into drive and arrived at the middle school in what felt like record time. I took a deep breath before I entered the school, trying to contain my excitement. I kept reminding myself with each step to stop smiling, but I was extremely proud of Kamdyn for sticking up for herself, and I was absolutely going to side with her.

"I'm Kamdyn Cordova's mother," I said as I stepped into the principal's office.

"Ah yes, Mr. Fuller is in his office. Go ahead and go in," the receptionist said as she pointed to an open door.

"Hello, Mrs. Cordova. I'm Mr. Fuller, principal here at the middle school," he said as he stood and introduced himself.

He was a middle-aged man, balding long before he should be, and clearly drank too many beers based on the size of the spare tire around his midsection. He wore a brown tweed suit and penny loafers. He kept a mustache and my instant thought was that it was to compensate for the inability to grow hair on the top of his head.

"Where's Kamdyn?" I asked, looking around the cluttered office.

"She's back in class right now," he said as he took a seat and gestured for me to take the one across from his desk.

"Okay. Well, how can I help you?" I said pleasantly.

"Well, there was... Uh... An incident today that I need to discuss with you." I felt my breath catch and excitement pulsed in my chest. "Your daughter, Kamdyn, got into a fight with another student."

"Brett Murray?" I suggested.

"No. Why do you think Brett Murray and your daughter would have been in a fight?" he asked with an odd expression across his face.

The look of confusion crossed mine because if she hadn't gotten into a fight with Brett Murray, then why was I in the

86

principal's office? The plan must have gone wrong, and she must have improvised, and suddenly, I became frantic. I had been prepared to chew out this principal, but if the plan hadn't worked out, then I might have to come up with a plan B of my own.

"There was an issue between them yesterday. But if that isn't it, why am I here?" I asked, needing to know the answer.

"Well, your daughter got into a fight with Zoe Miller," he started before I interrupted him.

"Zoe? That's her best friend."

"I don't think so anymore," he muttered under his breath.

"Okay, can you just get my daughter down here and tell me what the hell is going on?" I demanded.

He obliged and ten minutes later, Kamdyn sat next to me with a happy grin on her face. I was even more confused than I had been before and I had a burning desire to get to the bottom of this.

"What happened?" I asked Kamdyn, unable to wait on Mr. Fuller to get the conversation started.

"Okay, so I came to school today and everything was going just fine until third period, right? Well, that's the class I have with Brett. So when I walked into Ms. Turner's room, I saw Brett sitting at his desk writing a note. I didn't say anything to him and I just took my seat in front of him."

I nodded my head, trying to follow where this was going. "Ok."

"Well, right before Ms. Turner started class, Brett tapped me on the shoulder and passed me a note. It was for *me*. So I opened it and it basically said that he was sorry for yesterday. He had been cruel and that hadn't been what he meant to do. He felt pressure from the other guys on the basketball team, but he felt horrible about it because he really likes me," she said and her cheeks flushed.

Seeing her this happy erased any anger I had towards the situation and the humiliation the little shit caused my daughter, but my curiosity remained. One positive thing so far was that Brett had a decent set of parents if he could not only recognize what he did was terrible, but apologize for it. How many middle school boys would do that?

"So then I was super excited and wrote him a note back. Ms. Turner didn't see me pass it to him. By the end of class, Brett was my boyfriend, and I was super happy. So we left class holding hands, and he walked me to fourth period. Well, Zoe saw us holding hands. I thought she'd be excited for me and everything."

I did not miss middle school-days. Just listening to the drama was causing my head to throb behind my eyes. How did I ever survive those years? I did a double-check because I was sure she'd just told me she had her first boyfriend. Was I allowed to be excited or was I supposed to be upset because I'd been called into the principal's office? I was so confused.

"Okay..."

"So Zoe comes up to me and asks me what the hell I'm doing and I'm like all confused. Well, she says I shouldn't be holding hands with the boy *she* likes and that it's a betrayal of our friendship. But I've liked him forever and that isn't fair. So I told her that she needed to check herself."

"What did Brett say?" I asked with interest.

"Brett told her that he didn't like her and that I was his girlfriend. So then Zoe got really mad at me and threatened to tell all my secrets to the whole school, so I reminded her about girl code. But she told me that didn't matter anymore since we weren't friends because I stole the boy she likes. Then she like got into my face and was yelling, so I slapped her," she said, finally finished and waiting for me to respond.

"You *what*?" I asked in shock.

"I slapped her. Right across the face," she repeated as if she'd kissed her and not slapped her.

"Kamdyn!" I said with shock, horror, and extreme pride.

"What?" she asked, shrugging her shoulders.

I rubbed my eyes and felt the throbbing strengthen behind them.

"So what is the plan, Mr. Fuller?" I asked, not needing to know any more of the story and knowing he already had a punishment in mind.

"Well, she's going to have to write an apology letter to Zoe and serve five Saturday detentions. If she doesn't want to do that, she can be suspended for a week," he said calmly, almost looking bored.

I looked at Kamdyn who was looking at the floor and then back to Mr. Fuller and said, "We'll see you next week."

Chapter 9

I stood up, tugged at Kamdyn's arm so she would follow suit, and I marched us right out of his office. I didn't say a word until we were safely in the car and free from anyone who could be eavesdropping.

"Damn girl, that was badass!"

"Mom!"

"I'm proud of you for standing up for yourself, but please don't go slapping people on a regular basis," I said as I gave her a look.

"I won't. I promise."

"Alright, let's go home. Your dad and I will figure out your punishment later."

"Punishment? I thought you were proud of me?" she asked frantically.

"Oh I am, but it was still wrong to slap Zoe so you do still have to serve a punishment. I mean, you can't go unpunished when you're suspended from school," I said, thinking that through as I said it.

"Ugh... Mom!" she pleaded.

"Nope, none of that business. So tell me more about Brett," I said, changing the subject to a happier topic and thankful that my baby girl was confiding in me like she used to.

We spent the rest of the car ride home talking about Brett Murray. The smile on Kamdyn's face was worth every suspension they could give out, even if I was secretly disappointed she had caved and accepted his apology so quickly. I hung my keys on their hook and together, she and I made dinner.

Afterwards, as I did the dishes, she sat at the kitchen island and told her father everything that had happened. With my back to them, I smiled while I washed the dishes. This teenager stuff wouldn't be so bad as long as Kamdyn continued allowing us to know what was going on in her life. Kendall hadn't done any of that and Carter barely talked about anything other than sports.

I stayed up late finishing my book before I crawled into bed. I didn't work the next day and I looked forward to the chance to sleep in for once. Or at least the chance to go back to bed after I got the kids on the bus. I always felt I needed a vacation from a vacation!

I crawled back into bed the moment the yellow school bus drove down the road. I had just fallen back asleep when the phone rang. I ignored it. Who would be calling at 09:00 a.m. anyways? When it rang again a few moments later, I became irritated but continued to ignore it. Finally, when it rang a third time over the course of only a few minutes, I picked up my phone off the bedside table, intending to answer it. But the screen was blank. No message, no missed calls. Confused, I looked over at Parker's bedside table and saw his phone laying there just as it began to ring a fourth time.

"Hello?"

"Hey Kim, is Parks there?" a woman asked.

Parks? Who the hell was this woman? The phone number appeared on the screen and the name read "Madison Medical Company".

"Uh, no. He's in surgery. I can take your name and number and have him give you a call when he's done," I suggested, playing along.

"Wait, this isn't Kim?" she asked skeptically.

I tried to think fast and came up with the only other woman on the OR team who would be answering his phone. "No, it's Bethany. Kim is doing a special assignment today, so I've got Dr. Cordova's personal phone."

"Ah, lucky Kim! Well, why don't you tell Dr. Cordova to meet Renee for lunch in the call room at noon?" she said, too playfully for my liking.

"Got it. Meet Renee. Call room. Noon."

"Thanks doll!" she said and I almost puked in my mouth.

I ended the call. What. The. Hell. Was. That? *Who* the hell was that? Renee? I knew that our marriage hadn't been running at full speed like it had in years past, but an affair? Was this really happening? Had I misinterpreted the entire thing? No, I was sure I'd understood perfectly.

The last week or so had all been a lie when put into this context. Our marriage hadn't been revived, it was already dead inside to Parker. He had already moved on. This was going through the motions. My blood was boiling.

Usually, being angry made me sulk and gorge myself with ice cream while I had a good cry. But this time was different. This time, I didn't feel sad at all. I felt powerful. Vindictive even.

As the energy within me increased, I felt as cold as a rock in Antarctica. The only emotions I felt were anger and aggression. An idea brewed in my mind. I was going to go to that call room at noon and catch the cheating bastard in the act. I didn't deserve this. We made vows to work through anything. Clearly, Parker needed to be reminded.

Sleep was useless. I took a warm shower trying to relax myself a bit since I had a few hours to kill. Nothing I did worked though, so I ended up laying in bed staring at the ceiling for a few hours until it was time to go. I got up and put on my tightest skinny jeans and a size-too-small v-cut shirt that Carter was embarrassed to be seen with me wearing.

I arrived at the hospital with a few minutes to spare and planned my attack. Around the corner from the call room was a little nook with a desk. My plan was to hide under the desk and use the little sliver between the desk and the wall to record their interaction the best I could. Then, when they were both in there, I'd quietly use my key to let myself in and catch them in their adulterous act.

I only waited a few minutes until Renee showed up. She was short, had long auburn hair, and large full breasts. What did she have that I didn't? I instantly hated her, but I figured that was a pretty normal reaction for anyone seeing their spouse's mistress for the first time. I heard footsteps down the hallway and hit the record button on my phone.

"Hey there, Dr. Cordova," Renee said as she eyed Parker coming down the hallway.

Looking up and down the hallway, "You look gorgeous today." He put his hands around her waist and pulled her into him.

"How was your vacation?" she asked with a wink.

"It was relaxing," he said as he began nuzzling her neck.

"I'm starving," she said in this overly seductive voice.

He reacted by kissing her. KISSING HER? What the hell, Parker? The anger and aggression that had softened for a few hours returned ten-fold. I was ready for a full on fight, but I kept quiet and kept recording as she started to slide his lab coat off his shoulders, and he unlocked the call room door.

I flipped off the phone once they were in the room and stood from my hiding position. I was ready to fight for my marriage. I wanted to wait five minutes so I could catch them in the act and have evidence. However, I also knew Parker wouldn't last much longer than that so timing it had to be perfect. I stood close to the door and listened but didn't hear anything.

Briefly, the thought crossed my mind that maybe, just maybe, I wouldn't want to *see* this actually happening. Maybe knocking on the door and interrupting and then showing Parker the video was actually my best plan of action. At the end of my internal battle, I was more pissed off than before and I wanted to hurt someone.

I slid my key into the door handle and quietly unlocked it. I heard shuffling and a few quiet moans. No sick to my stomach feeling. No nerves. Anger and aggression. I turned the video recording on again as I walked into the room.

"What. The. Hell," I said after a moment.

Parker was undressed from the waist down and laying on top of a completely naked Renee. His full erection died the moment he saw me, and he began to scramble to his feet and head for me.

"This isn't what it looks like," he pleaded.

"It isn't? This looks pretty clear to me there, darlin'," I said calmly. Anger and aggression.

"Well, I mean it is, but it isn't," Parker stammered.

"Look, it's clear you're fucking another woman. I'm not sure what else it *could* be."

Watching him try to defend his actions caused the anger to surge inside me and I picked up a lamp on the table and threw it to the floor. It shattered into a million little pieces and the room darkened slightly. Renee flinched when it happened and continued scrambling to find all of her clothing and put it back on.

"Whoa! Kate, calm down," Parker pleaded with me.

"Calm down?" My face flushed red. "Calm? Down?" I asked again, louder and slower than the last time.

94

When would men learn that telling an angry woman to calm down only infuriated her further? Telling your wife to calm down after she just caught you screwing another woman was a step above that. I had ice in my veins and a taste for blood.

Renee practically ran for the door, mumbling something about a conversation for just the two of us. I let her off easy. I let her escape. She was just as guilty in this as he was. Anger and aggression. Parker quickly put his boxers back on, but I didn't move an inch.

Now, I had always been told that when dogs jump on you with excitement, you're to knee them in the chest. So when Parker approached me and attempted to give me a hug, I quickly lifted my knee up as hard as I could. It made contact right where I had hoped it would and by his reaction, I had definitely hit my target.

"Shit, Kate! Why did you do that?" he asked after he was able to catch his breath.

"I'd like to ask you the same damn thing, Parker."

"Fuck. I didn't deserve that."

"Really? If you put your dick in another woman, that's exactly what you deserve. Do you think I should just look the other way while you cheat right in front of me? Even the girls in the OR know you're having an affair. I look like an idiot. YOU put me there. YOU'RE the one who did this. Yes, you deserve to have my knee in your testicles."

My voice had started out steady and calm but had escalated to screaming. No tears fell, but every emotion inside me burst out as anger and aggression. Parker stood opposite of me, massaging his testicles, and praying they would survive.

"Look, Kate," he began, but I cut him off.

"Look, Parker," I screamed in a mocking tone. "I don't want your fake apologies. If you don't want to be married to me anymore, then do it the right way. Don't play these games. We're too old for this high school bullshit."

"It's not that easy, Kate. I love you. I really do."

"Great way of showing it."

"I am *in* love with you."

"What was last week? What was that all about?" I said, lowering my voice.

"What do you mean?" He said, his body language relaxing slightly.

"What do I mean? I mean the amazing vacation that we just had together. The one where we had sex every night. The one where we flirted and connected like newlyweds. Was all that fake?" I said with my volume rising again as I battled internal emotions.

"That was real," he said softly.

"Then what was *this*?" I asked as I motioned towards the bed.

"I don't know. I had needs," he said, shrugging his shoulders.

"Wow. Don't bother telling me about needs. Just go find some side piece to fulfill them. Got it." Anger and aggression returning.

"It's not like that."

"You keep saying that, but you haven't said exactly what it is like."

"I have a lot to explain." He looked at his watch when an alarm went off. "I have to be back in surgery. Can we discuss this at home?" he pleaded with me.

"Ah, I suppose. If I'm still there, that is."

I turned on my heel and left him alone in the call room, slamming the door on my way out. Several people had been hanging out in the hallway, probably having heard my yelling, and quickly looked away when I stormed out. In my head, I dared one of them to talk to me, but luckily, no one took me up on it.

I walked straight to my car chanting my mantra, anger and aggression, before climbing into the driver's seat and finally bawling my eyes out. I went straight home. I took a Benadryl and Motrin and passed out in bed. Sleep was my new best friend and I could think of nothing I wanted to do more. Well, except hurting Parker, but I was pretty sure he would feel the pain from my knee for awhile longer.

When I woke up later that evening, I heard a familiar voice and thought that I must be in some crazy dream land. I closed my eyes tight and prayed that I was just dreaming. Instead, when I opened them again, there she was. In all her glory, my mother stood at the end of my bed, demanding I get my butt out of bed.

Kathleen "Kitty" Henderson was all of five feet tall, but she sure packed a punch. She had been the "fun" mom growing up because, as a stay-at-home mom, she was always on our field trips, allowing slumber parties, or coming up with fun ideas. The one thing she didn't tolerate well, was being told what to do and wasting daylight.

The first question I had was where the hell she had come from. How long had I been asleep? Kitty lived four hours away. Had she scheduled this visit and I'd somehow forgotten to write it on the calendar? No. I'd have remembered if she was coming — that took preparation.

"Mom, what are you doing here?" I asked with one open eye.

"Parker called me. He said I needed to come spend a week helping you or something. I didn't question him, I just packed my bag, and started to drive. When my baby girl needs her momma, I'm going to be here," she said as she sat next to me on the edge of the bed.

"Mom, I don't need you right now though."

"Well, Parker seems to think you do. Do you know why he would think that?"

"Yes, I do. But I'm not ready to talk about it yet, let alone with you."

"Well that's rude," she said with her feelings sincerely hurt.

"Mom, I love you. But sometimes I have to fight my own battles," I said grabbing her hand and giving it a squeeze.

"Then I will stay and help with my favorite grandchildren while you fight your battles," she said with a smile and I rolled my eyes.

"You know the kids are grown and will probably ignore you, right?"

"Nah, they can't ignore their favorite grandmother!" she insisted.

In my family, my mother was the go-to woman when someone had a problem. She always had ideas or the solution to any problem. Admittedly, she was very skilled at it. She and my father had two children, me and my older brother, Kristopher. Kristopher chose to give his life to God at the age of eighteen and became a Catholic priest. When my father died a few years later, my brother just got weird. He spent less and less time with my mom and I until finally, he stopped doing it at all.

Parker's parents lived across the country, and we rarely saw them. Parker's three sisters lived down the street from them. His mother paid so much attention to Parker's nieces and nephews that it felt like our children never even existed. Sometimes though, they would send a birthday card to one of the kids, but not a single year went by where all three of them received cards. Parker had stopped getting cards when he turned thirty and I'd never received one. It wasn't just about the cards, but the feeling of being abandoned.

My mother had been the one bawling her eyes out at my wedding. She told me straight to my face that my marriage would mean her eternal loneliness. It was dramatic, but effective. Parker's mother couldn't make the wedding because one of his sisters was expecting a baby. Of course, that meant his dad couldn't come either.

My mother used to spend so much time at our house when we had first married and when the kids were born. But when Parker and I moved after his residency ended to accept a new orthopedic job, she was devastated. No amount of train tickets, hours in the car, or apologies would ever be enough for moving. Parker's mother had never even been to our house.

Having my mother here, now, was both comforting and irritating. Parker reaching out to her was annoying. Rather than talking to me himself, he just called my mother to come out and try to win me over. Screw that. He had cheated on me. And more than once! My mother being here would not weaken me. It did mean that I would have to continue sleeping in the same bed with him though. His entire plan was so transparent.

"Mom, I have to work tomorrow. And the next day."

"I know. I've already settled in the guest room. I'll be here when you get home tomorrow. We can talk then," she said as she patted my leg.

"What's for dinner?" I said with a groan, giving in.

"Now that's my girl," she said, heading to the door to go check dinner. "You'll see when you get out of that bed and get yourself dressed."

When I finally made it to the kitchen, all of my kids were sitting around the table playing cards with Kitty. Everyone was laughing and having a good time, totally oblivious to the absolute destruction of my marriage. I plastered on my fake smile and ran straight for the coffee pot. Luckily, my mother knew me well and had a fresh pot waiting for me. Some things hadn't changed, like my coffee addiction.

"What are you guys doing?" I asked, trying to sound upbeat and happy when inside I was a boiling pot of anger.

"Beating Grandma at Skip-Bo," Kendall proudly reported.

"Ah. Sounds like fun."

The oven beeped and I offered to get whatever it was out rather than interrupting their game. Opening the door, I was blasted with warm air and the most delicious scent that had filled my nostrils in quite some time. One of the best things about my mom coming to stay was that she always made my favorite meals. Nothing compared to her home cooked chicken pot pies. I melted as I stood in front of the oven door.

I carefully pulled the pies from the oven and set them on the stove top just as Kitty came over to check them. She placed a hand on my shoulder and whispered that whatever was going on would be okay. While I had been irritated when I was woken up, I was comforted having her here now. Truthfully, I hadn't seen her in a few months and I missed her.

Parker chose that moment to return home from work and my mother felt my body stiffen when I heard the garage door open. She squeezed my shoulder again before poking the pie with a toothpick and declaring dinner was complete. The kids began to put the cards away as Parker came inside.

100

"Whoa, is that my mother-in-law's famous chicken pot pie I smell?" Parker announced as he hung his keys on their hook and removed his shoes.

"Yes, sir," Kitty said, blissfully unaware of what he had done, as she kissed Parker on the cheek.

"Well it smells delicious. Glad to see you, Mom," he said with a smile.

"I'm glad to see you too because dinner is ready, and I didn't want to wait long to eat it. You and Kate need to set the table. Kids, go wash your hands for dinner please," Kitty instructed.

Not wanting to air my dirty laundry in front of my mother, let alone my children, I continued the fake smile and went to the cupboard to grab the plates. Parker came up beside me.

"How's it going?" he quietly asked.

"Don't ask," I said with tight lips.

We set the table in silence and everyone took a seat. A quick prayer was said and everyone began to eat, except me. I took one bite and thought I was going to puke. My mother's chicken pot pie, my favorite meal of all time, tasted horrible.

"Why aren't you eating, Kate," Parker asked.

"I'm not hungry," I lied.

"I saved an extra pie for you to take for lunch tomorrow. No worries, Baby Girl," Kitty said soothingly.

I didn't wait for dinner to finish before I stood and went back to the bedroom with a headache. The throbbing behind my eyes was making me sick to my stomach, dizzy, and lightheaded. I hadn't been back in bed long when I heard Parker come into the bedroom.

"Are you ready to talk?" he asked.

"About what? Your affair or the fact that you called my mother to come stay with us so I couldn't attack you?" I asked, trying my best to be quiet but feeling quite sure that any and all sound would echo off the bedroom walls.

"Look, I didn't mean to hurt you, Kate."

"Wow, I'm glad you thought about my feelings before you went and found yourself a side piece," I seethed.

"Kate, it happened by accident. We haven't been having sex regularly for years," he whined, but I interrupted him.

"So that gives you an excuse to have it with someone else? That's just sick, Parker. You probably should have acted like a married man and *communicated* your issues with your wife. Now there's a brilliant idea, right?"

"Look. It just kinda happened. It was wrong. I was wrong. I knew it was wrong, but I was thinking with the wrong head. Our vacation *was* absolutely wonderful and reminded me of what we had and what we can have," he said, reaching for my hand.

"But it didn't stop you from screwing her yet again, did it?"

"I really want to work on our marriage. I want to work through this. With you," he said the last part softly. "I don't know if you can ever overcome this, but will you try?"

"Well damn, Parker. Let me go bang the neighbor and then ask you for forgiveness. How do you think that will go?"

"I understand you're upset right now," he began before I interrupted again.

"Upset? Right now? Screw you. Don't you dare try to tell me how I'm feeling because you have *no* idea."

"You're right," he admitted.

"Hell yeah I'm right." I paused to think of my next jab. "Just get the hell out," I decided, pointing toward the door.

He quit trying and left the bedroom. I needed more time to decide what I wanted to do. For the kid's sake, I was trying not to make any hasty decisions. Hell, what had made him change his mind so fast anyways? Now that he'd been caught, he wanted to work on our marriage? Earlier, when he was banging the OR nurse he certainly wasn't thinking about our marriage.

It was just so much to take in. It had hardly been a week ago we were on an amazing vacation and having sex daily. I thought we had rekindled our marriage. And now I find out he's been having sex with one of his OR nurses? The throb behind my eyes was stronger than ever, but I knew that getting out of the house was the best medicine of all right now.

I quickly dressed and headed for the living room. I kissed each of the kids and my mother, but excluded Parker and hoped no one would notice. I grabbed my keys from their hook and practically ran for the car in the garage. I didn't know where I was going, but I knew I needed to be out of the house. Thankfully, no one asked.

I put the car into reverse and pulled out of the driveway. I went left out of the driveway, like always. I turned the radio on, found a country music station, and just kept on driving. When the surroundings became unfamiliar, I turned to the right and drove for another five minutes before pulling into the parking lot of my favorite all-night grocery store.

Sitting in a parking spot in the middle of the lot, I put the car in park and let the tears flow. Not just a few tears, a cry-your-eyes-out kind of cry. A got-my-shirt-wet type of cry. In one day, my entire world had come crashing down around me, and I was helpless to stop any of it. I was used to being the woman who fixed things and people. Here I was, the woman needing the fixing.

When I finally had no more tears to cry, approximately one hour later, I put the car back into drive and went home. I parked the car in the garage and hung my keys on their hook. The house was much quieter than when I'd left and I didn't bother to locate anyone. Straight to my bedroom, straight into the bathroom to change my clothes, and then straight into bed.

Thankfully, Parker had taken the hint and was *not* in our bed. The alarm would sound far too early in the morning to justify talking to anyone tonight.

Chapter 10

For once, I was looking forward to being at work. With a house full of lies, I knew I didn't want to be there. Eventually, my mother would force the truth from me, but I didn't want to talk about it. I was just glad that I had someplace to go and could avoid the inevitable confrontation a little bit longer.

I was energetic when I got to work. Maybe it was the two cups of coffee I'd had that morning because it was easier to dodge questions when I had a coffee mug to my mouth. Or it could be because I'd spent more than twenty years working my butt off in the emergency room, waiting for my time to be in management, and the time was so close I could taste it. I wouldn't let Parker's indiscretions stop me from my own dreams. Anger and aggression, I reminded myself.

As my last day shift before my return to nights, I accepted my assignment and headed to Sam to get report. Sam had always been a nurse I enjoyed working with. He'd been working the night shift for as long as I could remember and had always had my back.

"When do you come back to the dark side?" he asked as I approached.

"Tomorrow night," I said with a smile.

"Sweet. I'll be here!"

And suddenly my first night back didn't seem as daunting as it had earlier, but I also knew the drama factor of the night shift patients was an entirely different ballgame. But as karma had it, I was in store for an entirely dramatic day shift and just didn't know it.

Sam was pleased to report off on the two patients that would carry over onto my shift — a lady with an ear infection that hadn't bothered to go to her own doctor because it had been too inconvenient and another lady with an ingrown toenail who claimed that she thought it was an emergency at four in the morning. Sam and I both rolled our eyes as we discussed the ridiculousness of the toenail emergency.

Finally, he bid me goodnight and bolted for the exit, leaving me to the ladies and two empty rooms. I finished drinking the third cup of coffee before I went to introduce myself and discharge the ladies. As I waited for a patient to be placed in one of my rooms, I sat quietly and took in all the sights, sounds, and smells of the department.

To my dismay, I only got to do that for a minute before I was alerted that a patient was being placed in my room and I headed off to greet him and complete a more thorough assessment. I expected to see an adult, but obviously I'd completely misread the date of birth because before me was a six-year-old.

"Hello there. What brings you in to see me?" I asked as I knelt down to his level.

"I swallowed the quarter!" he proudly proclaimed.

"You did? I don't think you're supposed to do that."

"Well I had to. My friend dared me and you don't back down from a dare," he said excitedly.

"I see." I glanced at the mother who was rolling her eyes and trying to keep her mouth shut.

"Well, does it hurt at all?" I asked with enthusiasm, trying to keep his attention.

"Nope!"

"Okay, well. The doctor is going to come in and ask you more questions. Then, you'll probably get to have an x-ray. Have you had an x-ray before?"

"Nope!"

"Well, they are going to use this machine to look inside your body! It's *so* cool. That picture will show them where the quarter is."

"How do they get the quarter out?" he asked curiously.

"Well, it depends on where it is," I explained.

I gave him a last smile before I left the room. And that was how my last day shift began. And just as I sat down, another pediatric patient was brought to me. Was I a kid magnet today or were those the only patients we were seeing?

When the ten-year-old boy sat on the stretcher, his hand was covering his eye. When I asked why he was there to see me for, he removed his hand and I saw the bleeding of his eyeball. I think if he hadn't been scared, he'd have been crying.

"How did it happen?" I asked.

"Well, I was picking on this girl in class, and she got mad and threw a pencil at me," he admitted.

"What did I tell you about picking on people?" the mother asked angrily.

"I know, Mom. I know," he said, shaking his head.

"I ought to smack you right now, but I think you learnt a thing or two already, huh?" she said with a twisted grin.

"Yep," he said, wincing when he tried to make a face at her.

I finished my charting and left so that the doctor could come in to see his eye, and pretty much put money on the fact that we would be seeing the ophthalmologist soon.

Returning to my computer, I saw a beautiful bouquet of flowers sitting next to my keyboard. Colorful orchids, daisies, lilies, and tulips were arranged with baby's breath in a circular glass vase. The other nurses ogled over the display and wondered anxiously who it was from, but I knew it was from my husband. Opening the card, I immediately recognized the handwriting and the simple words, "I love you".

I let the card fall into the nearby trash can before I moved the flowers to the break room for everyone else to enjoy — I didn't want to see them. They felt as fake as our marriage. I just wanted to focus on my job and *not* think about what had happened the day before. I didn't want to think about Parker. I didn't want to think about my marriage. I didn't want to think about relationships. I didn't want to think about anything other than how I could help my patients.

When my next patient was brought back, I was relieved to see that he was an adult. Without looking at his chief complaint, I went to the room and logged into the computer. He looked perfectly fine, but you would never know what was going on underneath the gown without asking.

"What brings you in today?" I asked casually.

"I think I have the flu," he said with a groan and covered his abdomen with his arms.

"What makes ya think that?"

"I feel so weak, I keep puking, and I can't stop using the bathroom," he let out another low groan.

"How long has it been going on?" I asked without flinching.

"A few days." Another groan.

I wanted to roll my eyes, but I refrained. I was determined to wait for the eventual lab work before making my diagnosis of man flu. As I waited for the doctor to see Mr. Man Flu, I made my way to the light with my kid's x-ray clearly showing a quarter in his stomach.

I asked the doctor about the eyeball injury and was told that ophthalmology had been paged already and would have to evaluate. Instead of standing around, I went to check in with Avalon, but I couldn't find her.

I sat down at my computer and began to look at the status of my patients. The kid who ate the quarter had discharge paperwork to be signed and supplies to be explained to the mother. I thought that seemed rather fun, so I hurried to the supply closet for a container.

"Alright, Buddy. No more quarters, okay?" I said as I looked at him with a smile.

"Wait! You're sending me home?" he asked confused.

"Yep."

"But we didn't get the quarter out yet," he protested.

"Well, that's going to be your mom's job," I said as I gave the mother a little grin.

"How is she going to do that?" he asked before the mom had a chance to ask.

"Well, every time you have to poop, I need you to poop in this thing here. We call it a hat. Then, your mom is going to have to dig through it with a fork looking for the quarter. When it comes out, you can stop," I said, looking at the mom for her understanding.

"What if it doesn't come out?" she asked, worried and grossed out at the same time.

"Doctor says if it doesn't come out in a week or two to follow up with your pediatrician for further guidance."

"That's gross," he said as he laughed.

"Do you want a sticker?" I asked, ignoring his comment.

"No, I don't need stickers anymore. I can't wait to tell my friends about my mom digging through my poop though!" he said as he jumped excitedly off the stretcher and began putting on his clothes.

"I don't think you need to tell anyone about me digging through your poop," the mother said she grabbed his shirt and turned it right side out.

"Okay Mom," he said and I knew that really meant he planned to tell everyone anyway.

Once he was gone, the ophthalmologist had arrived for the kid who had been stabbed by the pencil. I returned to the computer to quickly finish charting on the discharge. Man flu was going to be getting blood work done as soon as the lab came, so I sat at my computer and patiently waited for someone to need something.

When lunchtime rolled around, the break room had a cake and ice cream set up for me, wishing me well on the "other side". I was going to miss working with these people all the time, but I knew I wouldn't be far away. Only another clock away.

After lunch, Man Flu's labs were back and showed just as I'd expected — he had the man flu. All his whining about dying was futile. He just needed to go home and rest on the couch and have some woman baby him and soon enough he'd be feeling better.

When I got home that afternoon, Parker was still at work and the kids were still at school. The house was quiet but my mother was in the kitchen baking. I was a lot like my mother. I cleaned as I went along and despite having baked several sweet treats, my kitchen remained sparkling clean.

An apple pie, chocolate chip cookies, and freshly baked brownies were sitting on racks to cool. My mouth immediately began to water and I couldn't help but smile. Memories flooded me and suddenly, I was overwhelmed with emotion. I hadn't been prepared for the emotions to come to the surface so fast or so forcefully. Without a word, I rushed to my bedroom, claiming I needed to change my clothes. My mother knew how to make me talk.

After a few short minutes, I heard a soft knock on the door and my mother's voice. It was warm and comforting as she asked if she could come in. This time, I allowed her in. She sat on my bed and began watching me as I changed.

"How was work today?" she asked, trying to stir up conversation, but I knew that wasn't what she really wanted to talk about.

"It was good. The staff had cake and ice cream to celebrate my last day shift. It was pretty sweet of them," I said recalling it fondly.

"You must have made a great impact on them."

"I'm only moving to night shift. They act like I'm leaving the department."

"Well, maybe they needed an excuse to party."

"I think that's much more likely," I said with a little laugh.

There was a long pause before she continued, "Are you ready to tell me why I'm here?"

"Oh Mom," I said with a deep sigh.

"No, oh Mom me. I dropped everything and came right here and the curiosity is killing me," she said as she patted the bed next to her, signaling her demand that I sit down. "What is going on?"

"Parker cheated on me," I spit out before I have a chance to change my mind about telling her anything.

"He did *what*?" she says with a gasp.

"I caught him with his pants down. One of his OR nurses," I said as all the tears began to fall from my eyes.

Rather than speak, she pulled me into her for a big hug. I allowed myself to melt into her. I collapsed like I had as a child because having my mother hugging me was the medicine my soul needed. Finally, she pulled back from me and used her sleeve to wipe the tears from my eyes.

"Baby girl, what are you going to do?"

"I don't know. He wants to work things out," I said softly.

"But what do *you* want?" she asked as she brushed my cheek.

"I love him, Momma. I want to pretend it didn't happen, but I don't know if I can do that," I admitted with a new wave of tears.

"Listen, if your love is strong enough, it can overcome anything. I believe that. But, and this is a big but, you have to rebuild that trust. And that takes time and work. Work *he's* going to have to put in." Her mom-advice had never let me down, and I was sure it wouldn't now.

"I don't want to be with anyone else but him," I confided in her at last.

"Then you have your answer," she said with a sweet smile.

One of my favorite things about my mother was her caring heart. I'd heard of co-workers who had caught their spouse cheating, or had done the cheating, and their in-laws never forgave them. I knew in my heart, my mother would support me no matter what, and she would work to forgive Parker if that is what I wanted to do.

"What do I do now?" I asked.

"Talk to your husband."

We made our way back to the kitchen and when everyone was finally home, my mother and I had prepared an amazing feast for all to enjoy. It suddenly felt like everything in my world was right again. My house felt like a home. I felt the love around the table as I watched my family talk about their day, laugh, and tell stories. I had an inner peace and I knew that despite what Parker had done, if he really wanted to work on our marriage, I would let that happen.

112

Coffee. I smelled coffee. Coffee and bacon. I rubbed my eyes, took in my surroundings, and felt that coffee might be the best thing for me considering the throbbing behind my eyes had already started. I glanced over at my clock and saw it was nearly eight o'clock.

My first thought was that I'd forgotten to set an alarm and my kids were missing school. Then I remembered that my mother was in the house and Parker had already gotten up and gone to work. That's when I realized I was alone in the house with my mother, and that the coffee and bacon was all mine. I scrambled out of bed, threw on a robe, and went straight to the kitchen.

Sure enough, breakfast was on the table for me and sitting next to my mother as she read a smutty romance novel. She smiled when she saw me, introduced me to my breakfast, and returned to her reading. I scarfed down the bacon and began to slowly work at the coffee. Coffee was something that deserved to be worshiped, not chugged, unless necessary.

"What are we doing today?" I asked after I'd drunk half my cup.

She set her book down delicately and watched me for a moment before speaking.

"I thought we'd go run some errands."

It was the most boring and dreaded answer I expected from her. Whenever she was in town, like me, she insisted on following her routines, and this must have been the day to run errands. I had zero desire to go with her, but I also wanted to spend time with her. My face must have told her this because she then sighed, laughed, and told me she was kidding.

"You need to relax a little, my lovebird. Live a little."

I couldn't help but smile. It had been forever since she'd referred to me as her lovebird. She picked up her book and returned to reading. I decided to join her, so I grabbed my book from the library and returned to the table where we continued to read for the next three hours.

After we'd had lunch, I tucked myself into bed for a nap in anticipation of my first night shift in ages. I didn't sleep well, and I was quite sure I heard every movement made within the house. Finally, I'd given up.

Chapter 11

Per the assignment board, I was on the "blue" team. Next to me was Sam and Mia. Mia had the most beautiful dark skin I'd seen, long wavy black hair, and bold brown eyes. She was naturally a beautiful woman, but her personality accentuated the looks that her momma gave her. I didn't know her too well, but I was interested in getting to know more about her.

I saw that I already had three of four rooms occupied and quickly took report on those three patients. Since all three were fairly new, I took a moment to introduce myself quickly to each of them. Dr. Moon had already seen them, so until she wrote orders, there wasn't much I could do for them.

Dr. Gwen Moon was my favorite night shift doctors. She had been working the night shift her entire career and loved every minute of it. Still in her forties, she had kids living at home and her husband was a stay-at-home father. She was kind, patient, and loved to laugh. She was also physically fit and was always ready to tackle an unruly patient or family member if needed.

I sat at the bank of computers with Sam and Mia chatting about how our day had gone, the amount of sleep we did or didn't get, and what we brought for lunch. It felt like being in elementary school again, and yet so normal.

"Are you excited to start the preceptor position?" Mia asked.

"Definitely. I've worked in the ER for over twenty years. I'm long overdue."

"Overdue? Does that mean you're old?" Sam joked.

"If I'm old, what does that make you, smart ass?" I shot back.

"How does Dr. Cordova feel about your promotion? Did you do anything fun to celebrate?" I froze when Mia asked this question.

"Naw, not really. We haven't really had much time to celebrate with his OR schedule lately, but he's happy for me," I said.

"Liar!" Sam said under his breath.

"And what exactly does that mean?" I said angrily.

"Oh nothing."

"Oh nothing, my ass. Spit it out, Sammy Boy."

"Alright you two," Mia said as she tried to put out the smoldering fire.

"I just heard a rumor is all," Sam said sheepishly.

"A rumor?" My temper was rising rapidly.

"It's nothing."

"Fuck that. What rumor?" I demanded.

"I heard that Dr. Cordova was caught with a nurse from the ortho floor in the call room," Sam said as fast as he could.

Mia sat stunned that Sam would call me out like that. I sat silent, debating whether to admit it or deny it. What if I pretended I hadn't known? Did everyone know that an affair was happening except me?

"Kate, as your friend, I wanted to come right to you when I heard. I'm so sorry," Sam said with honest compassion.

"Thanks, Sam. My marriage is in the shitter right when my career is finally where I want it to be heading. How's that for irony?"

"Oh, Kate," Mia said, moments too late.

Mia placed her hand on my forearm and then brushed a strand of stray hair from my face. While it was something a friend would do for a friend, it felt intimate in a way. Because I wasn't sure how to interpret it, I brushed it off as nothing.

"Please don't say anything to anyone," I pleaded to both of them.

"Not a worry," Mia quickly said.

"You can count on us for that, but know that rumors spread like wildfire and just about everyone has already heard the gossip," Sam said.

"I know. I just hate it. Can't anything be private?"

"Girl, you know no one can keep their mouth shut around here," he said as he nudged my shoulder.

I'd known Sam long enough to know what kind of friend he was. A damn good one. He was trying to be realistic on my behalf and I appreciated it once my anger subsided. An alert popped up on Sam's computer screen before he had a chance to continue.

"Oh shit. Patient in 12 is having chest pain again. Gotta go," he said as he quickly jumped up from his swivel chair and headed in the direction of room 12.

It seemed like a good time to check my own screen and I saw that Dr. Moon had begun putting in her orders and my time for chit-chat was up. Prioritizing, I went to the med dispenser and grabbed the right meds for the patient in room 8. Then, I grabbed the supplies for an IV and headed into her room.

I explained to the patient and her family what I was planning to do, and everyone agreed to the plan. For being in her eighties, the woman had some amazing veins, and I was able to start the IV within moments. After I finished with the first flush, the son stopped me and asked to be told about the medication I was giving her. I repeated what I had said before but before I could connect the syringe to the IV, he stopped me again.

"Do you really think we should be giving this to her?"

"Of course not, but I've always wanted to know what it felt like to murder someone, ya know?" I said with a serious look.

The son's jaw dropped to the floor and the daughter began to laugh, praying I was actually kidding. I pushed the medicine, threw the syringe in the sharps box and left the room without saying another word. Why do people come to the ER for help and then ask stupid questions like that?

Back at the computer, I charted the details of starting the IV and the administration of the medicine and then looked at the orders for room 5. Dr. Moon had written an order for 500 mg of acetaminophen. The patient's chief complaint was that his dog had eaten forty Percocet, and he was out. I laughed and thought to myself how much fun this was going to be.

"Alright, sir. I have the Tylenol Dr. Moon ordered for you," I said pleasantly as I pulled the curtain back and stepped into the room.

"Tylenol? I'm allergic to that shit," he said quickly, shaking his head back and forth.

"You are? Oh shit. It's not listed as an allergy in your chart. Anything else you're allergic to?"

Was he aware that the Percocet he was seeking contained Tylenol? Inside my head I was dying from laughter, but I played along.

"I'm allergic to Tylenol, Motrin, and another one with a T."

"Got it. I saw on your chart that your dog ate forty Percocet tonight?"

"Yeah, that's what I need more of. She got into my pills and ate what I had left! Now I'm hurting," he said as he faked a moan and reached for his lower back, clearly forgetting that he'd complained of right arm pain when he checked in.

"Aren't you worried about your dog?" I said, continuing my serious face.

"My dog?" he asked and I worked very hard to not bust out laughing.

"Your dog. You know, the dog who ate forty Percocet tonight. Those forty Percocet would kill a human. I'm sure your dog is probably going to be dead when you get home unless you got her to the vet right away," I said.

"Oh no, the dog will be fine," he said confidently.

"What kind of dog is it?" I asked.

"It's a mutt. I don't know what it is. Someone dropped it off at my house a few years ago and I kept it," he said plainly.

"Well that's good. Let me go check with Dr. Moon on what else she can give you since you're allergic to Tylenol," I said.

"Yeah, see if she can just give me the Percocet like I usually take," he pleaded.

I walked out of the room laughing to myself. This patient was an idiot. Mia saw me shaking my head and asked what was so funny. When I told her my encounter, she suggested I go back in with the same pills and offer him the generic version of Tylenol, acetaminophen. That was a pretty good idea, and so I gave it a try.

"Alright, I talked to Dr. Moon. She suggested you try these acetaminophen instead. They have some of the same active ingredients as the Percocet you've been taking and should fix your pain. We can't get the Percocet after midnight, but like I said, these have some of the same active ingredients," I said with my best sales pitch.

"Wow, something new! I'll try them!" he said as he quickly swallowed the two pills.

"I'll come check on you in about thirty minutes, and we'll see if they made a difference for ya," I said as I snuck out the door.

Mia was standing by, having overheard the proposal to the patient and immediately gave me a high five. It wasn't exactly lying though since acetaminophen *is* an active ingredient in Percocet. For the sake of a good laugh, I told Dr. Moon about it, and she about fell off her chair laughing.

"Hey, check out this x-ray. What do you think all these things are?" Sam asked as Mia and I walked by the light box.

The light box, near the bank of doctor's computers, illuminated an abdominal x-ray of a patient who had refused to take off her fanny pack. The doctor had instructed the tech to just take the picture anyway with the fanny pack to the side as good as he could get it and that he'd see how it looked. Having gotten an adequate view of the abdominal cavity, the rest of us began playing the "guess what that is" game and having a good laugh.

"That lady must have liked collecting pens," I mentioned as I pointed to an area with about twenty of them.

"I think those are pencils. Look how well the lead shows up," Dr. Moon said as she picked herself up off the floor.

When I returned to my Percocet seeker, I found him fast asleep on the stretcher and knew my ploy had been a success. I sat down at the computer and entered my progress note: "Patient resting peacefully with eyes closed. Tylenol effective at relieving pain."

When I returned to the first room, the elderly woman was lying on the stretcher but did not appear to be breathing as well as when I had left. Her breaths were slow and deep followed by a pause and then, when she'd finally breathe, they would be fast.

Oh shit, I thought. Had the medicine caused her to start the dying process? I quickly, but calmly, took a new set of vitals and found that her oxygen level was far too low and immediately started her on oxygen. Her heart rate was up and down and then up again. I hooked her up to the heart monitor and called to the techs to get monitoring set up. I excused myself to alert Dr. Moon of the change in condition.

Rather than just take my word for it, she came to the patient's room to see for herself the patient's condition. As she did a re-assessment and requested some STAT orders to be placed, the family watched my every move.

"Your nurse did this to her, ya know?" the son said with hate in his voice.

"What? The nurse didn't do this. The fact that she's at an advanced age has done this to her," Dr. Moon said quickly.

"No, she gave her that medicine you ordered. I asked if we should be giving it to her and she said she just wanted to kill her," the son said, evil twinkling in his eye.

Dr. Moon shot me a glare that could kill and then returned to the patient's family. "Your mother came into the emergency room having chest pain, but her EKG looked pretty good. Due to some of her other symptoms, I had Kate give her heparin. Heparin is a blood thinner. It's to prevent stroke, heart attack, or a pulmonary embolism. It would *not* have caused these symptoms," she said in my defense.

"Whatever. It's pretty coincidental, isn't it?" the son said.

"Look, if you aren't going to listen to what Dr. Moon suggests, then why did you bring her in?" I snapped.

"Hush," Dr. Moon snapped at me quickly. "One thing that we need to discuss is how you would like us to do treatment in the event that your mother *does* have a heart attack. Do you want us to perform CPR, or chest compressions, and attempt to keep her alive?" Dr. Moon asked the family with sincere empathy.

"Yes, keep her alive at all costs!" the son said quickly.

"Yes, keep this poor old woman alive. How much is her check that you're cashing?" I said before I realized I'd spoken my thoughts instead of keeping it to myself.

My hand quickly shot to my mouth and I excused myself and left the room. Shit. What had gotten into me? Twenty plus years of effectively using my filter and then, right there, it decided to fail me? Maybe I needed another cup of coffee? Was everything with Parker affecting my work or was it the switch to night shift?

I went to see the orders for the patient in room 6 just as a new patient was brought back to room 7. I needed to get myself in check really quick before my mouth got me fired from the job I hadn't even really started yet. I asked Sam to cover for me quick and I headed straight to the coffee pot.

Unfortunately, the coffee pot was empty. I paced a few steps before Mia found me.

"Are you okay?" she asked.

"I'm not sure what is wrong with me," I admitted.

"Sam told me I should check on you."

"Yeah, I just have this pounding behind my eyes and I lost my cool with a patient's family."

"Kate, I don't know you all that well, but that doesn't seem like you," she said as she took a step closer to me.

"Yeah, I appreciate that. I'll be alright. I just have to get back into the groove of night shift. A few nights on the floor and I'll be ready to start my new role."

Was I trying to convince Mia or myself? I was shocked I'd said that to the family, however true it might have been. I'd seen some really pathetic stuff, but I'd never lost my mind and said my thoughts out loud. A range of emotions fluttered through me but I couldn't seem to organize them or make sense of what was going on.

When I returned to the floor ten minutes later, Sam had gotten my new patient settled and had taken over the elderly woman's care. The new patient was a middle-aged man with severe pain to his pelvic area and lower back. He complained of burning when he did pee, but said he was having difficulty going at all despite feeling like he always had to go. Classic kidney stone pain.

I approached the man to introduce myself, but he was laying curled in the fetal position moaning loudly when I entered. A woman who I assumed was his wife sat in a chair by the bed trying to comfort him and failing. She gave me a weak smile when I entered, but tried to give me the details she'd already given to Sam. I asked the patient if I could start his IV now so that when pain medicine was ordered, I could get it going as fast as possible. The patient said nothing, but held his arm out.

Tourniquet applied to his upper arm, I searched for a vein without finding anything worth jabbing a needle into. I tried the other arm and again, found nothing of value.

"Have you been drinking any fluids lately?" I asked, looking at him directly.

"No," he moaned.

"I can tell. You're dehydrated beyond belief. This IV is going to be difficult so buckle your seat belt," I said, trying to lighten the mood.

"Look, I don't give a shit what you do if it eventually stops this pain. Just, please stop talking to me," he pleaded between painful moans.

"Got it."

I gave his arm another look, found a possible contender in his hand, and poked him. While I was apparently sucking at life, I was successful at starting his IV because I saw a flash of blood right where it was supposed to be, and was able to get it placed without the difficulty I'd imagined. I wanted to cheer and clap, but I didn't think it would go over well.

"Alright, I was able to get it in. I will check with the doctor and see what we can do to get you some pain relief," I said as I left the room.

"Thank you," the wife said quietly.

My pager came to life and alerted me that CT was on its way to get the middle-aged man, and I was pleased that something was going right for a change. Everything else in my world was out of place, but for a split-second, I was the badass nurse I'd always been.

I was only allowed a few hours of sleep before I was rudely woken up, again, by my mother. I didn't need to be taken care of nor did I need her micromanaging my schedule. How long did she say she was staying again?

"You're wasting daylight hours," she said as she threw open the blinds, practically blinding me.

"Whoa, Mom. Did you have to do that?"

"Yep. Get your butt out of bed. I made lunch plans for us," she said cheerfully.

"I'm not hungry."

"I didn't say you had to eat. You just have to go. Now get up or we'll be late."

She made herself perfectly clear, I had zero choices in the matter. I'd allowed this woman into my home, and she had taken over. I was kicking myself for giving her a house key when we first moved in.

"You do realize I worked all night, right?" I asked, but it was futile as she was already out of the room and down the hall.

Arguing would be pointless, so I threw on clothes and went with her to our arranged lunch date. It hadn't been anything exciting or special, so I was confused as to why I couldn't be at home in my warm, fluffy bed sleeping.

When we returned from lunch, Parker was sitting on the couch next to Kendall. Seeing us walk in, Kendall quickly jumped up and asked if she could talk to Parker and I. Alone.

Why was Parker home in the middle of the afternoon? Was this an intervention? Everything about this moment was causing red flags to be raising and instantly, I was anxious. The throbbing behind my eyes returned with a vengeance.

Kitty excused herself and headed to the guest room. Rather than sitting by Parker, I sat in the chair instead of the couch. Kendall looked nervous. I couldn't imagine what was so important that she was staging a meeting with us, but I was about to find out.

"Mom. Dad. I asked to talk to you guys because I got some information today that I need to share with you," she said, anxiously.

Chapter 12

I could feel my heartbeat increasing the longer it took to just spit it out. Parker looked just as anxious as I felt. With everything that had happened over the last few days, either I needed a Xanax or a stiff drink. Or both.

"Spit it out, Kendall," Parker finally said.

"I'm pregnant," she said as her hands raised and covered her mouth.

"What?" Parker roared to life.

"What the hell were you thinking?" I asked on impulse.

"Stop!" Kendall said firmly. "It wasn't done on purpose!"

"Who is he? Where does he live?" Parker asked, putting on his shoes and his face turning a deep shade of red.

"Dad, you aren't going to go kill anyone. Your grandbaby will need her grandfather," she said.

Parker, at hearing the word grandfather, continued, "Not if I can help it! Someone impregnated my daughter!"

"Now Parker, it takes two to tango," I reminded him. "Who's the father, Kendall? Tell us about him," I said, trying to be the calm, realistic parent.

"Fuck that," Parker said.

"Wait a minute, did you say *her*?" I asked, the word registering in my head.

"Everyone, please calm down," Kendall insisted.

I started to survey her body from head to toe. She was a grown woman. She was probably five feet eight inches, medium-sized breasts, narrow waist, and a set of hips. And, now obvious to me, a rounded stomach. How had I missed this? I used to be so close to Kendall. Where had I gone wrong?

I clearly hadn't been spending much time with her or I'd have known this. She would have confided in me months ago. And the more I thought about it, I could recall her wearing some frilly one piece on the cruise while at the pool rather than her standard bikini. I thought she'd been maturing, instead, she'd been hiding her growing stomach.

"How far along are you?" I asked.

"Please sit down and I'll give you the details," she demanded. "I am twenty weeks this week. I met with my obstetrician today and that is when I found out that I'm having a little girl. Before you freak out more, I found out I was pregnant last week."

Parker sighed heavily, "Too late for an abortion."

"Parker!" I chided quickly.

How could he have jumped right to terminating the pregnancy. It wasn't like it was Kamdyn giving this announcement. It was Kendall. Our eighteen-year-old daughter. She was an adult. Decisions like this were hers and hers alone. Well, maybe the baby's father, but not Parker's or mine.

"This is going to ruin her entire life. What about school?" he fumed.

"What about school, Dad? Why can't I have a baby *and* go to school? Technology will allow me to go to school online! This isn't 1950," she pleaded.

"Kendall, who is the father?" I asked again.

She looked down at her feet and began playing with her hands, "I don't know."

"What. The. Fuck?" Parker said, raising his voice loud enough that Kitty came running out into the living room.

"What's wrong? Is everyone alright?" she asked, frightened.

"Everyone is fine, Grandma. I'm pregnant."

"Pregnant? Well, congratulations, sweetheart," she said as she crossed the room and gave her first granddaughter a hug.

"Kitty! This is *not* a good thing," Parker said as he directed his gaze directly at my mother.

"Oh hush up. In my day, girls got pregnant all the time at this age, and we turned out just fine. In fact, I was only nineteen when I got pregnant with Kate," she said as she meet his gaze and narrowed her eyes.

"It's not the same thing. You were married. You had a support system," Parker replied.

"And so does she, dammit!" Kitty roared back at him.

Finally, Parker admitted defeat and sank back down into the couch. I tried my hardest not to smile. In that moment, watching Kitty put Parker in his placed was highly satisfying to me. I was pretty upset that Kendall had gotten pregnant and didn't know who the father was, but I certainly would never turn my back on her.

"Kendall, do you have any idea who the father *might* be?" I asked compassionately.

"Well, kinda."

"Kinda?" Kitty asked.

"I had a one night stand. I'm pretty sure he's the father. The problem is that I don't know who *he* is," she admitted.

"Oh boy," Kitty said as she sat next to Parker on the couch.

"I'm so sorry," she apologized.

"Sweetheart, while disappointed in you, we still love you very much, and we will always be here to support you," I said, rising from the chair and giving her a hug.

Tears began to softly, quietly stream down her face and I felt her body release the tension it had. My precious daughter was melting in my arms, becoming my baby girl again. This wouldn't be an easy road for her, but she would manage just fine.

"Whoa, what's going on? Who died?" Carter said as he charged into the room and stopped in his tracks.

"Everything okay?" Kamdyn said from behind him.

"You want to tell them?" I softly asked Kendall.

"Tell us what?" Carter said as he looked from person to person.

"Hey guys. I'm pregnant. Surprise!" she said unenthusiastically.

"Holy shit!" Carter said with his mouth falling to the floor.

"Carter Daniel!" Parker snapped quickly.

"What?" he asked as he shrugged his shoulders then took off for his room.

Kamdyn gave her sister a hug and went to her room, announcing she had homework to work on. Parker sat down on the couch next to Kitty and I gave Kendall one last squeeze before pulling away. I quietly whispered in her ear that when everything settled down, everyone would be supportive, and she had nothing to worry about. She kissed my cheek and mumbled about having to get back to her apartment.

What type of reaction had she expected? Would it have been different if she knew who the father was? No matter what, I had twenty more weeks to adjust to the idea that I was going to be a grandmother whether I liked it or not.

I sunk back down into the chair and sighed heavily as Kitty announced she wanted to take a nap before dinner. Then, I was alone with Parker. After a few moments of silence, I looked at him and began to laugh. Seeing my laughter, he too began to laugh. What else could we do? The last few days of my life had been hell and all I could do was laugh because I didn't have any more tears to cry.

Finally, I got up from the couch, reached for his hand, and led him to our bedroom to have a more private talk. After thinking everything over, avoiding it altogether, and fighting myself, I was ready to break down the wall. I wasn't going to give in, but I'd at least talk.

"I want to talk," I said softly when the door was shut behind me.

"Thank you," he said with a deep sigh.

"I'm really hurt," I said plainly.

"I know you are. I didn't want to hurt you, but I know that I did. I can't make excuses because there aren't any. I completely disregarded our marriage and disrespected someone I value immensely."

"Hell yeah you did."

"Maybe it was a wake up call or something. I want to work through it and save our marriage, if you'll allow me to. I mean, everything on vacation was amazing and I want that again."

"I want this marriage to survive too. I can try, but I know it won't be easy to erase those images from my memory and to forgive you, but I can try. That's all I can really say. It's going to take work."

"That's all I can ask for."

"But I have to know *why*."

"I don't want my reasons to sound like excuses because you deserve better than that," he admitted with his tail between his legs.

"I need to know what was going through your head. I need to know how we can avoid this in the future. I need to know what we have to work on," I pleaded with him.

"We lost our intimacy for a long time. Years ago we focused on our careers, then our kids, and then ourselves. When we have had sex, it's been because it was convenient and not because we both wanted it," he said.

"I know," I admitted.

"What happened on our trip, that was the us that I've missed. But I felt like it was just because we were on vacation. Before that, it would be a convenient fuck in the shower, not making love," he continued.

"Was Renee an easy fuck or did you fall for her?" I crudely asked, dreading the answer either way.

Without any hesitation, he said, "An easy fuck."

I didn't cry or scream like I thought I might. I wasn't angry and I wasn't feeling aggressive. To my surprise, I was feeling excited. It was entirely foreign to me because I knew it was 100% inappropriate to feel like that, but it felt like I had no control over my own body. I reached for his hand and gently placed it on my breast.

"Kate, what are you doing?" he asked with surprise.

"You don't want to?" I asked as I lifted off my shirt.

"Are you sure you want to do this?" he asked softly.

"Didn't you say we needed to be more intimate? We don't have to if you don't want to," I said as I slid my bra off my shoulders and unhooked it.

"Oh I do. But is it the right thing to be doing?" he said, torn between wanting to have this intimate moment with me and letting everything between us settle first.

"You aren't exactly known for doing the right things lately. So should you really be the one asking that?" I pulled the pony tail out of my hair and shook my head.

"Kate, you're gorgeous," he said almost breathlessly.

I tugged at his shirt, removing it with a smooth over-the-head motion. As I began to throw it on the ground, he grabbed my wrists and pulled me into him, turning the tables on me and taking charge. I gasped quietly as I was caught off guard. He quickly twisted and turned, tossing me playfully on the bed. He then tugged at my pants and tossed them aside.

The sex had been passionate, aggressive, and filled with desire. We hadn't had sex like that for over a decade, and I was reminded just why I had enjoyed it so much. We laid side by side on our backs in our bed as we tried to catch our breaths. Each time Parker reached over and softly caressed my naked breasts, electricity shot through my body and I jumped with pleasure.

"That. Was. Amazing," I finally said.

"Yeah, it was. When was the last time we did *that*?" he asked before he leaned over and began kissing my neck.

"I don't even know, but can I have more?" I asked with a moan escaping from my mouth.

When he felt full, he stopped nibbling at my neck and went into the bathroom. I laid on the bed for a few more minutes and thought about the actual conversation we'd had prior to the mind blowing sex. I would accept some responsibility in the relationship breakdown and I would work on my part, but he should have come to me with the problem rather than seeking extra company. Confusion clouded my mind — I wanted to hate him, but I loved him deep down.

I was going to forgive him and work past this. I would do my part as long as he was doing his. I was genuinely going to have to stop playing the victim and focus on what I could control instead. What would it take to get past this though? Why did I think that I *could*?

I groaned at the thought, but rolled myself off the bed and went to join Parker in the shower. As much as I wanted to lay in bed and enjoy the exhaustion of my muscles, I had to get myself ready for work.

All the joy I had was sucked from me the moment I began drawing up the assignment board at work. Why was it so hard for people to come to work on a regular basis? I would be on the floor again, and I was not happy about it.

My saving grace, as always, was working next to Sam. I needed his comedic relief more than anything. Knowing everything that I've been going through the last week, he approached with two steaming hot cups of coffee and I immediately knew we were going to have a good night.

After the first few gulps, I felt ready to tackle anything and sat at the computer to get started. Even though I had received report, I wanted to read everything for myself so that if something happened, I could spring into action and the patient's care would flow seamlessly. Four rooms, four patients.

I debated in my head if I preferred coming in to empty rooms and filling them up or coming in to full rooms and emptying them. Admittedly, I wasn't a morning person. There was something satisfying about emptying the rooms and there was certainly more drama with the patients on this shift than the previous one.

"So Sam, what's new?" I asked as I read the computer screen.

"I've been seeing someone," he said with a boyish grin.

"Ooo-la-la. Give me details!" I begged.

"Well... His name is Trevor."

"Trevor, eh?"

"Trevor. That's all you'll get for now. I want to see where things go before I start sharing all the juicy details," he teased.

"Well, I can appreciate that! Wanna help me start an IV on a kid?" I asked with a laugh.

"Only if you'll help me hang insulin first," he countered. "That's fair."

After the insulin was hung and the IV had been started, I was able to discharge two of my patients. In a rare moment of quiet, I sat in one of the empty rooms and just listened. I heard the most interesting conversations. The unit clerk was secretly dating one of the PCAs, Sam's new relationship with Trevor was discussed, the latest in cell phone technology, and what we were missing on prime time television while we were at work.

I was just about to leave the room when I heard someone mention my name and I froze. I quickly debated if I wanted to hear what people said about me or not, but ultimately decided that, of course, I did. I tried to listen carefully to the words as well as to determine who the speaker was.

"I can't believe he did that to her! Such bullshit," voice #1 said.

"I agree. She's such a good person. She didn't deserve that," voice #2 responded.

"Probably because she's boring. They've been married forever. Probably wasn't putting out anymore," voice #1 said.

"That or the sex was boring. Either way it wasn't right," voice #2 said.

"But *her*? She's so trashy. She's willing to let anyone put their dick in her pussy," a third voice chipped in.

"I feel bad for her. Just when she gets her preceptor job, he goes and does that shit. Now everyone is talking about it. It's just wrong," voice #2 said.

"I don't know that I can look at him the same way anymore," voice #1 said.

"Shit! I can. He's fucking hot!" the third voice said. "Now that she's working nights, he probably has a new girl over every night. Hell, I'd go home with him. He makes a boat load of money!"

"Nikki! That's not right! You're so bad!" voice #2 said.

With a laugh, voice #3 added, "Of course I am! He wouldn't have to cheat on me. At least I could keep the spice alive in the bedroom!"

I rolled my eyes. Great! My co-workers thought I was pathetic. I was pathetic and my cheating husband was hot. Is that what everyone thought about me or was it just the young kids behind the desk scribing orders? I couldn't walk out of the room now and face them. First, I didn't want to know who it was that felt that way about me. I didn't even know who Nikki was. Second, I was mortified that people felt sorry for me.

And then there was the entire topic of people thinking about my bedroom skills. Ugh. That was none of anyone's business. It happened behind closed doors for a reason. I immediately send a text to Parker. He had to find a way to fix this. I was so close to crying, but didn't want to look even more pathetic that I already did.

I paged Sam to the room, and he arrived with a look of confusion. I was freaking out and needed someone to talk me off the ledge. Sam was the only person I could trust. When he saw my distressed face, he began to freak out, thinking the worst.

"What is up? Say something! You're freaking me out," he admitted.

"I came here to listen to everyone talking. Like recon. Anyways, the girls at the desk just had an entire conversation about me! They feel sorry for me! They had an entire discussion of my husband cheating on me. Of my bedroom skills, or lack thereof. How can I face my coworkers knowing that everyone feels pity for me and thinks I'm awful in bed?" I blurted out in a quick rush of words.

"Oh Kate! Not everyone feels sorry for you!" he said sympathetically.

"Don't lie to me! You can tell me the truth! They feel sorry for me. They said I was a bore. Ugh." I fought back tears.

"I'm being serious. Please don't stress about it. You know as soon as the next crazy thing happens, Dr. Cordova sleeping with Renee will be old news," he said and the words stung as soon as they left his lips.

"Please don't say that," I begged.

"Kate, I promise. This will all blow over," he pleaded.

"And when do you suppose the next great scandal will take place? I have so much on my plate and feel like I could explode at any time. I can't handle this too," I admitted.

My pager came alive with the message that I was receiving a new patient. I was in no mood to take care of patients, but I knew I had to put my own pride and personal problems aside. I needed to be a leader and show that what happens outside of work wouldn't impact my work performance. I painted on the happy face, left Sam standing in the dark room, and went to greet the new patient.

Just before I stepped into the new room, I heard a commotion from behind me and spun around. That's when it happened. That's when I realized Sam was actually my best ally in the entire world. Sam wasted no time after I'd left the room in creating the perfect plan to end the conversations about me. The perfect plan to get everyone to move on to the next big gossip drama.

Sam emerged from the room and loudly made a brief announcement to everyone that they needed to watch him make a statement. Just about everyone turned around, patients and staff, and watched him as he waltzed across the emergency room to where the doctor's computers were lined up. Several doctors were busy typing away and not paying attention to anything else, but Sam didn't seem to care.

He tapped Dr. Nathan Frost on the shoulder and stood waiting for him to turn around. When Dr. Frost did, Sam grabbed his hands and helped him to his feet. Dr. Frost looked somewhat confused and Sam said something quietly under his breath. Then, to the amazement of everyone watching, Sam leaned down and passionately kissed him.

Those watching began to buzz animatedly and pulled cell phones from their pockets to start the gossip mill. Sam had been right — my husband cheating on me was now old news. Sam had literally caused a scene to make me feel better and to make sure that everyone forgot all about my husband sleeping with his nurse. My heart melted with love for Sam. How would I ever be able to thank him?

Chapter 13

I stepped into the new patient's room and saw Reggie sitting on the stretcher. I rolled my eyes and knew exactly how this visit was going to go. Part of me felt comfort in the now familiar routine of Reggie's care and the other part felt irritation that we would be caring for him for the exact same issue for the billionth time.

"What do I owe the pleasure, Reggie?" I asked sarcastically.

"Well, I was out to dinner tonight and didn't feel right. I think my sugar is high," he said as if it were no big deal.

"You keep this up and you're going to need dialysis before the end of the year," I mumbled.

"Nurse Kate, I know. I can't help myself though," he said.

"You can't help yourself?"

"No, those little cupcake things are divine," he said, smiling at the memory in his head.

"Are you serious?"

"Yeah, and thinking of them makes me hungry. Any chance I can get a sandwich?" he asked seriously.

"No way in hell," I said as I walked straight out of the room to get the glucometer, shaking my head.

Sam was sitting at the computer when I sat at mine. I had to resist the urge to give him a big hug and a peck on the cheek. My heart overflowed just looking at him.

"That was epic. Thank you," I said to him.

"My pleasure. Thank you for giving me a reason to finally do that," he said leaning in and bumping our shoulders together.

"How long has it been going on? And what about Trevor?"

"His code name is Trevor. It's been going on for a few months now. He's wanted to tell people for months but I wasn't ready. Today I was. So I went for it," he said as he glanced up at Dr. Frost and winked.

"I'm glad. So happy for you," I said sincerely.

And I was. How could a girl ask for a better friend? Anyone willing to put themselves out there to save my butt would be classified as a winner in my book. On the flip side, Parker would still be hearing about the humiliation he caused me in my own department the next time I saw him. A text wasn't effective at getting my anger across.

When I went to check on the kid I'd started the IV on, she was fast asleep on her mother's chest. I was immediately transported back to the day that my own Kamdyn had been quite sick and required an IV in the emergency room. She had fought so hard during the procedure that once it was over, she fell asleep on my chest for hours. What I wouldn't give to go back to those days of being the person your child runs to.

I was quickly brought back to reality when my personal phone rang and I saw Parker's phone number and picture flash across my screen. I quickly debated between answering and letting it go to voicemail, but for the sake of hoping no one was injured, I answered. Why else would he be calling me in the middle of the night? Had he seen my text?

"Hello?"

"Um... Kate?" his voice came out shaky.

"Yes," I said with a little panic. "What's wrong?"

"Nothing. Sorry, nothing is wrong. I just wanted to tell you I have a case that's going to go late tomorrow and wanted to know if you wanted to bring me dinner when you got up, and we could eat together?" he asked, hesitation in his voice.

"I'm not sure about that," I admitted.

I felt guilty for saying no. I'd spent the last twenty-something years telling Parker yes and look where it had gotten me. And now, only several days after I caught him with his pants down, he was wanting to pretend that nothing had happened and have dinner like we used to when we were first married. Just because we'd had sex didn't mean all was forgiven.

Or was calling me in the middle of the night his idea of trying to repair our relationship? Was it just a response to my text about the staff talking about me? Why was I assuming the worst of everything? I had more questions than answers. I also wasn't usually the person to lack self-confidence like this. The throbbing behind my eyes made another appearance and I closed my eyes.

"Okay, it was just an idea," he said desperately.

Okay, he was trying and I shouldn't be difficult. But why should I make it easy? And why was he calling me in the middle of the night to ask me about dinner? The questions just kept streaming into my mind, one after another without an opportunity to answer them.

"Wait. Will *she* be there?" I asked.

"Yes. Unfortunately, I can't get around that," he said. I was happy he was telling the truth.

"In that case, yes. I get up around four o'clock. I could be there at, say, five? But right now I need to get back. I have a new patient," I said.

"Okay, thank you," he said. Before he hung up, he quietly added, "I love you, Kate."

I would show up and have dinner with my husband just to save face. I didn't want to let that homewrecker think she had succeeded in stealing my husband or ruining our relationship. I wondered if he'd talked to her since I caught them. Had they seen each other at work or had they talked on the phone? Maybe sent each other text messages?

She may have had him for a short time, but he was *mine*. Forever and always. He was always mine. I would fight for him. I might still be angry and upset, but I would always fight for him. I would always fight for our marriage. Of course, that was as soon as I stopped being so wishy-washy. Where had that version of Kate come from? I was annoying myself but I couldn't stop it.

I was glad he had thought of it though. Since we wouldn't see each other in the morning, it was nice that he was taking the extra steps to actually spend time with me. I could appreciate the effort even if I was playing hard-to-get and working through my anger.

My next patient came in complaining of shortness of breath, but was having no problems telling me about all the things I should be doing as I applied the nasal cannula under his nose and turned on the oxygen. Several times he reminded me that he had chronic obstructive pulmonary disease, COPD for short, and that something was *obviously* wrong since his nebulizer hadn't made things better for him. I tried to avoid rolling my eyes.

"Don't turn that oxygen up too high. I'm a retainer, ya know?" he said, referring to the belief that increasing his oxygen would lead to a higher carbon dioxide level and cause him to stop breathing at all.

"Do you smoke?" I asked as part of my assessment, ignoring the comment about being a retainer.

"Yeah, sometimes," he said casually and I, again, tried to prevent my eyes from rolling.

"How many packs do you tend to smoke in a day?" I asked, knowing damn well he didn't only smoke "sometimes" as he said.

"Oh, only about a pack these days," he said as if one pack per day was not a big deal.

"I see," I said as I continued to chart.

"What does that mean?" he asked defensively.

"What?" I asked, pretending I hadn't heard or understood his question.

"What does that mean?" he repeated, enunciating his words more clearly this time.

"If you stop smoking, you'd be able to breathe. But you already know that, don't you," I said as I continued my computer charting.

I typed "patient in denial about causes of symptoms and continues to smoke one pack per day on average, but likely more" and smiled to myself. I found smokers, drinkers, and drug seekers usually under exaggerated their actual use. Based on the smell coming from him, he probably smoked a cigarette in the car on the way to the emergency room. He was probably one of those guys that believes that smoking a cigarette will help him breathe rather than make it harder.

"I just can't breathe," he said and let out a forceful exhale.

"Well, for someone who can't breathe, you seem to be doing a lot of talking," I commented quietly.

I finished my assessment, rechecked his oxygen levels, and then left the room to find another patient being brought to my empty room. I began to wonder if I'd ever get to use the bathroom, let alone take a lunch break. But after this many years, I knew that those things were a luxury and not a privilege.

"Have you gone to lunch yet?" Mia asked as she walked past with my new patient in a wheelchair.

"Nope, not yet."

"Let me get this guy settled, and we can go together. I'll get Sam to cover your rooms, okay?"

Thirty minutes later, Mia and I sat down to lunch in the cafeteria. With my mother being in town, I hadn't really talked to anyone about all the things going on, so this thirty minutes was refreshing. Mia wasn't a judgemental type, and she was a good listener. She was also quickly becoming someone I reached out to. If Sam trusted her, I trusted her.

"So what are you going to do?" she asked after I told her about Kendall.

"I'm not going to do anything. I'm just going to be the best grandma you've ever seen. That's what I'm gonna do," I proudly proclaimed.

She laid a hand on my forearm and spoke, "I know you will be."

I let her hand linger for a moment longer than usual before I pulled my arm away and began to pack up the remnants of lunch and made a comment about having to get back. I wasn't sure if she was just being a good friend or what. I didn't want to think too much into it. Just because she preferred women didn't mean she was into me. I wasn't that narcissistic.

When I got back to my patients, the kid with the IV had been admitted and moved to the pediatric floor. Reggie was still demanding food, and the COPD guy was still pretending he couldn't breathe while spewing run-on sentences that made me winded just thinking about them. I also had a new patient where the kid had been. Would this night ever end?

The new patient was absolutely trashed. He claimed to have only had three beers, but there was zero possibility of that being the truth. The girl who had brought him in said she'd picked him up at a party and when he puked in her car, she'd brought him in. That alone seemed rather odd. If I'd picked up a guy and he'd puked in my car, I'd have kicked him out rather than driving him straight to the emergency room.

"Just so I'm understanding this, he called and asked for a ride?" I asked, trying to understand the story and the relationship between the two.

"Well, he found my profile and reached out to me," she said.

"Your profile?"

"Yeah. On the dating app YOLO," she said as she typed into her phone and then turned it around to show me.

"YOLO?" I asked skeptically.

"Yeah, ya know? You only live once." She then put her fist in the air and yelled, "YOLO."

I cringed. She wasn't kidding. This was a real thing. This was proof that I was getting old!

"You can upload your profile and it has a spot to put what type of relationship you're looking for and then if you like someone, they can reach you," she explained.

"So you don't know each other? He just reached out to you and you just went to pick up a stranger?" I asked, feeling scared for the next generation.

My own daughter was about as old as this girl and I prayed she had more street sense than to go to some random guy's house to pick him up in the middle of the night. A sickening thought crossed my mind. What if that's how she'd met the man she got pregnant by? Ew. I tried to shake the thought out of my mind and focus on the task at hand.

Momentarily, I thought of asking her to search for Kendall to see if she did have a profile. Finally, some common sense came to me and I kept my mouth shut. Maybe the old Kate was still inside my body after all?

"So when you got to his house, he was drunk?"

144

"No, he wasn't at his house. He was at a party. When I got there, he seemed pretty cool. But when he got into my car, his eyes like rolled back and stuff, and he started puking."

"Okay, let me make sure I'm on the same page. He reached out to you on... YOLO..." I lifted my fist into the air as she had when I said it. "And you went to a party where he was and thought he was pretty cool? What made you guys leave the party?" I asked with genuine curiosity.

"He wanted to go somewhere more private, ya know?" she said with a wink that made me sick.

"What made you want to bring him here versus taking him home and putting him to bed?" I returned the wink.

"Well, I don't know where he lives and like, what if he's a mass murderer or something?" she said, not even realizing how dumb her entire logic was when she'd gone to a stranger's address to pick up a stranger but then wouldn't take him to her house because he was a stranger.

"Never mind. We're gonna run some blood work and find out what's going on. You didn't see him drink anything, right?" I asked one final time before I left the room.

"Nope."

I couldn't help but shake my head. I also prayed that my children wouldn't be as stupid and made a mental note to check their phones for that YOLO app. At the computer, I found that Reggie was having a second round of blood work done and my COPD patient was having a second breathing treatment.

"Hey Kate?" a unit clerk called to me from her computer in the center of the unit.

"Yeah?" I responded as I walked closer to her.

"Your patient in 10 would like to know if he can go out for a smoke," she said with a knowing smile.

I quickly looked away after I acknowledged her statement. She was one of the girls who had been talking about me. I could only imagine what was being said in her head when she smiled at me. Was she picturing how pathetic I was in bed or how boring I was? I quickly tried to erase the thoughts from my mind.

"Oh Lord, help me now," I prayed as I walked towards room 10 to give him a piece of my mind.

"I heard you want to go for a smoke?" I asked the moment I stepped into the room.

"Yeah, can I do that? It'll help me breathe," he said as he removed the nebulizer mouthpiece for a moment to speak.

"Are you kidding me? You need your head checked. You're delusional if you think smoking will help you breathe. Smoking is what got you here in the first place. With all due respect, give it up," I said with a deep breath of my own. "That shit is going to kill you. Do you really want to suffocate to death?"

Maybe it was harsh, and maybe it was cruel to take the deep breath he craved right in front of him, but wanting to go smoke while you were unable to catch your breath was ridiculous. Next, the drunk guy would want another beer.

"Mia, if you could only see one type of patient for the rest of your career, which would it be? The COPD-er who wants to smoke, the diabetic who won't give up sugar, or the drunk who only had three beers?" Sam said when I returned to the computers, and we both laughed.

When I finally saw the day shift nurse, I was filled with joy. I was beyond ready for the night to be over and to get back home and back to the warm bed calling my name! AnneMarie had assigned one of the new graduates to relieve me, so I knew there would be a million questions, and she'd take notes, but at this point I didn't care. I saw the light at the end of the tunnel, and I was running for it at full speed.

"Good morning, Kate," Jenna said with enthusiasm.

"Yeah, something like that," I mumbled.

"Well, let me get my notepad, and we can get started, okay?" she said as she began to dig through her carefully packed bag.

"Just let me know when you're ready," I said, unenthused.

"Okay, I'm ready."

"Alright, the patient in 7 is Reggie."

"Oh, I know Reggie. He'll be happy to see me," she said with a sing-song voice that I wanted to smack right out of her.

"Cool. IV in right AC, insulin hanging. Wants food. Any questions?"

"Uh, let me see. What was his sugar when he came in?" she asked sweetly.

I rolled my eyes, but answered anyways, "531."

"Wow, that's pretty high. Any other symptoms?"

"That was a while ago now, can you look it up?" I begged.

This girl clearly hadn't worked a night shift in her life. My goal was to give her the essential information that she wouldn't be able to glean from a chart and get the hell out of the building, not socialize about how sad it was that the patients were here in the first place and give her a play-by-play of each patient's stay.

"Yeah, I suppose that's a good point. Room 9?" she finally said after considering my request for a moment.

"Drunk. Wants food. Just waiting for him to sober up and then it's a bus token back to wherever he came from," I said with a yawn.

"Harsh. Okay. Room 8?" she said judgmentally.

Where was the rule that I had to be nice? I generally tried not to scare the newbies, but I was tired and stressed. I didn't have time for this chit-chat. Every moment spent with her was a moment stolen from time in my bed.

If she worked in this emergency room as long as I had, she would understand. I gave it a year before she began to act just like I was. It's not that all drunk patients are bad, but when the same ones come in week after week, you begin to get a little immune to them. In fact, I once promised a drunk that if he would stay out of the ER for an entire month, I'd buy him a steak dinner. He was back the next night. If he had been smarter, he'd have just used a different emergency room, but not a chance. He claimed our turkey sandwiches tasted better than the other hospitals.

"Lastly, you have the guy in room 10 who is here for COPD. He wants to smoke," I said, thinking I was done and could finally leave.

"He wants to smoke? Is he serious?" she asked and I prayed I didn't have to stay and have an entire conversation with her.

"Yep, dead serious. Have a good day," I said as I grabbed my pen and headed for the break room.

The alarm chimed right at four o'clock that afternoon and despite wishing I could just silence it and go back to sleep, I wouldn't let that happen. Taking dinner to Parker was much more important than sleep today. Reminding myself of my best intentions, I rolled myself out of bed and dragged myself into the shower.

When I emerged fifteen minutes later, I was much more prepared for the task at hand. It was so much more than just taking Parker dinner. It was Parker making an effort. It was

Parker showing that he still loves his wife to the same people who knew he'd had an affair. And it was Parker showcasing his wife in front of the woman he had an affair with. And like hell would I let this chance to waltz into that department looking like a million dollars to deliver some dinner pass me by!

For the first time in a long time, I carefully applied makeup, was picky about what clothes I put on, and styled my hair. My usual wardrobe featured scrubs or pajamas, sweat pants or running shorts if I was lucky. I usually put my hair in a messy bun and I most certainly did *not* put on makeup. I had found a pair of skinny jeans in the closet, threw on a black fitted shirt, and a pair of black heels. I thought I looked pretty good. I gave myself a final look in the full-length mirror before leaving my room to have my mother approve.

With Kitty's jaw on the floor when she saw me, I didn't even have to ask for her opinion. It was either really good or really bad. Personally, I didn't want to know, so I didn't ask. I told her I'd be back in a bit, that I was taking dinner to Parker, gave her a peck on the forehead, and held my head high as I lifted the keys from their hook.

Twenty minutes later, my heels were tapping against the floor of the surgical unit as I carried dinner in one hand and my heart in the other. I stood at the welcome desk in the waiting room until the unit clerk returned to her desk and paged Parker. He emerged from one of the locked doors, greeted me with a kiss right there in front of everyone who was watching, and took the dinner bags from my hands. He placed his free hand in mine and led me to the staff break room where we could enjoy dinner together.

"You look beautiful," he said as we passed through the door.

"Thank you. You look handsome in those surgical scrubs," I teased.

My mind immediately flashed to the body underneath those scrubs. The surgical scrubs he wore were a little snug along his biceps and broad shoulders. His pants hung low on his waist and the sight of his ass made my blood pump a little faster in my own body. I felt a surge of warmth inside me and fought the urge to take him to the call room myself.

"If you wear that outfit again, I'm not sure I can control myself," he whispered in my ear.

Renee sat in the break room eating her own dinner and stopped with the fork in mid-air when Parker and I entered hand-in-hand. Parker gave her a nod and the air in the room became awkward. I smiled in her direction and made sure my chair was extra close to Parker when I sat down.

Parker and I chatted about the kids while we ate dinner while Renee pretended we didn't exist. I tried my best to be flirtatious, but I was a bit rusty. Several times when I'd laugh, Renee would shoot me a side glance, but I kept on enjoying my dinner with my husband. When we finished eating, we cleaned up the table together and I kissed Parker.

As we headed out the door, I called out, "It was nice to see you again, Renee. You look good with your clothes on."

Her eyes narrowed and if looks could kill, I'd have been dead on the spot.

Chapter 14

At the end of the week, Kitty was wanting to stay, and I was ready for her to leave. My life wasn't going well, and she thought she could fix it. The thing she didn't remember was that this was only one small blurb in a fabulous life. I'd managed to get myself to this point and I'd managed to get myself out of it too.

Sure, my husband got caught cheating on me and my eighteen-year-old daughter was pregnant, but there were far worse things in life than that. I had a roof over my head, food on the table, and I accepted the night shift preceptor position. On top of that, I had three beautiful children, supportive friends, and amazing family.

What did she think she could do? She couldn't fix my marriage. That was between Parker and me. She could try to distract me, but that wouldn't solve anything. On top of everything, I was so confused about my own feelings. Until I figured *me* out, how could anyone help me figure out *us*?

Kitty went to each of the children, lined up by age, and kissed them on the forehead and told them to behave. When she got to me, she hugged me and whispered into my ear to call her if I needed *anything*. I wouldn't be calling her. I could stand on my own two feet. When she got to Parker, she faked a kiss and pleasantries, but I saw her pinch him hard. I stifled a laugh.

None of the kids were aware anything was wrong between Parker and I. Parker slept on the couch in our room, but as far as the kids were concerned, there was absolutely nothing wrong with anything. I was thankful that my mother had kept everything quiet. She wasn't one to keep quiet, but I was glad she had the decency when it came to this, something major, she had kept quiet.

And then, just as she'd arrived, she was gone. As I watched her little car drive off down the lane, I was torn between being happy she was gone and maybe missing her just a little bit. The kids barely waited until she'd gotten into the car to run back inside to their important little lives. I rolled my eyes at the world and went back inside myself to get ready for work that night.

When I arrived, I was back on the floor thanks to an employee calling in sick. Again. I swore that no one has a work ethic anymore. I also had a note from AnneMarie that she wanted to meet with me in the morning before I left. Now I was left to wonder all night long what I'd done wrong and why I was being called to the "principal's office". I didn't have time to focus on that though since it was a Saturday night and all hell was breaking loose.

Now that I was making the assignments, I had purposely kept myself far from triage. I'd also purposely assigned myself to a team between Sam and Mia. If I was going to have to work the floor, at least I was going to enjoy the people I was working with.

I gulped down an extra cup of coffee before my shift had even started and took report from Betsy, the cute, dark haired day shift nurse. She wasn't her normal bubbly self tonight, which was a bad sign from the start. She was leaving me with four full rooms. Rooms full of jerks. Her term, not mine. And to add salt to the wounds, it was a full moon.

I braced myself when I entered Room 5 to meet the sixteen-year-old boy who had gotten overly intoxicated at a party. Word was we had yet to reach his parents. I laughed inside because he reminded me of Carter, and then I cried because he reminded me of Carter. When I entered, he completely ignored me as he continued to talk on his phone. I was used to this, and personally, I'd rather he didn't talk to me while I worked anyway. I took his free arm and began taking his blood pressure, checking his IV site, and documenting on the computer. Of course, his blood pressure was a little too low and his IV site happened to be red and swollen. I finished charting and left the room, hoping he'd just finished his call by the time I returned with new IV supplies.

My wish was *not* granted, and he was now arguing with someone when I returned. I gave him my best "mom look" and he quietly told the person he had to go and hung up. I barely spoke as I told him what I was going to do. I made it perfectly clear that if he didn't cooperate, I'd call security in to help me.

"It doesn't work like that, ya know?" he said.

"What doesn't?" I asked, not understanding.

"You can't just call security. They won't just let you do whatever you want to me. I have rights, you know?" he said.

I looked him dead in the eye and said, "Try me."

I wasn't going to let a drunk little smart ass get under my skin. But I would treat him like I would my own child. If he wanted to press his luck, I'd grab a bigger needle to start the IV in his hand rather than the small one I had intended for his arm. He didn't fight. He just narrowed his eyes and watched my every move, which was fine by me.

As someone who wasn't really superstitious, I had never believed in the black cats, walking under ladders, and crazy people emerging from their hideouts on a full moon. Until I began working in the emergency room, that is. Without fail, a full moon left even the most confident nurses preparing for the craziest of things to happen.

When the schizophrenic woman who had swallowed safety pins arrived with police on either side of her, I looked towards the sky and said a cursed prayer. I'd given up asking how or why many years ago. Frankly, no one ever had an answer. I simply did my job with as few words as necessary and went on my way.

When my next patient told me he was confident he had worms in his stomach but couldn't say how they got in there, I went straight to the break room and poured myself a large cup of coffee. I had to wait for this guy to poop in order to prove him right or wrong.

"How's your night going?" Sam asked casually in passing.

"It's a full moon," I said, and he quickly agreed.

That night I also managed to care for an elderly woman who went on a shoplifting rampage, slipped, fell, and broke her hip. Another was bitten by her cat when she attempted to give it a bath. And finally, I had a woman who insisted that her baby wasn't breathing but presented with a life-like doll.

It was when we received the call that the medics were bringing in a woman who had been stabbed in the chest, that all hands were on deck. Generally, we had several more nurses attending our trauma rooms than our other rooms, but when we received calls of critical patients, everyone did their part to give the patient the best chance at life.

Because my patients were stable and waiting for imaging or blood results, or a bowel movement, I stepped up and offered my services. A special trauma code was called which brought staff from the trauma department, radiology, unit clerks, PCAs, nurses, and the emergency room physician to the room prior to the ambulance arriving at our back door.

I heard the sirens approaching as I waited at the back door with Helen, one of our seasoned trauma nurses. The engine was barely off when a medic exploded from the back of the ambulance and the stretcher was wheeled out, revealing a heavy set woman clutching at her chest and moaning.

We rushed her to our trauma room and began doing a more thorough assessment as staff began shouting out their findings and the physician responding with verbal orders. From an outsider's perspective, it was chaos. For me, it was what I lived for.

She continued to moan as an IV was started, blood was drawn, and the wound assessed. It was during this time that the monitor leads went flat and the alarm began to sound. Someone shouted out that we were losing her as the physician jumped into action and cracked her chest open further and began to hand pump her heart.

Something in me began to see the entire scene in front of me in slow motion. The noise became a blur and the lights brightened. Maybe it was an out-of-body experience or something? I stood frozen by the patient's feet as nurses and doctors moved around me, working to save her life.

Metal paddles appeared and were used to shock her heart several times between the hand massage from the physician. The patient made no noise and her hand went limp and fell off the bed. The room continued to swirl around me. This had never happened to me before.

Suddenly, the room went black and I knew nothing of the surrounding scene.

My eyes fluttered open and for a brief moment, I panicked. Why was I laying on the floor in the trauma room? Why were people rushing around me? What the hell had happened? I tried to stand but I felt a hand preventing me from doing so and someone softly telling me to relax. Was I dead?

"What is going on?" I asked the soft voice.

Mia came into my view and said, "You passed out, sweetie. Just lay down for another minute or so while I get you some water, okay?"

I listened and rested my head on the folded blanket under my head. I felt a sharp throbbing behind my eyes and I thought my head might explode if I stared up at the bright lights, so I quickly closed my eyes and squeezed them shut. When Mia returned, I refused to open them. I felt a straw push at my lips and I reluctantly took a sip.

The cold water burned as it went down my throat. I vaguely remembered trying to help save a woman's life, but there was no patient on the stretcher above me. I slowly opened one eye and watched as Mia fumbled with a blood pressure cuff.

"Can I get up now?" I asked, still unsure what had happened.

"Let me take your blood pressure first," she directed.

For a second time, I laid my head back on the folded blanket behind my head and shut my eyes as she inflated the cuff around my arm and then slowly released the air. Slowly the memories of what had been happening before my world went black returned to me. I saw Dr. Frost crack open a woman's chest and massage her heart with his gloved hand.

I opened my eyes again and looked at Mia, then asked, "Did she live?"

"No," she said quietly, shaking her head.

"Did I pass out?" I hesitated to ask.

"Yeah."

"What the hell is wrong with me?" I asked before I had a chance to stop myself.

156

The question had been meant to be a thought, but my mouth opened and the words flew out before I could stop them. Why were so many strange things happening to me? I'd been doing this job for a very long time and my gut told me *something* wasn't right. It was completely out of character for me to say the things I'd been saying to patients and to pass out in the middle of a trauma. Where had cool, confident Kate gone?

"Babe, I don't know," she said as she brushed a strand of hair from my face.

The act felt strangely intimate. Was I attracted to Mia or was I imagining things again? Everything in my life was confusing as hell. I just wanted to go back to normal. Back to my routines. Back to a life I understood and had control over.

I quietly knocked on Kamdyn's door. I knew she was in there as I had seen her getting off the bus through the window in the library as I read. I also heard the bedroom door close a short time later which signaled she had entered the "Kam-DEN" as she liked to call it. I had been waiting for the perfect moment to talk with her about so many things, but had realized that there probably would never be a perfect moment.

"Yeah?" she called.

"Can I come in?"

"Yeah."

Opening the door, I glanced around her room. Everything was perfectly organized, her bed was made, and nothing littered the floor. She was sitting at a small desk against the far wall with an open book in front of her. The light pink walls were the only remnant of the nursery that this room had once been.

"Have a minute to talk?" I asked as I stepped into the room and sat on her bed.

"Do I have a choice?"

"Not really."

"Well, then yes, I have a minute. What do you want to talk about?"

"Everything. Boys, school, the things going on around here, your friends..."

"Really, Mom?" she said, rolling her eyes.

"Really. I've noticed how you've been more distant since you started dating Brett and I know you well enough to know that *something* is bothering you. I also know that you don't always want to talk about it, but as your mom, it's my job to try," I said sympathetically.

"No, it's not," she said.

"Yes. Yes it is. Sometimes I wish it wasn't because sometimes I don't want to talk about the unhappy, unfun, and difficult things either, but I know that we have to," I said.

"So you're obligated?" she said with a sassy tone.

"Not exactly. I *want* to talk to you, but I also know it's hard to talk about difficult things at times."

"I see. So what do you think is going on?" she asked, now probing me for answers.

"I don't know. That's why I'm here. How are things with your friends? Things with Brett?" I asked, trying desperately to start the conversation.

"Mom! I'm *not* going to talk about that with *you*. I'm just not," she said as she threw her arms up and stood from her chair and began to pace the room. "I don't know why you're doing this. If I had something to talk about, wouldn't I come talk to *you*?"

"I suppose you might. Most teenagers don't want to talk to their parents though. I know that I really didn't want to go to my mom, but I always felt better when I did because she always had great advice," I pleaded.

"You're just saying that."

"Nope. Not just saying it. I'm speaking the truth. Come sit down and talk to me. Really talk to me. I probably know more about what you're going through than you think."

She took a seat next to me and for a flash of a moment, she was my baby girl again. I just prayed that whatever she had to say to me wouldn't devastate me. I hoped that her father and I weren't the cause of her distress.

"Okay, fine. You won't quit until I talk, so I might as well just get it over with. I like a boy. I don't know if he likes me or not," she said with a weight coming off her shoulders.

"Brett?"

"Garrett."

"What happened to Brett?" I asked, thinking it hadn't been too long ago when she'd started dating him.

"Oh Mom! He's old news," she said as she rolled her eyes.

"Okay, so why do you think Garrett likes or doesn't like you?"

"I think he does like me too, but he's not going to make the first move and I'm too afraid to do it too. Like what if I do it, and he *doesn't* like me back? Then I'm going to humiliate myself in front of people," she said, clearly stressing over this decision.

"Why not just pull him aside and tell him?"

"What would I say? It's not like I can just come right out and tell him."

"Back in my day," I laughed, "We used to write each other notes and pass them between classes. Then, the other person had time to think about it and write a response. Have you thought about going old school and writing a note?" I suggested.

"No, Brett wrote me a note telling me he liked me, so I can't just write one to Garrett. Besides, what if he showed it to his friends," she said as she thought it over in her head.

Smart girl. Making sure that when you confess to something big, something personal, you don't have any proof that it was ever said or done. Where did this girl get all these smarts? By her age, I certainly hadn't learned all that. Of course, I grew up in an era without the internet destroying lives every day.

"At some point you have to take a chance," I said as I smiled at her.

"I can't. I can't. Not after what happened with Brett last month," she said, realizing her error and covering her mouth immediately and her eyes growing wide.

"Oh boy. What happened with Brett last month?" I hesitantly asked.

"Oh Mom. Middle school is complicated. Eighth grade is complicated. Can't I just skip ahead to ninth?"

I laughed, "Of course not. It's going through all of this stuff that makes things better in ninth," I explained.

"Well, I hate it. All the kids are so immature. I feel like I can't win no matter what I do."

"Prepare to have that for a while," I lamented.

"Well, when Brett was my boyfriend he sat next to me on the bus. He kept flirting with me and I flirted back. Then one day, he asked if he could touch my boob. I didn't know what to say, so I ended up saying yes. Next thing I knew, his hand was under my shirt, and he was touching my boob," she admitted.

I cringed inside. My baby girl wasn't such a baby anymore. Boys were after her boobs, and I was powerless to stop the

160

little pricks. At that age, boys only think with their penises and I prayed that fondling my daughter's breast was all this boy did to her.

"If you didn't like it, you should have told him no," I encouraged.

"But that's the problem. I *did* like it. I liked it a lot. I've never felt like that before. I don't know. I can't explain it."

I could have died right there. Not only was she no longer my baby girl, she was entering womanhood. Clearly I had done a piss poor job of explaining the birds and bees to my two other children and I wasn't sure if I should be attempting it for the third time or if I should leave it to Parker. Then, of course, I remembered how he felt about monogamy lately and thought that maybe I *was* the best person to educate her about sex.

"Okay, so how does this involve this Garrett kid?"

"Well, I told Brett that I liked it. So then every day on the bus, he would feel my boobs. And then one day, I wanted more. We agreed to meet one day at his house, but I chickened out. When I didn't show up, he told everyone that I had big nipples," she started to cry.

"What's wrong with big nipples?" I asked.

"I don't know. You tell *me*. I figured it was a bad thing since he was saying it just to get back at me," she admitted.

"There is nothing wrong with having big nipples," I laughed quietly.

"There isn't?" she asked hopefully.

"Absolutely not. I see them all the time, and they come in all sorts of sizes. Don't let those boys convince you there is anything wrong with your body! And I'm not just saying that because I'm your mom. I'm being serious. I'm saying it as a nurse."

"How do I convince Garrett? I want him to touch my boobs too," she admitted, completely missing the fact that I did *not* want to hear about this or guide her in how to get boys to want to be sexual with my baby girl.

"Wow, I'm not sure how to answer that," I said awkwardly.

She sighed heavily, "I guess I'll just have to tell him there isn't anything wrong with my nipples and see what he says, right?"

"Something like that."

"If he does like me and wants to do more than touch my boobs, what do I do?"

And this is where I shuddered and debated what to answer with. I had to choose my words carefully and I knew that in the end, I'd be blamed for anything that went wrong. It was a battle I couldn't win. With my new mindset of just saying whatever comes to the top of my head, right or wrong, I went for it knowing I'd regret it later anyway.

"Well, you do what feels right."

She bounced up and gave me a tight hug. Then, she announced she had some homework to finish and asked to be left alone, but I caught her picking up her cell phone as I left the room. I prayed she wouldn't be sending nude pictures to boys. Maybe she was going to search for pictures of boobs to determine that her nipples were perfectly fine, if she hadn't already. All I could do was shake my head and return to my book. My head was pounding again.

When Parker came home from work late, the kids and I had already had dinner. I was soaking in a warm bubble bath while the kids were doing whatever kids do. I was pretty sure Kamdyn was still in her room since she had only come out for dinner and then immediately returned. Carter had been brought home from practice by Jayden's mom, taken a shower, ate dinner, and then rushed off to his own sweet paradise in the basement.

I only knew Parker was home because I had received the doorbell alert that someone was near the door on my phone. He would have to fend for himself for dinner because I wasn't getting out of this bathtub. I had three more chapters left of my book, and I was going to read each of them before I went to bed.

Parker peeked his head into the bathroom and smiled when he saw me. I looked up and smiled sweetly. It was weird — I wasn't sure how I was feeling that particular moment. Maybe a mixture of happiness, sexiness, and anger. Even though I was angry with him and hurt, I was still happy to see him. And I was still drawn to him. I was sick of being so conflicted and without any control over my emotions.

"Hey beautiful," he said with a big smile.

"You're just saying that because I'm naked, aren't you?"

"No, but it's not a bad idea," he teased.

"I see. Do you work tomorrow?" I asked.

"Why do you do that? Why do ya gotta bring work into it? There goes everything I was imagining I could do to you. When I compliment you, you always brush it off," he said angrily.

"Sorry. It's an old habit that needs to die," I responded.

"I hope to clean out that closet in the basement," he said before closing the bathroom door.

I was angry with myself for how that exchange had gone. He was right. It was *that* behavior that had driven us apart in the first place. My avoidance of anything sexual or intimate. Why had I done that? Why did I feel I needed to? Was something wrong with me? Putting my book safely on the top of the toilet, I got out of the tub and dried off.

I stood looking in the mirror for a few minutes. I could see stretch marks across my abdomen from three pregnancies. I had a scar near my belly button and one on my side from having my appendix removed many years ago. My breasts hung lower than they used to. My butt wasn't very perky anymore either and had cellulite.

Parker had loved me through each year of my body changing. He'd traced my stretch marks with his finger while his other hand gracefully laid on our newborn daughter as she breastfed. It was the breastfeeding that caused those breasts to hang so much lower than they used to. When Parker looked at my body, he saw memories and not imperfections.

Those three chapters could wait. I walked confidently into our bedroom to seduce my husband.

Chapter 15

I hated having to fill in on the floor, but when I entered the triage room, the stench of the patient stole my breath! It was a combination of old urine, booze, sweat, and vomit. I could see the leftover food still in his beard. I noticed his boots were muddy and falling apart. His hair was greasy and I could see the caked dirt under his fingernails.

How you react to a patient like this really defines what type of nurse you are. A good nurse will wish that she has the ability to give him a bath, feed him, and find him proper shelter. A worn out nurse, more like myself, thinks "here we go again, another homeless drunk". A newer nurse might think that she can change him. I've been each of these in my career at one point or another. Today, I was the irritated nurse who only wanted clean patients.

"What brings you in today?" I sighed heavily.

"I have a headache," he quietly replied.

"Maybe you shouldn't have drank so much."

He looked up and said, "I haven't drank in ten years, ma'am."

It was bullshit. All bullshit. I could smell the booze on him. I knew he'd been drinking. I was sure he was hungover and hungry and had decided that the emergency room was the best place to go to sleep this off. The shelter wouldn't take him in this condition.

"On a scale of zero to being hit by a car, how would you rate your headache at right now?"

"A seven," he offered realistically.

"When did your headache start?"

"About an hour ago."

"Have you taken any Tylenol or Motrin?"

"Yes."

"How long ago?"

"About an hour ago," he repeated.

I wanted him to drop the act and tell me the truth. Clearly, he was telling me the scripted answers he had memorized. I had the PCA come in and take his vital signs. His blood pressure was definitely elevated, but most of these guys never filled their hypertension meds anyway.

"Any other symptoms?" I asked.

"I've been seeing double over the last few days, but I didn't think that was anything to worry about," he said slowly.

"You said your last drink was ten years ago?"

"Yes, ma'am."

"Any medical history I need to know about?"

"I haven't seen a doctor in ten years, so I'm really not sure."

"Do you take any medications?"

In my head, I was screaming for him to tell me the truth. To tell me that he drinks a fifth of vodka every night and smokes a pack of cigarettes every day. I wanted him to fess up and admit that this wasn't really a headache. I wanted him to be just another homeless drunk.

"No, ma'am. Just the Tylenol I got from my neighbor tonight."

His neighbor? Maybe he lived in one of those tent cities where everyone camps out in some park. My mind began to wonder briefly, imaging him knocking on a pretend tent door and asking for some Tylenol. Would the neighbor invite him in?

"Have a seat in the waiting room, and we'll get you back to see the doctor as soon as we can."

"Thank you, ma'am," he said as he shuffled back out the door.

I noticed as he walked he leaned slightly to the left. He must have an old injury to that leg, I thought. I'm sure living on the streets was a difficult thing, and he'd been jumped for booze or something once. I didn't spend much time thinking about it before I called the next patient back.

My next patient was here to be seen for a stomach ache. I was sick of seeing patients for stomach aches. It felt like everyone was a whiny baby tonight. Do people really wake up in the middle of the night and just decide to visit the ER for the stomach ache they have had *all* day?

"I'm not sure when it started, but I stayed home from work today," the woman replied.

"Any nausea, vomiting, or diarrhea?" I asked politely as one can when asking about these gross body functions.

"Not really. I thought I was going to puke once, but I didn't."

"What have you had to eat today?"

"I had left over pizza for breakfast but felt sick, so I went back to bed. Then, I went to Taco Bell for lunch. Then, the stomach pains started, so I had leftover lasagna at home for dinner. I haven't eaten since then." I wanted to smack the woman.

"Have you had this stomach pain before?"

"Once in a while I get it real bad, but I haven't had it in a while," she said, clutching at her stomach.

"Have you ever had an ultrasound on your gallbladder?"

"Never."

"Okay, here is a cup for a urine sample that the doctor will want. You can put it in this bag when you're done and bring it to the desk. We will get you back as soon as we can," I said, sending her to the packed waiting room.

Even though I disliked triage, I had always kept a smile on my face and tried my best to enjoy it. I was their first impression of our emergency room, and I felt it was an extremely important assignment to have. It wasn't saving lives in a trauma room, but it was still important. My irritation and aggravation right now were alarming.

A patient room became available and I looked over the list of waiting patients to determine who to bring back next and headed for the waiting room. I always dreaded this part when there was a packed waiting room because inevitably, someone would have a bout of self-righteousness and think that people should see the doctor in the order of arrival.

"Yavonne?" I called out.

"Wait a minute! I've been here for over an hour and that woman just got here!" called a short, hairy man from the corner.

Here we go again. I worked hard to restrain myself, but lately this was becoming more and more difficult. I took a deep breath and turned toward the man as, who I assumed was Yavonne, stood and headed in my direction.

"Sir, this isn't your family physician's office. There aren't any appointments, and we don't see people based on when they arrive. We see people based on the severity of their needs," I said as I tried very hard to keep my voice steady.

"Well that's bullshit," he said as he stood up.

The woman who had been walking towards me spoke, "I don't know what this Yavonne chick is here for, but I agree with this guy. My grandmother has been waiting for three hours to be seen and it's unacceptable."

Okay, definitely not Yavonne.

"Anyone who feels our system is an inconvenience can easily go across town and use the ER there. But here, we will see everyone based on acuity and I cannot guarantee a short wait because, as you can all see, there are lots of people who need our help tonight," I said, continuing my steady voice.

"Bullshit," someone called, but I was unable to see where it came from.

"Look. I don't give a shit who you all are. All I care about is what you are here for. If you think your flippin' hangnail at 02:00 a.m. is really that big of a deal, you're a selfish person. Someone in this emergency room is *dying*. Did you hear that?" I paused for dramatic effect. "Dying. If you think you are more important than us trying to save that life, then get the hell out and don't let the door hit you on your way out."

I got off my soapbox, called for Yavonne one more time, and when the young girl approached, I took her to the empty room. The waiting room was full of energy but I didn't give a shit. I hated selfish people. People that clearly had no compassion for others. I was proud of myself for the restraint I'd shown, but I was also pissed that I'd stooped to their level. I was so quick to become angry. So quick to feel attacked.

Once Yavonne was settled in her room, I returned to the triage area and saw that three new patients had arrived during that debacle. My joy overflowed. So did my sarcasm. If the mood in the waiting room was as dark each time I went to call someone back, I might not survive my night.

As I was triaging the next patient, there was a commotion from the waiting room. As I made my way out there, I kept thinking the patients were having an uprising. Instead, I noticed that my fake headache man was on the floor. Quite dramatic for a headache, I thought. I quickly took a new set of vital signs, and his blood pressure had gone through the roof.

I called to the back for a stretcher, and we got him back to a room that had just cleared. Of course, at that point my job was done, and I returned the triage area and resumed triaging the patient I had been before the interruption.

Later, it was from Sam that I learned that the headache guy had actually been having a stroke, not just a headache. And he was now unconscious, and they were unsure if he'd wake up. They had called his family to make decisions about his care.

"How did you find his family?" I asked, interested.

"What do you mean? We looked at his emergency contact list he gave at registration," Sam said.

"Wow, I thought most homeless people didn't have family anymore."

"Homeless?" Sam asked, confused.

"Yeah, isn't he homeless?"

"Uh, no. He lives a few blocks away from me. He's always making sure that the kids get to the bus stop safely, mowing neighbors yards when they are sick, and he'd drop anything to help anyone," Sam said, irritated I'd insulted his friend.

"Wow, I totally got that one wrong," I said, shaking my head.

"Yeah, you sure did."

Upset with myself, I wanted to follow Sam. I hadn't meant to upset one of my best work friends. I didn't have many friends at all these days, but Sam was one of them. I cursed at myself.

But on my way back to triage, I couldn't help but hum the tune to "Another One Bites the Dust". Was it wrong? Oh yes. Did it stop me? Oh no. I'm not sure what had gotten into me, but I was emotionally void at this moment.

I called the next patient into the triage area and was surprised when the man was escorted by a uniformed police officer. The man, wearing handcuffs, refused to sit down.

"I can't."

"Why not?" I said, eager to hear the answer.

"I got into a fight with my woman, and she called the pigs on me. I got real nervous they would find my stash, so I shoved my three bags of coke up my ass so they wouldn't find them, but my woman ratted me out," he said, as if this were just another day.

"Excuse me? You shoved what? Where?"

"Ugh. Open up your ears. I shoved three baggies of cocaine up my ass," he repeated slowly and loudly.

"Wow. I thought I'd seen enough dumb for one day but I think this one takes the cake," I said more to myself. "So why can't you take a seat?"

"If I sit down, those baggies will burst and I'll be dead. Do you have Narcan on hand?" He was 100% serious.

"First, this is an emergency room. Of course, we have Narcan available. We use it daily, in fact. Second, you have the same chance of shitting yourself every time you sit down as you do having the baggies burst when you sit down. Sit your ass down. Please," I said slowly, firmly, and loud enough that others outside the room might be able to hear.

He sat down. Nothing burst and he didn't die doing so. I got his vitals and then sent him and the officer, who was trying desperately to keep from laughing, to a room. I pitied the doctor who would have to dig those out, but I shook my head and laughed once he was gone. No one ceased to amaze me anymore.

By 07:00 a.m., there were still patients in the waiting room to be seen. I gladly handed off responsibility to Adel when she arrived. It appeared that the day shift was going to start off busy as hell, but some days were like that. I, however, planned to start my day off tucked deep under the covers.

First, I had to meet with AnneMarie since I hadn't been able to make our last meeting. I found her drinking coffee at her computer and took a seat across from her.

"What's up?" I said.

"I'm gonna make this short and sweet since I'm sure you're tired. I've had a few complaints from patients about the way you've been treating them. It's completely out of character for you, so I'm going to count this as a warning. Please try to control your mouth," she pleaded.

I just nodded and headed home. I didn't have anything to say.

Around 02:00 p.m., my phone started ringing and in my sleepy haze, I answered it. I don't know why, but I don't think I'd been in very deep sleep. Most likely, I answered it because the screen read "Franklin High School" and that could only mean trouble with Carter.

"Hello, Mrs. Cordova?" a woman asked.

"This is she," I said, my mind flashing straight to the previous phone call I received last month and praying this woman wasn't sleeping with my husband.

"This is Principle Ruggles. I'm calling regarding your son, Carter." While I felt relieved the woman wasn't sleeping with my husband, I was instantly worried about Carter.

"Oh boy, what has he done?"

"Well, I'd like to discuss that with you and your husband, in person, if possible."

"Okay. When did you have in mind?"

"Today or tomorrow if possible?"

"I can meet with you today, if you'd like," I kindly suggested.

"That would be excellent. In the meantime, your son has been suspended from school until our discussion. I will see you this afternoon," she said quickly before hanging up the phone.

It was the word "suspension" that jolted me from my sleepy state and made me completely awake. I could only imagine what Carter could have done to get himself suspended. Growing up, he'd been such a sweet, caring boy. It was around age fourteen that he began to become a little asshole. I thought it was just a stage, but with each passing year, he became more and more difficult to manage.

I really needed Parker to be the one spending time with him. To start laying down the law. To show him how a man is supposed to act. I called Parker's phone and left a message with Kim, the "fabulous" traitor surgical assistant, to have him call me when he was out of surgery. She said his schedule was clear when he finished the current case, but I knew exactly how that kind of stuff went.

I threw myself in the shower, dressed in a pair of jeans and a "mom" t-shirt before heading straight to my favorite device in the entire house: the coffee pot. After the first cup, I was feeling a bit more clear and ready for the meeting that I was dreading. I filled my travel mug to the brim, grabbed my keys from their hook, and drove to the school.

To my surprise, when I arrived at the principal's office, Parker was already there. Dressed in surgical scrubs and his lab coat, I couldn't help but swoon for a brief moment before remember what he had done and feeling sick to my stomach again. I thought I'd already moved past those feelings, but they took me by surprise.

Carter was supposed to be at baseball practice, but here he was, sitting next to Parker. The two men in my life, causing trouble and giving me headaches.

Mrs. Ruggles opened her office door, called for us to come in, and Parker and I took seats on either side of Carter. The office was small. Not only was it small, she had shelves stuffed with folders, binders, books, trinkets, and trophies. The walls were plastered with degrees, letters of recommendation, and pictures of her own kids. Instantly, the temperature in the room went up five degrees and I felt panic begin to rise inside me and the nagging pain start up again behind my eyes.

"Now, Carter, would you like to tell your parents why I've called this meeting and why you've been suspended?" Mrs. Ruggles asked, keeping a stern face.

"Not really," he admitted.

"Alright then, I don't have time for games. Dr. and Mrs. Cordova, your son was caught kissing and fondling a young lady this afternoon in the ladies' bathroom," she said with a completely straight face.

I rolled my eyes and said, "What the hell, Carter?"

Parker looked at Carter and for a moment, I thought he was going to give the kid a high-five, but instead said, "Carter, what were you thinking?"

"He wasn't thinking. Duh," Mrs. Ruggles said as she rolled her eyes.

"Clearly. Carter, what do you have to say? Anything?" I asked.

"Nope," he said smugly.

I wanted to smack the smugness right off his face, but felt that CPS might end up getting called if I unleashed my current pent-up aggression. I didn't even know where it had come from, but I was feeling enraged and I wasn't sure if I had control of it.

174

"Alright then. Carter will be suspended five school-days starting tomorrow, he will write a 500-word essay about his transgressions, as well as perform ten hours of community service. I expect that those can be completed next week while he is off," Mrs. Ruggles said.

"Yep," Carter said.

"Sounds good to me," Parker said. "Are we done?"

"If you have no objections, then yes."

Parker and Carter both stood and turned straight for the door before I'd barely grabbed my purse from the floor. As I started for the door, Mrs. Ruggles stopped me.

"Kate, can I talk to you in private for a moment?"

"Uh, sure."

I closed the door and sat back down. Mrs. Ruggles, or Jess as I preferred to call her, and I had been friends for many years. Kendall and her daughter had been on the same soccer team many years ago, and we'd built a solid friendship. When it came to Carter, we tried to keep things professional.

"Kate, what the *hell* was he thinking?"

"Who? Carter or Parker?" I said with a gossipy tone.

"Either, ugh. Their smug faces just pissed me off."

"Try living with them. I'd like to say Carter isn't a spitting image of his father, but clearly he is. They look alike, talk alike, and unfortunately, are now acting alike. Parker's mother warned me many years ago, but I insisted that I brought out the best in him. WRONG."

Jess laughed before adding, "Men! I just don't know how to get across to that kid. He gives me a headache."

"Tell me about it! I've had a headache every day for the last two weeks. And while I think it's too soon, I might even be starting menopause. My hormones are so fucked up right now.

I'm angry all the time and I find myself wanting to rage at situations I used to be so chill about."

"Really? Shit. If you're almost there, that means I'm almost there. I'm not ready for that. I hate getting old."

"Me too. I need more wine to survive teenagers," I said with a deep sigh.

"Red or white," Jess said with a laugh.

"Kendall came home and told us she's pregnant," I said.

Jess gasped, "Are you serious?"

"Oh yeah. Not only is she pregnant, she already knows she's having a girl!"

"Damn, Kate. You got *shit* going on. I thought I had it bad when Leah moved across the country for college and left me alone with Mav. Mav hasn't started actually acting like a teenager yet. He just hides in his room reading books."

"Books? Like what kind of books?"

"*Text*books. Who does that? My kid? He's too smart for his own good. I wish he'd get some sunlight in his life," she said laughing.

"How's the hubby?" I asked, secretly hoping she was having it as rough as I was and knowing damn well she'd never admit it if she was.

"Ha! I divorced him last year. Told him if he couldn't get his shit together, that I was done. He didn't get his shit together, so I left. Well, I kicked him out, but you know," she said without a hint of sadness.

"I'm sorry to hear that," I said sincerely. Maybe she was more honest that I had thought.

"Naw, it's life. I'm so much happier now."

Was that true? Would I be happier without Parker in *my* life? I wasn't sure of that answer but maybe it was something I needed to explore. I had a lot of feelings I needed to explore but the reality was that I simply didn't want to. I didn't want to face the truth. He cheated on me and I'd caught it all on camera.

But I told him I wanted to work through things. I did. I was pretty sure I did want to work on our marriage. I wouldn't be happier without Parker. And I was able to calm myself down and redirect my thoughts.

"I'm glad to hear that. I'd love to stay and chat, but I have to go kick my son's ass. Can we get together soon for that glass of wine?" I offered.

"Glass? Try the whole damn bottle!" she said with a smile.

"Truth," I said with a laugh as I left her office.

Chapter 16

I was actually happy to be back to work a few nights later. While there was drama at work, it wasn't personal. The patients could hate me all they wanted, they didn't live with me. I hadn't been feeling well for a few weeks now and I wanted to say it was all related to stress, but the longer it went on, the more I thought that maybe I needed to see a doctor about everything. That idea scared me. I was always the one who had my shit together.

"Hey girl, how are you tonight?" Mia asked.

"Ah, things have been better."

"Wanna talk about it?" she asked.

"Lets see, I caught my husband having sex with another woman. My eighteen-year-old daughter announced she's pregnant and doesn't know who the father is. My son was caught in the women's bathroom at school fondling and making out with a girl. I mean, thank God for Kamdyn, right?" I shook my head.

"Damn girl," she said as she came behind me and began rubbing my shoulders. "She doesn't know who the father is?"

"Right! And I completely forgot to ask who the girl was that Carter was caught with. He's suspended for five days, has to do an essay and community service."

"That's just from the school though, right?"

"Oh yeah. I think Parker wanted to high-five him though, so not sure how effective the punishment will actually be though. He's kicked off the baseball team, but he didn't care since the season is pretty much over anyways."

"I'm sorry."

Mia's hands on my shoulders were magical. The way her thumbs dug into just the right spots and melted my muscles. I felt the tension disappearing with each circular motion. The way her hands worked across my shoulders sent electrical impulses down my spine and somehow, the entire massage felt almost erotic. I accidentally let out a moan.

"Whoa, that good?" she asked laughing.

"I guess I needed that more than I thought," I said, embarrassed.

"Isn't that what they all say?" she asked with a seductive undertone. "Well, that isn't exactly what I came to see you for, but glad I could make you feel a little better."

"That sounds dangerous. What's up?"

"Brent is feeling sick, has a slight fever, and needs to go home. Any chance you can come take over his team?"

All the electric charge in my body fizzled out, and I was left with irritation. Brent was such a wuss. It seemed like at least once a week he was sick with something and couldn't possibly do his job. I think, if anything, he was allergic to work. Normally, I would be compassionate towards a sick employee, but Brent was on my very last nerve.

"Ugh, yes. I need a break from this computer anyways. Let him know I'll be right out."

When I got to the floor, Brent was sitting on a swivel chair, drinking a soda and laughing with Donna. Deep down, I knew the truth. He wasn't sick at all. Maybe he had a hot date or something, I didn't know. What I *did* know was that he wasn't sick.

"Brent, what's wrong?" I said as I approached him.

"I'm not feeling well," he said, his whole demeanor changing.

"Yeah, I don't buy it," I said with my hands on my hips.

"What?"

"I don't believe you're really sick. If you are, you're going to need a doctor because you're sick every damn week. In fact, you're making *me* sick... sick of your shit," I said.

His mouth fell open and he was quiet. Donna, who had been laughing at the exchange also grew quiet and then slowly headed back towards her group. I continued to stand with my hands on my hips waiting for his response.

"Okay. I'm going home. I'm not dealing with this shit. I don't feel good," he insisted.

"Good. May I have your keys and badge, please?"

"You're firing me?" he asked in anger.

"Yes. You've had too many absences," I said defiantly.

"Screw you," he said as he removed his name badge from his scrub top, grabbed his keys from his pocket, and threw them at me.

The badge and keys hit me in the stomach and then fell to the floor, but I didn't adjust my gaze. I saw patients standing at their doors watching, but I didn't move. In my head, I was counting to ten, hoping that he'd just leave peacefully so I wouldn't have to call security to escort him off the property.

Lucky for me, he left quietly. I sat down at the computer and gave myself a quick report on the patients that were now left in my care. All four of his rooms had patients, so I had plenty of things to do since he'd not only gone home early, but he'd clearly not been keeping up on his nursing tasks during the time he was supposed to be working. My head was spinning when Mia sat down at the computer next to me and asked if I wanted help.

"Do I? Of course! I don't even know where to start with these people," I said as I stared at the screen.

"Well, whatcha got?" she said optimistically.

I explained that I had a patient with an abscess to his scrotum who had just arrived, a patient with chest pain who was waiting for the doctor to return, a patient with a laceration to his forehead waiting for stitches, and a car accident victim waiting for x-ray results. She offered to assist with the laceration while I went to assist with the scrotum.

"I can't wait!" I said sarcastically.

"You know that's not my thing," she said with a laugh.

I wasn't sure if she meant the scrotum or the abscess but either way, I laughed along with her and headed for the room. When I opened the door, I paused because sitting on the bed with a look of pure embarrassment was one of the most attractive men I'd seen in ages. He was older with salt and pepper hair, a strong jawline, and a little scruff where a beard might grow. His biceps were toned and I could only imagine that everything else would follow suit. Instantly, I caught my eyes searching his left hand for a ring, but I found none.

"Hi. I'm Kate and I'll be your nurse tonight," I said with a sweet voice.

"That's a blessing because I really didn't want to do this with that guy that was in here earlier," he said with relief.

"No worries."

"To be honest, I'm not sure I'm ready to do this with a hot nurse either, but definitely not with a dude nurse," he said with a smile.

I watched his eyes travel the length of my body and suddenly felt myself become excited. The doctor came in then, thankfully, and I had the gentleman lay back and expose himself. I couldn't help but chuckle a little at his discomfort, which I knew was the wrong thing to do. Luckily for me, the guy was already in a mortified mood and clearly had the same bad sense of humor that I did because he kept cracking dirty jokes and laughing along with me.

"When I made plans tonight, I never imagined I'd have a hot nurse holding my balls while a doctor sucked on them," he said with a hearty laugh.

There it was again. He'd called me hot. The excitement returned and I had to turn my head to prevent anyone from seeing my cheeks flush. I couldn't recall this ever having happened to me before, but suddenly I was turned on. It was completely inappropriate. Not to forget, the guy was having an abscess drained from behind his testicles. I'm sure that sex was the furthest thing from his mind.

"It's your lucky night," I added.

Dr. Navarro was patient as he squirmed with each laugh, but he never broke his concentration and continued to work without saying a word. I caught myself noticing things like the man's well groomed pubic hair, the size of his manhood, and the muscle tone of his thighs. I was enjoying this way more than I should.

When the wound was cleaned out and packed, Dr. Navarro placed a new dressing over it. Then, he excused himself to go write discharge instructions and a prescription for antibiotics.

"Well, that was fun," the man admitted.

"You call *that* fun?"

"No, but it will make a great story later!"

"I'll give you that," I said as I started to leave.

"I can think of more fun things to do though," he hinted as he locked eyes with me.

"Oh yeah?"

"I think you know what I'm talking about. And I'm pretty sure you were thinking about it while the doctor was here fixing me up," he suggested with a raised eyebrow.

"Is that so?"

182

"I saw your eyes. You liked what you saw," he said with a mischievous smile.

It was happening again. I was being hit on by a good-looking man and was feeling butterflies in my stomach. In all my married life, I'd never contemplated straying from Parker. In the last month, I'd actually thought about it twice! Again, I was asking myself what the hell was wrong with me.

"I'm married," I said quickly, knowing that I was blushing again.

"So?" he said with a wink.

"Let me go check on your discharge paperwork," I said as I quickly left to get his discharge paperwork.

"How was the abscess?" Mia asked when I sat down next to her.

"I don't want to talk about it," I said. "How about that laceration?"

"Deep."

As soon as she said the word, my mind flashed back to the man's groin area. To his suggestion of a fun time. How I wanted it to be deep inside me. Then, I tried my best to scold myself for thinking it and erase the thought from my mind.

"Thanks again for your help."

"Anytime, Kate."

I grabbed the discharge paperwork from the printer and headed back into the lion's den. Part of me hoped he'd pounce on me while the other part hoped he'd keep this civil. Part of me wanted him to devour me while part of me wanted to just hand him the paperwork and go.

"Alright, here's your discharge instructions and your prescription for Keflex," I said as I tried my best not to look at his devilishly handsome face.

"Is your phone number on there in case I have questions?" he asked and my cheeks flushed.

"Are you asking for my phone number?"

"Uh... Yeah, I am," he admitted with a boyish smile.

I felt my body twitch with excitement when he cracked his smile. He wanted *my* phone number. He wanted to call me. It was beyond inappropriate in many ways to give him my phone number, and yet I found myself writing it on the discharge papers and handing it back to him.

When the weekend arrived, Parker and I both had been scheduled off. Originally, we had planned a getaway a few hours north to a cozy bed and breakfast that I loved, but now everything was up in the air. With everything that had been going on, I really just wanted to go on a date with Parker and then come home and sleep in my own bed.

As I sat reading in the library, Parker came in and sat in the other chair. He was freshly showered and had used my favorite cologne of his. Wearing those jeans and t-shirt that I loved so much, I wanted to crawl into his lap and nestle my head on his chest, but I fought that urge.

"I canceled our reservations, but I was wondering if you'd like to do something else instead?" he asked hesitantly.

"What did you have in mind?"

"Was thinking maybe dinner and a movie?"

"I could be convinced."

"Great. Let's leave at four, just like we'd planned to leave for the bed and breakfast?"

"Sounds like a plan. I'll go get ready," I said as I set my book down and headed for the shower.

Two hours later, Parker and I were at my favorite restaurant downtown. Just like when we were on vacation, everything felt like it had many years ago. Conversation flowed effortlessly and I saw a glimmer in his beautiful eyes. Why had our marriage broken down to the point that Parker had cheated on me? I imagined another woman looking into those eyes, thinking exactly what I was thinking now and I felt the waves of jealousy and anger return.

"Can I ask you something?" I asked as he reached for my hands across the table.

"Anything," he said with a smile.

"Do you miss her?"

He looked at me with a blank stare before responding, "Why would you bring that up, Kate? We're having a great time. We're trying to work on our marriage and questions like this aren't helping." He shook his head and took his hands back.

"Because I want to know. It matters to me," I explained.

"No, I don't miss her, Kate. Is that what you want to hear?" he asked aggressively.

"No, don't just tell me what I want to hear. Tell me the damn truth," I said quietly but sternly, looking him straight in the eyes.

"This is ridiculous. Do you want to work on us or focus on the past?" he asked, still avoiding the original question.

"I want you to answer the question."

I felt my phone vibrate in my pocket and being the paranoid person I'd become, I quickly read the text message.

"Hey Parker?" I asked, looking up from my dessert.

"Yeah?" he asked with a mouthful of cheesecake.

"Did you remember to tell Carter we weren't going away this weekend? Or Kamdyn's friend's mom when you dropped her off?" I asked, my eyes wide.

"Shit! No, I totally forgot. Why? What's your message say?"

He didn't answer the question and it would have to wait. I kept reading the text message in my mind as Parker paid the bill, and we walked to the car. The throbbing behind my eyes returned and I pressed my fingers into my temples, trying anything I could think of to stop the pain.

"What's wrong?" Parker asked.

"The throbbing behind my eyes."

"Again? You really need to have that looked at," he said with concern.

"I know."

"Did you hear back from the neighbor yet?" Parker asked.

The text message at dinner had been a screenshot from a parent of Carter's friend, announcing a party at *our* house. I immediately texted our neighbors in an effort to get more information. I didn't know what was going on at home, but Parker and I were about to find out.

The moment I opened the door, a teenager brushed past me. A teenager I didn't know. I shot a quick glance at Parker, but he just shrugged his shoulders. Parker then grabbed my shoulders and pulled me out of the way as a teenage boy chasing a teenage girl ran our direction and nearly knocked us over as they ran through the door. Like the Christmas song, they were laughing all the way.

That was the moment I realized that the pounding I heard when we pulled into the driveway wasn't just my headache increasing but the sound of a bass drum from a speaker system. Parker noticed it too because as I looked at him, I saw his face change from one of concern to one of anger. Our son was throwing a party in our house. Still thinking we were gone for the weekend, he had arranged this. I thought my head might explode from the pressure building inside it, anger raging through my entire body.

I didn't remove my shoes nor did I hang the keys on their hook. I stormed into the house and looked around. Nearly every surface of my kitchen was covered in dishes, drink cups, plates, and napkins. There were teenage boys with sitting on our couch with half naked girls on their laps in the living room. The lamp next to the couch was missing its shade.

"Where the fuck is Carter?" Parker said as he grabbed a boy by the shirt.

"Dr. Cordova? Uh... I... I don't know..." he said in a squeaky voice.

"Find him," Parker demanded through gritted teeth.

Overwhelmed with emotion, I headed straight for my bedroom. I'd seen enough teenage angst movies to know that kids could be hooking up in my bedroom. I prayed that it was all for Hollywood, but feared that it was probably reality. I'd never gone to a house party like this. Even if I had been invited, I probably wouldn't have gone because they usually ended in trouble.

I could hear Parker screaming at teenagers to get out of our house and calling for Carter. I could hear teenagers scrambling in fear, doors slamming, cars starting, and tires screeching down the road. The music stopped abruptly and I took a deep breath to mentally prepare myself for what I might see when I opened the door.

Throwing the door open, I found two naked teenagers getting frisky in my bed. Headache or not, I screamed at the top of my lungs for them to get out of my room, to get out of my house! As they fumbled for their clothing, I began stripping the sheets from the bed and swearing at them.

For a moment, it felt like I was funneling all of my anger towards Parker cheating on me into our own bed. The teens had already picked up their clothes and ran but I continued to rage a battle on the bed linens. A switch had flipped inside me, and I was out of control. The party was long forgotten and it was just me and the bed.

It was when I grabbed the lamp and threw it at the window that Parker came rushing into the bedroom. The lamp lay shattered on the floor and our bedroom window had a large crack running from corner to corner. He took a step towards me cautiously as all the anger and aggression left my body and I fell to the floor. I laid there sobbing in the fetal position until Parker was by my side comforting me.

"I've got to get this house back under control, Kate. Will you be okay if I leave you for a few minutes?" he asked softly.

"Yes," I said as I blew my nose into the sleeve of my shirt.

I heard Parker yelling at more teenagers until he was completely over it, and began yelling that there were cops outside. The words had barely left his lips when teenagers began emerging from nooks and crannies all over our house and fleeing like cockroaches. It was quite effective.

When everything was quiet again, Parker found me in the exact same position as I'd been in when he left me. He quietly asked me to come to the living room to deal with our own children. I dreaded this. I felt too weak to fight with Carter, but I knew it was my job as a parent go chew him a new one.

Parker reached out a hand and helped me up off the floor. I felt sick to my stomach and the throbbing behind my eyes was as strong as it ever was. I swallowed to prevent the bile in my stomach from rising up my throat. I was dizzy and lightheaded. Did I really have to do this now?

While I had prepared myself for an intoxicated Carter, I hadn't prepared myself for Kamdyn. She sat next to her brother with her head hanging low. My baby girl. She wouldn't have been involved in this, I thought. Surely, she had been found asleep in her bed when Parker went room to room checking for more teenagers. She was supposed to have been at her friends. That's where Parker had taken her. I blinked my eyes several times trying to clear the double vision I was seeing.

"Explain," Parker said with a firm face.

"What do you want me to say?" Carter said as he rolled his eyes and shrugged his shoulders.

Before I had even registered how disrespectful his response had been, Parker had grabbed his arm firmly and pulled him to a standing position and was now within inches from his face. My head pounded and my knees felt weak. I kept telling myself to stay standing.

"What the fuck did you say to me?" Parker yelled.

"I don't know what you want me to say," Carter said defiantly.

Smack. The sound of Parker's hand across Carter's face was enough to collapse the last bit of resolve I had and I crumbled to the ground as I blacked out from the pain.

"Mom?" Kamdyn yelled as she knelt beside me, shaking my shoulders.

"Huh? What happened?" I asked as I opened my eyes.

"Kate, are you okay? You passed out," Parker said as he pulled my upper eyelids open and shined a mini flashlight into them that he happened to pull from a drawer in the coffee table.

"Wow, my head is pounding," I said as I closed my eyes again and rubbed my temples.

"How long have you been having these headaches again?" Parker asked.

"I don't know. I just want to sleep."

"Kamdyn, will you help your mom into bed, please?"

"Come'on, Mom," she said as she helped me stand up.

Carter sat quietly on the couch, looking irritated and not concerned. As I looked around my trashed living room, all I felt was hatred. I'd never felt hatred in my life. I wanted to run through the room and smash things. My weak legs dizziness were preventing that.

"Wait, Kamdyn. We need to change the sheets on the guest bed, and she can sleep there," Parker said as he flew past us towards the guest room. "The window in our room is broken."

"Mom, I'm sorry," Kamdyn quietly said.

"Not now, Kamdyn," Parker said firmly.

I felt guilty leaving Parker to handle this on his own, but I had little choice in the matter. I was too weak to fight battles anymore. What was happening to me? Where had all of my strength gone? I had practically raised three children alone and worked a full time job while Parker was building his career. I ran the household and everyone's schedules. I was super mom. But this Kate, the one who faints when the going gets rough? The one who gets a throbbing behind the eyes every time the smallest bit of stress appears? Where had *she* come from?

Was I finally ready to admit that *something* serious was going on with me? Was I finally ready to go see my doctor about it? Or would I just keep ignoring the symptoms and pretending everything was alright? And at what cost? My job? My family?

Chapter 17

When Parker was finally ready for bed, he carefully carried me back into our bedroom and gave me a Motrin. He had patched the window, cleaned up the mess I'd made, and put new sheets on our bed.

When I asked where Carter was, he informed me that while he was helping me to bed, Carter had run off somewhere. However, Parker insisted I not worry about it at the moment.

"How am I not supposed to worry about it?" I asked.

"I will handle it. I need you to get some sleep," he said as he rubbed my back.

What had gotten into Carter lately? What was happening around me? What was happening *to* me? Was this normal? My head hurt too much to think about it, so I did the only thing I could — closed my eyes.

In the morning, Carter still wasn't home. One moment I was filled with rage and the next I was worried. When I went to the kitchen for coffee, I noticed it sparkled. Who had cleaned it? *When* had they cleaned it? I heard a noise in the living room and peaked in, seeing Kamdyn picking up trash from the coffee table.

"Did you clean the kitchen too?" I asked.

"Yeah," Kamdyn said quietly as she looked up and saw me for the first time before quickly hanging her head.

"It's a good start," I mumbled as I returned to the kitchen and began making a pot of coffee.

Before it was finished brewing, the garage door opened and Carter walked in. Without words, he tried to walk past me but I put the kibosh on that.

"Sit. Now." I was firm and direct and pointed towards the chair at the island. "Where have you been?" I asked when he took a seat.

"I was at Jayden's," he said quietly.

"You are in a lot of trouble. I don't know what's gotten into you, but this behavior is completely unacceptable. In fact, it's complete bullshit." His eyes grew large and he stared at me.

"I don't know what to say," he said, surprised with my lack of restraint.

"What is going on with you?"

"I don't know. I wanted to hang out with my friends," he said as he shrugged his shoulders.

"And by that you mean making a mess in our home? There were kids having sex in my bed!"

"I'm sorry."

"You completely disregarded our rules. You disrespected your father and I. Unacceptable. You better listen carefully. As long as you live under *my* roof, you *will* do as I say. You *will* be respectful of my rules. And if you don't like them, there is the door," I said through clenched teeth, my eyes narrowed like laser pointers as I looked directly into his eyes.

He was silent.

"That's all I know to say right now. You're fucking grounded. No going out, no sports, no phone, no nothing. Grounded."

He didn't argue. He didn't speak. He got up from the chair, set his phone on the island, and went straight to his bedroom. The familiar throbbing returned behind my eyes, and I was pleased to see the coffee was done. Once I'd drank the first cup, I was ready for my second.

"Whoa there. You're going to turn into a coffee if you don't slow down," Kendall teased as she waltzed in the garage door.

"What are you doing here?" I asked surprised to see her.

"Uh, we have breakfast plans, remember?"

"Oh yeah," I lied. I excused myself and went to get dressed.

"So you guys had a party here last night, eh?" Kendall said when I returned.

"We aren't talking about that," I said as I gave her my best side eye. "Just get in the car," I demanded.

Thankfully, she obeyed.

My hopes for a nap or at least silence were quickly squashed when I walked in the door to the house and saw Kendall sitting on the couch with friends. I placed my keys on the kitchen counter and removed my shoes.

"Hey mom," Kendall called.

I was curious as to why she was in *my* living room when she had her own apartment across town. Had I missed something? As I got closer to the living room, I saw the coffee table filled with snacks and drinks. My expensive throw pillows were lazily tossed on the floor.

"What are you doing here?" I asked, trying to keep my tone cool.

"What do you mean?" she asked, sounding very confused.

"What do I mean? You have your own apartment now. I figured that meant you'd be hanging out with your friends at *your* place from now on."

"Oh Mom. You're funny," she laughed.

"I am?"

"Yeah. I told you and Dad last month that I was moving home for the summer. We even talked about it at breakfast the other day. We'd only signed a nine-month lease, remember?"

"Ooohhh. Yeah." Has something so big and so important literally escaped my mind that fast?

I shook my head and headed straight for my room. No peace and quiet for me. I felt the tension headache budding behind my eyes and decided a nice, warm shower might relieve the pressure.

After my shower and a few minutes of rest, I emerged from hiding and headed to the kitchen to begin dinner. I checked the calendar first and saw it was blank. Kamdyn and Carter would be arriving home on the bus anytime now and I'd have to start the fight over homework. School would be over soon, so I had that to look forward to.

Like clockwork, they came in like an army charging into battle — loud and aggressive. Instantly, that familiar pain in my head returned and Kamdyn saw me cringe.

"What's wrong, Mom?" she asked.

"My head hurts."

"Why don't you go lay down. I can order a pizza for dinner."

"Okay."

I didn't put up a fight because the pain was so intense I felt nauseous. I dug through my medicine drawer and found my bottle of Imitrex and swallowed the pill frantically. I crawled into my bed and cried. I didn't even think I was crying about anything specific, just crying.

When Parker came home a few hours later, I was still laying in bed with a pillow over my head. I didn't feel like talking, so I didn't bother to remove the pillow when he came in. He quietly changed his clothes and then snuck out of the bedroom without disturbing me. Part of me was irritated he hadn't even bothered to check on me and the other part of me was pleased that he'd just left me alone.

Once he was gone, I threw the pillow across the room and stewed. What the hell did I expect? What did I want from him? Why did my head hurt so damn much? It hurt too much to think about it all.

When I finally crawled out of my makeshift fort I'd created in the bed, I took another shower and went to the kitchen to pack my lunch. I stopped dead in my tracks. Glancing around the room, my spotless kitchen was covered in dirty dishes, empty boxes and containers, remnants of some baking experiment, and Kamdyn's slime ingredients. The sound that left my mouth was shrill enough for the neighbors to hear, I'm sure, but it did the trick as all of my children came running.

"What's wrong, Mom?" Kamdyn asked before realizing what I was seeing.

"Don't worry, Mom. We'll clean it up," Carter said as he shrugged his shoulders.

Just looking at my kitchen was giving me a panic attack and I didn't want a repeat of what had happened last time the kitchen had looked like this. No way would I be packing my lunch in that kitchen. I would order out or I'd take a walk on the wild side by testing out the hospital cafeteria. I yelled goodbye to anyone who was listening and reached for my keys. Except the keys were *not* on their designated hook.

I frantically began looking for them. I always put them on this exact hook. Without fail. Had someone taken my car? I opened the door to the garage, but there sat my car, parked right where I'd left it. Where were my keys?

"Has anyone seen my car keys?" I finally yelled.

"I think they are on the counter," Carter yelled back.

I scanned the disaster of a counter and finally laid eyes on them. By my clock, I was already running late for work or I'd have marched my happy butt into the living room and given those little shits a piece of my mind. It wasn't funny to mess with my car keys, nearly giving me a heart attack.

I questioned my sanity when the alarm went off at five o'clock that morning, but I shut it off and sat on the edge of the bed. My attempts to wake up were met with such resistance that I would have just gone back to sleep except for the fact that Parker was prodding me to get my butt out of bed and get myself ready.

The annual hospital-wide charity softball tournament was usually one of my favorite days of the entire year. Each department assembled a team and then battled it out for a champion. Of course, it was all for the sake of charity. It was a highly advertised event and was generally well attended by the public.

This would be my tenth year as the team's second basewoman. I played a little back in high school, but that was all. I just wasn't the competitive type. Parker on the other hand, was always competitive. In fact, it was his competitive spirit that got me playing in the tournament in the first place. He had joined the team from the ortho floor and couldn't wait to battle against me. It took him quite a few years to wear me down, but once I played in the first tournament, I was hooked.

The atmosphere when we arrived at the field was just like it was every year — jubilant. Vendors were set up between fields, food trucks were waiting in the parking lot, a news camera was set up near a press box, and teams wearing various colored t-shirts were assembling all over the place. It was a warm sunny day and I could already feel sweat dripping down my back.

When I looked at the geeky, boyish smile on Parker's face, it was hard not to fall in love with him all over again. His toned thighs peaked out from under his loose basketball shorts and his biceps threatened to bust the sleeves of his orange team shirt. I could just picture in my head the abdominal muscles he'd spent hours defining in the gym contracting and expanding as he moved his pelvis in a rhythm that sent pleasure shooting through my body. My husband was damn good-looking.

"Good luck, Cordova!" Parker said after he gave me a kiss and headed to meet his team.

"Yeah, you're going to need it, Doc," I called after him.

The tournament began with teams playing on four different fields. The emergency department team played the medical-surgical floor team and won by a mercy in four innings. Parker's ortho floor team also won, but by only one run against the adult medical floor. I was just glad the first game was over because the hot sun was beating down on me, and I was dripping with sweat. The familiar throbbing behind my eyes began and I tried to drink as much water as I could, thinking I was becoming dehydrated.

As the second round began, the sun was blazing down on the players and I was sweating from every spot on my body, even the places that I didn't know you could sweat from. Even my sunglasses couldn't stop the glare from the summer sun. However, I didn't let it affect my game. I ended up getting walked in the last inning and became the winning run when my teammate hit a pop up and I crossed home plate.

Parker's team lost in the second round, and he joined me during a break for lunch before the third round began. We had walked just up the street to a sweet little café and sat on the same side of the booth. Something about it felt so romantic. I knew we were trying to work on our marriage, but I'd assumed it had just been words. It was refreshing to see Parker really making an effort.

He had been so kind and compassionate to me since his little affair was discovered. Even though I was mad and making this difficult, he hadn't wavered in his demand to work through it and fix our marriage. With the chaos in our lives and the constant headaches and mood swings, he had been my rock the last few weeks. I knew I needed him. My life just wasn't complete without him.

When round three began, I wasn't nearly as peppy as I'd been for the first two. I missed an easy pop up in the fourth inning and I never made it on base. We ended up losing to the trauma care unit, but I was okay with it because I was way too tired to continue anyway. Usually, I'd have been yelling, screaming, and putting up a good fight. But not this year.

"You did a great job today," Parker said as he drove us home.

"Thanks. I did better than you," I teased.

He reached his hand over and held mine for the remainder of the drive, and I let him. I turned the radio to the station we always listened to when we first began dating and it played the same songs we used to listen to. This moment felt right in every way. I was transported back to a time with so much less stress. When we were just starting our careers and working towards starting our family, it was like this. Things were easy between us.

"So who won?" Carter asked when we walked in the door.

"I did," I proudly proclaimed.

"We didn't even play each other," Parker argued.

"Doesn't matter. I won," I repeated.

Carter just shrugged and headed for the basement.

"I'm going to shower," I said as I lifted my eyebrows in Parker's direction.

He picked up the hint and followed close behind. After a shower and dinner, I crawled into bed to read. I had a meeting with AnneMarie the following afternoon and just thinking about it was causing me stress. The throbbing behind my eyes remained and I finally gave up reading and just went to sleep.

In the morning, when I woke up, my head continued with a slight throb, but nothing I couldn't work through. I showered and dressed. I wasn't sure what I was going to do with my day, but my meeting with AnneMarie was at two o'clock. I decided to read until my meeting and then go from there.

When I knocked on AnneMarie's door, she invited me in and I sat in the chair across from her desk. I wasn't sure what we were meeting for, but I hated that our meetings meant me getting up and coming in rather than her getting up in the middle of *her* night and coming in to meet with *me*. Being realistic, I knew that would never happen.

"How are you, Kate?" she asked.

"I'm fine. You?"

"I'm well. Look, I wanted to sit down and talk with you about a few things," she began and I felt the throbbing of my head immediately intensify.

"Okay."

"I know you've had a lot of stress going on at home lately," she started before I cut her off.

"So?"

"Well, I want to make sure you're okay with everything."

"You called me here in the middle of the day to make sure my private life was okay?"

"Okay, let's get right to it then. Yes and no. I've noted a few things and I wanted to talk with you about them. We've known each other for many years. I know the way you work. I know the things you usually do. The person people are describing to me isn't you," she said bluntly.

"Like what?"

"Well, some staff have mentioned the way you've talked to patients. In fact, I had three complaints *last week* regarding the things you said to patients."

"Oh."

"Kate, I know you. You can't tell patients to fuck off. You know that. I'm just trying to figure out what is going on with you."

"Nothing is going on with me!" I said, my voice rising in anger.

"Look, please just watch what you say to the patients. And if you're going to fire a nurse, don't tell him you're sick of his shit, even if you are," she said, irritated.

"Well, I'm being honest."

"Honesty is the best policy, but sometimes you can use a little more discretion when you tell the truth," she said.

"That's no fun."

"No fun? What the hell has gotten into you?" she said with a concerned look.

"I guess I don't know *what* you're talking about," I said as I stood from the chair.

"Kate, you're not yourself. Clearly *something* is going on," she said as she put her hands on her hips.

"AnneMarie, I don't know what you *think* is going on, but my personal life is personal and it stays at home. I'm doing my damn job and if it's not good enough for you or anyone else, then find someone else to do it!" I yelled back at her.

"Whoa, you don't have to yell. I'm not trying to upset you. I'm just trying to get to the bottom of everything," she said as she stepped from behind her desk.

"Clearly you think *something* is happening so just say it. Stop pussyfootin' around it."

"Fine, we can do this your way. Is your husband's infidelity affecting your work performance?" she said bluntly.

"What? Fuck no! How has my work performance not been acceptable to you?"

"Kate! It's the way in which you say things, your decision-making abilities, your temper, and the like. The other day you were in triage and kept an adult with a headache and hypertension in the waiting room!" she said with frustration.

"He was having a headache!" I screamed at her.

"Yes, due to a stroke!"

"Are you questioning my ability to take care of patients?" I finally asked.

"No, I'm just trying to find out why the sudden changes in everything about you," she said calmly.

"Well, when I have a problem, I'll let you know. Until then, let me do my job."

"I can't do that. I have a department to run. I'm putting you back on the floor until further notice. It's just not the right time to have you teaching other nurses when I'm struggling to trust you on your own."

"Such bullshit," I said as I kicked the chair in front of her desk. "If you're putting me back on the floor, then I want to come back to day shift. No use being on night shift."

"As much as I'd love to do that so I could keep an eye on you, I can't. I need you on night shift," she said.

My blood was boiling. I'd never felt so angry. My eyes burned and the pulsing behind them grew stronger. If I had been a cartoon, steam would be pouring from my ears. I wanted to break something.

She just shook her head in disappointment and pointed towards the door. I didn't know what she wanted to hear from me. And while I knew that I was changing, I didn't know why and I didn't know how to stop it. And I wouldn't admit it to anyone, let alone AnneMarie.

Chapter 18

Words would come out of my mouth and even *I* would be shocked. Even knowing that the behavior was wrong, I was powerless to stop it. And then there were the constant headaches I kept having. Foods I used to love tasted like garbage. My vision would be blurry at times. I felt angry most of the time. I laughed at all the wrong things, cried over nothing, and was angry and aggressive, all of which were out of character for me. Maybe the stress *was* getting to me?

I couldn't focus on one thing at a time and sometimes I struggled to think of words. I couldn't remember simple things that I'd always done. And despite the fact that my husband had cheated on me, all I wanted to do was have sex with him. Every chance I got.

We had gone from hardly ever having sex to his cheating on me to not being able to keep my hands off of him. Was this really a stress response? Was it menopause? Or was I just going crazy?

As a nurse, I knew there was more to it than just something simple. However, denial was my best friend. I was Kate, owner of the perfect life. I had the great marriage, three amazing kids, an amazing house, and an amazing career. My life was perfect, so what the hell was this?

I was eager for a night out with friends from work and practically ran out the door when the clock hit six o'clock on Saturday night. Parker was working late but said he'd try to make it if he could. They were, in fact, his friends as well as mine. I just wanted a chance to have adult fun and relieve some built-up stress that was taking over my life.

The bar, Highjinx, was located in the trendy part of the city. The bar was almost always filled to the brim with younger hipsters, but tonight it was filled with nurses, techs, residents, and doctors. Word of our night on the town had spread like wildfire through the ER, much like a good rumor.

I loved the tiny bar, the wooden floor creaking as you walked through, and the high table tops with bar stools scattered throughout. The music was never too loud so you could actually carry a conversation with the people around you. My favorite part was the drink menu though.

I stopped at the bar and ordered my usual and then made my way toward the back of the bar where a table full of co-workers had already gathered.

"Kaaatttteee!" Tyrell's loud voice boomed when I approached, and he pulled me into a side hug.

"Tyyyyreeellll!" I hollered in return as I squeezed around his midsection.

"Alright, enough PDA!" Adel said happily.

"You tell jokes," Tyrell scolded.

I looked around for Avalon, but she wasn't here yet, so I sat down next to Adel and Nora. I noticed Mia across the table eyeing me, but pretended I didn't notice. She and I had been spending more time at work talking and I enjoyed her company, but I wasn't sure if she didn't see it as something more. I saw Sam sitting next to Mia.

"Where's Parker tonight?" Nora asked, noticing his absence.

"Work. That's where he always is, isn't it?"

"Well, I guess when it's time for my knee replacement, I know who to call," she joked.

Nora was about thirty years old, skinny, and single. She was athletic and enjoyed hiking. There was no way she would need a knee replacement anytime soon. I'm sure her bones were as strong as diamonds. I also noticed that she kept her eyes trained on Dr. Ellis, who was a second year ER resident.

"How long have you guys been here?" I asked, thinking I was right on time but noticing everyone seemed a few drinks in already.

"Oh, a few of us came early and had dinner first," Adel said.

"Where was *my* phone call?" I asked with a laugh. "Now that I work nights, I'm just not part of the club anymore, am I?"

"No, you abandoned us!" Nora laughed.

"Well, I tried to come back to you guys, but AnneMarie put the kibosh on that. I'm probably stuck on nights forever!" I said with an evil laugh.

"Wait. What? What about being a preceptor?" Nora asked.

"Well... Let's just say that's not working out for now," I said, avoiding the true answer.

"Kate? That can't be true!" Adel said, looking concerned. "You're an awesome nurse. Why would AnneMarie do that?"

"She said I've been inappropriate with patients, and she can't trust me," I said flatly.

"What?" Nora and Adel gasped.

"Is she serious?" Tyrell finally piped up.

"Dead serious."

"Someone must be playing a joke on you," Tyrell said.

"I'm not so sure guys."

"What do you mean?" Nora asked, looking extremely concerned and taking a long sip of her cocktail.

"Well, a lot has been going on the last few months," I began before Adel interrupted me.

"Hell no. Parker's fuck up isn't the reason for all this, is it?" Adel sputtered.

"Of course not. But I don't know. Something is wrong with me lately and I don't know what the hell it is, but I'll figure it out. Maybe it's a good thing I'm stepping back a little right now," I admitted as I finished off my drink.

"What are you talking about, Kate?" Adel said supportively.

"I don't know. Just something inside me feels... off." I sighed heavily.

"We all have moments like that," Sam added as he came up beside me. "You can't just quit like that."

Everyone agreed with Sam. He'd picked an opportune time to enter the conversation. He was the only one who had been working beside me when all these alleged incidents occurred. He was the one I told about the drama at home. Was he the one reporting my behavior to AnneMarie?

I didn't wait for anyone to add to the conversation. The last thing I needed was for more gossip to center around me or for anyone to feel sorry for me. I was thirsty and needed another drink. ASAP. As I headed to the bar, I noticed Mia leave the table and follow me. No big deal. I hadn't even spent time with her outside of work, but I enjoyed her company. I ordered a second strawberry margarita from the bartender and heard Mia behind me.

"Make it two," she said.

I smiled pleasantly towards her. When the bartender delivered the two frozen margaritas, Mia promptly presented her card to the bartender and paid for both of our drinks. I tried to stop her, but it was no use. She touched my hand as I had dug for my own debit card and assured me it was her treat. Just like when she was rubbing my shoulders, I felt this surge of electricity run through my body when she touched me.

We returned to the table, but Mia did not return to her seat — she sat right next to me. Adel gave me a look, but I brushed her off. What was wrong with Mia sitting next to me anyway? Did we have to divide into day shift and night shift or something? Mia was newer, but why not use this opportunity to get to know her?

"So, Mia, right? What did you do before you worked in the ER?" Adel asked, trying to be friendly but clearly faking her smile.

She smiled and said, "I worked at a golf course in Florida before I went to nursing school. I fell in love with the ER during my rotation and here I am!"

"A golf course?" Tyrell said. "Can you play?"

Mia and Tyrell spent the next hour talking golf while Nora, Adel, and I spent that time peppering Sam with questions about his doctor boyfriend. It was around ten that Avalon sent me a text message that she couldn't make it, and we all switched topics. This group, minus Avalon, were my entire work world. They made going to work worthwhile. They were my second family. And being with them felt wonderful.

Around midnight, everyone began to say their goodbyes and slowly leave for the night. Every time I began to do this myself, Mia would strike up another interesting conversation and encourage me to stay for another margarita. I agreed and was now sipping my fifth margarita and the familiar headache had begun. I was so sick of the headaches, but I was becoming accustomed to them. I searched my purse for the Motrin I kept stashed in there and swallowed four of the little maroon pills.

When my margarita was half gone, I noticed that the last of the gang was leaving and just Mia and I remained. As we sat at the table nursing the last of our margaritas, I felt her hand settle on my thigh. I froze. My heartbeat quickened. I'd never done this sort of thing. I was a married woman. Married to a man. How was I supposed to react? Her hand didn't move as I took a long sip from my drink.

This is the exact thing I had feared. She had felt more of our conversations than I had intended. The so called problem was that I wasn't sure I wanted to stop what was happening. Each time she touched me, the electrical impulses started and if I was honest, I liked them. Lately, when I looked beyond the anger and aggression I almost always felt, I was sexually charged.

"Are you okay?" she asked.

"Yep." I didn't look at her when I said it.

"Are you sure?" Maybe I'd said it too quick?

"Yeah, why wouldn't I be?" I finally turned and looked at her as I said it.

Her eyes were bright green and soft. Her lips were a deep shade of red, plump, and moist. Her hair carelessly fell across her oval face. Damn she was beautiful.

I pushed her hand off my thigh. Then, I slid my bar stool closer to her and sat back down. Close enough our shoulders touched. I knew this woman, but I had never known her like this. I'd never known any woman like this. I had to decide what my next move would be, but thinking wasn't something I was doing lately. I was better at acting on impulse.

I reached for her hand and placed it back on my thigh. I turned to her, grabbed her face between my hands, and kissed her on the lips. I felt her hand squeeze my thigh and I felt her tongue begging my lips to part. I pulled back suddenly and she looked surprised.

"What was that?" she asked.

"Isn't that what you wanted? Isn't that where this was going?"

"Uh... yeah... but I wasn't sure if this is something *you* wanted."

"I wasn't sure either," I said as I placed my hand on the hand still resting on my thigh. "But I am sure I want to do it again."

Her maroon lips parted with a smile and her teeth sparkled. The bright green of her eyes melted away and the only thing I saw on her face was a look of desire. I felt the heat rising inside me. She stared at me for a moment before leaning in and kissing *me*. Except this kiss was forceful, and included her hand moving further up my thigh. Even though her lips were still on mine, my moan was audible.

The electrical pulses inside me were now starting a fire. I wanted her hands on my body, touching me everywhere, teaching me new things. I wanted her hands to explore every crevice of my body. Then, as if a sign from above, the band began to play Marvin Gaye.

"Can we get out of here?" she whispered breathlessly.

I didn't reply. Instead, I grabbed my purse and headed for the door. I did it without thinking, or hesitating. When I got to my car though, my brain had begun functioning again and I realized what was happening. I was about to go home with Mia to hook up. I was married. I was straight. Wait, was I straight? The fire inside me quickly extinguished as I worked through everything in my head.

"Mia, I can't do this." I blurted out before she got into her car.

"What?" she asked, turning around to make sure she'd understood me, her back leaning against her driver side door.

"I can't do this. I'm married." I stepped in front of her and looked into her beautiful green eyes and became unsure again.

Instead of saying anything else, she kissed me again.

I parked my car in the garage and quietly crept into the house. I flung my keys on the counter and removed my shoes. The clock in the kitchen read 01:30 a.m. when I glanced at it on my way past. Parker would be fast asleep by now.

That burning desire for hands to be exploring my body had died down when I was standing in front of Mia, but on my way home, my mind kept playing vivid images of Mia or Parker doing various things to my body. I needed Parker. I needed *his* hands.

I tip-toed through the hallway, carefully making my way toward my bedroom when a familiar noise stopped me. Had I heard that correctly? I admit, I had been fairly intoxicated at the bar, but I had sobered up quite a bit. This wasn't a noise you mistake for something else. I could clearly hear the pleasurable moaning of a woman coming from somewhere down the hallway.

From where I stood, my bedroom was at the end of the hallway, Carter's bedroom on the left, and Kamdyn's on the right. Which room was the sound coming from? Either my husband was having another affair or one of my children had an unapproved visitor in their room. None of those scenarios was favorable. I felt the familiar throb behind my eyes returning and a budding rage building in my chest.

I contemplated my next move in my head and decided to proceed with stealth-mode-Kate versus loud-make-it-stop Kate. I was going to catch someone in the act, and they wouldn't be able to deny it. I wouldn't be loud and let them know I was coming. This was a sneak attack. I crept slowly and quietly down the hall, my ears perked up listening for the noise. All of my senses were heightened. As I worked my way down the hallway, I could hear rhythmic tapping noises in addition to the moans.

I stopped outside the door where I was confident the noise was coming from. I felt vomit rise in my throat. Did I really want to witness this or was it better to just discuss it in the morning? No, it had to be stopped and addressed right this minute. My hand reached out for the door knob and I took a deep breath, preparing for a reaction and a fight.

"What the hell is going on?" I asked as I threw the door open.

A flash of skin, flying covers, and a nude woman hit the floor. Nice. Caught in the act, his gut instinct was to *throw* the poor girl on the floor? She landed with a thud and I saw her scramble to grab at her clothes. I flicked the bedroom light on and the room lit up like the house from National Lampoon's Christmas Vacation.

Chapter 19

"Mom!" Carter screamed.

"Carter!" I screamed back.

"Get out of here! This is my room!"

"Excuse me? This is *my* house and every room in it belongs to your father and me!"

I heard my own bedroom door fly open and Parker practically ran down the hallway after hearing the screams.

"What is going on?" Parker asked as he surveyed the scene. "Holy shit," he said as he registered the answer to his own question.

"Dad, tell Mom to get out of here," Carter directed, still trying to cover his own naked body with his bed sheet.

"I'm not telling your mom to go anywhere! And who is on the floor?" Parker asked as the girl slowly rose from the floor, now at least wearing undergarments.

"Hi. My name is Becca. Nice to meet you?" she said meekly and unsure.

"Becca, we need to call your parents," I said angrily.

"Mom!" Carter began to protest before Parker cut him off.

"Carter, I don't want to hear it. You know the rules. You've been pushing my patience and our limits for a while now. I'm done."

My blood was boiling when I said, "Put on your damn clothes and meet us on the couch in five minutes. That includes you too, Becca!"

Parker and I headed for the kitchen where I made a pot of coffee for the both of us. When I left the bar, this had been the farthest thing from my mind. I wanted to come home and screw my husband. Instead, I was standing in the kitchen, fully clothed, arguing with him what we were going to do about this entire situation. Then we argued over who would be the one to call Becca's parents. In the end, I "won". I always won when it came to things like this.

"Hello, my name is Kate Cordova. I'm so sorry for waking you up in the middle of the night like this, but I just found your daughter in my son's bedroom," I said as kindly as I could.

"WHAT?" the angry voice on the other end of the line roared.

"Yeah. I was hoping you and your wife might come to collect her and join us for a quick chat."

"You can count on that. What is your address?" the man asked, waking up a little more but not calming down any.

After giving him our address, I poured Parker and me cups of coffee and headed for the living room. The two teenagers sat on the couch trying to look innocent, but I could see Carter was angry and Becca appeared mortified.

"I'll just walk home," Becca said softly.

"Oh hell no you won't," I said a little too loudly.

"Mom!" Carter began but was cut off by his father.

"Shut up Carter. I don't even know where to start with you so my recommendation is to just shut up right now."

I hadn't seen Parker this angry in a long time, except the night he slapped Carter and I'd passed out, but I admired the crease in his forehead and the way his dimples appeared when he had this angry face on. His cheeks flush and his lips become fuller. I didn't like seeing him angry, but I admitted he was definitely sexy as hell when he was.

Becca's parents arrived fifteen minutes after I'd placed the call. I was sure they had jumped out of bed, thrown on the nearest clothes, and sped all the way to our house. That is until I learned they lived one neighborhood over. Then, it became obvious why it had been so easy for Becca to sneak out late at night and make it to our house without needing a vehicle to do so.

As mad as Parker and I were, Becca's parents were even madder. The look on her parent's faces when they entered our living room spoke volumes and I thought for sure this might be dramatic. In fact, I thought for sure Parker and I might even end up in a fight by the end of the night.

"What the hell is going on, Becca?" her father's voice boomed.

She didn't say anything. She kept her head down and her hands folded neatly between her legs. I'm not sure that Carter was thinking properly as he stood up in an attempt to defend her. Honestly, I thought that facing a pissed off father was brave. Or stupid.

"Sir, this is all my fault," Carter began before he was cut off.

"I'm sure it is you little fuck stick. What the hell? You think you can lure my innocent daughter to your house in the middle of the night and then do what exactly?" the father asked.

"Whoa whoa whoa," I said. "Fuck stick? Is that really necessary?"

His anger turned toward me. "Yes, it really is. You should have taught your son some fucking manners and to keep his dick in his pants."

At this point, Parker roared to life, "You need to back up. You don't get to talk to my wife like that. Or my son."

"You do realize your son has violated my daughter, right? Or the fact that she's only fourteen? I believe in this state that

214

would make this statutory rape, if I'm not mistaken," the father asked.

"Yep, I'm fully aware of the severity of this entire thing. But you also don't see us calling your daughter names, do you? Last I checked, it takes two to tango," Parker said.

"And with what I saw, she certainly wasn't being taken advantage of!" I chimed in.

"And what exactly did you see that makes you think that?" the mother said, finally taking her chance to speak.

"If you must know, when I opened the door, your daughter was on *top* of my son, riding him as if he were a rodeo bull," I said, feeling sick the moment the memory returned to me.

"Becca, is that true?" the father asked, turning to her.

Her head bowed further as she spoke barely loud enough to be heard, "yes sir."

When it felt like we were beating a dead horse, I finally suggested we discuss this further in the morning. While I saw the father begin to argue this, the mother gently grabbed his hand and pulled him back towards the door. Becca followed like a beaten puppy. Part of me was nervous about what would happen when they returned home, but the other part of me didn't care.

I glanced at my watch, and realized it was nearing 03:45 a.m. Parker declared that he was going to shower and head into the office since there wasn't a point in getting back to sleep. I, on the other hand, was exhausted and couldn't wait to fall into bed.

As I began to peel off my clothes in the bedroom, I felt a hand on my back. After twenty-one years of marriage, I knew exactly what that hand was wanting when it reached for my back. My mind quickly flashed to Mia and the bar. Her hand on my thigh. Our kiss. The electrical impulses returned to me, the warmth returning between my legs, my nipples standing hard and firm, and I immediately had my answer for Parker. I turned around and allowed the hand to rest on my breast. I closed my eyes and let that hand roam my body. Then, both hands twisted me onto the bed to a position on my back and I felt the weight of Parker gently lower on top of me. Except in my head, it wasn't Parker.

He began kissing at my neck and I kept my eyes closed. My hands running the length of his back as he kissed and brushed up against me. I felt him pull at my shirt and leaned up slightly to allow it to be removed. I felt his hand reach to the hook of my bra while I felt his mouth suckling at my breasts.

My back arched with pleasure and my nails lightly dug into Parker's back. As soon as I felt Parker's excitement brush against my pelvis, all thoughts of Mia disappeared and my desire for Parker was front and center. I found myself rushing to remove his shirt as my need to feel him within me grew.

I pushed him back and reached for his pajama bottoms, but he beat me to it and removed them. Then, he placed his hands along my sides and slid them down my body as he kissed a trail from between my breasts to south of my belly button. I felt hot breath on my groin and I wished that my panties weren't still on.

His hands tugged at the panties I had on and in moments, those pesky panties were on the floor. Without clothes, I felt a shiver of cold surge through my body and be quickly replaced with a new wave of need. His hands grabbed my wrists, and he pinned them above my head as Parker returned to me and I felt him asking for permission between my legs.

I reached my head up, kissed at Parker's neck, and wrapped my legs around his torso. With a quick motion, I felt him plunge deep within me and my breath caught in my chest followed by a low moan escaping my body as I felt him retreat again. He paused before he dove deep within me a second time and I felt like there was nothing more I needed in the world than him and I connected.

My head was pounding before I even walked in the door at work a few days later. A cup of coffee wouldn't solve what I had going on up there. I felt pressure behind my eyes and felt like someone had my head locked in a vice grip. Maybe I was coming down with a cold? By the time you have spent as much time in the ER as I have, you pretty much feel immune to most all viral illnesses, so a cold seemed a bit out of reach, but never impossible.

When a girl, maybe ten years old, arrived to my empty room screaming, I felt like my head would explode. She clearly didn't feel well and I could see she had a fever before I even touched her. Her cheeks were cherry red, her hair pulled back in a messy ponytail. She clutched at her right side.

"What's brought you in tonight?" I asked the mother as she began to change her daughter into a gown.

"Her right side started hurting about an hour ago and it's only gotten worse," the mother explained.

"Okay, I'm going to get the doctor to come in and check on you quick. Can I take your temperature really quick first?" I asked as I offered a thermometer towards the girl's mouth.

Even with a throbbing behind my eyes, a wave of compassion flooded me. This girl had classic symptoms of an inflamed appendix and I couldn't help but put myself in this mother's shoes. To feel helpless as your child is hurting was the worst of all pains.

The girl opened her mouth and when the thermometer beeped, it read 101.8 degrees. Fever. I grabbed a washcloth from the linen drawer, applied cold water, and offered it to her for comfort. I knew it wouldn't fix the fever, but it might be enough to comfort her for a short time.

As I left the room to let the doctor know the girl was ready to be seen, I was stopped by a man with a frantic look across his face. His face was pale, his hair messy, and his eyes wide. I instinctively took a step back when his hands reached towards me.

"Can I help you, sir?"

"Do you have any Jameson?" he asked, blowing his stale breath in my face as he spoke.

"Excuse me?" I said with a disgusted look.

"Fine. Do you have any Fireball?" he said as his right eye began to twitch.

I glanced toward Sam who was at his computer and then back to the man.

"How about some Pam?" I offered with a twisted smile.

Sam turned around in his chair and gave me a confused look.

"Pam?" the man asked, interested.

"Yep. Pam." I repeated.

"What's Pam?" he asked, moving even closer to me, a little bit of saliva flying off his lips in my direction.

Disgusted, I looked at Sam, smiled, and at the same time we said, "DiazePAM!"

While we began to laugh, the color of the man's face turned red, and he began to back away slowly. He wobbled as he walked and I wondered where he had come from and what exactly he was here for. I looked at his wrist and saw a patient bracelet, but had no desire to get close enough to check it.

"You're a witch!" he finally screamed before turning and running back to a room on another team.

Sam and I exchanged looks and continued laughed before I continued on my original mission of getting help for my young girl with abdominal pain. Once I'd reported her status to Dr. Navarro, I went back to the room and explained that I was going to start an IV.

I had the girl sit on her mother's lap with her mother's arms wrapped around her upper body tightly. The girl continued to scream and cry, and I tried to work as fast as I could. I knew I had to get the IV placed before my head exploded. I applied the tourniquet to her upper arm and began to search for a good vein. When I found one, I cleaned the site and began the process of starting the IV.

Suddenly, she whipped her arm back, which elbowed her mother hard in the breast. The mother screamed and dropped her grip on the girl. The needle was still held securely in my hand and poked into her skin in a random place, at which point she screamed and began to flail her arm.

Irritated, and no longer seeing the comparison to my sweet Kendall, I snapped at her, "Will you hold still before you hurt someone?"

"That f'in hurt!" she screamed at me.

Her mother and I exchanged looks in shock.

"So did jabbing your elbow in my boob!" the mother finally said with a dirty look.

The girl crossed her arms across her abdomen and curled up into the fetal position on the stretcher.

"Alright, we can play it the hard way if you'd like. I'll be back with reinforcements, and we *will* start the IV. It's the only way we can get you out of this pain right now," I said with a nasty tone.

I didn't even give her a chance to respond before I left the room. I know it shouldn't have surprised me that much that she had acted that way, but it was irritating when I was trying to help her nonetheless.

Of course, just as I sat at my computer to start charting the IV attempt, triage assigned the incoming ambulance to one of my free rooms. I quickly charted what I could and grabbed the nearest free nurse, Daisy, to help me get the IV in before the ambulance arrived. This time, I would hold, and Daisy could start the IV.

We exited the room sweaty and exhausted from fighting the battle, but victorious. That girl might only be ten, but she was strong! My ambulance patient had been settled in the empty room by one of the other nurses while we were placing the IV and so Daisy offered to chart the IV while I went to assess the new patient.

The ninety-four-year old woman lay motionless on the stretcher, breaths uneven and shallow. Three children stood around her bed, anxious and attentive. The nursing home where she lived sent her to the emergency room at the request of the family, who insisted there was something wrong with her. Lab work drawn this morning at the nursing home showed absolutely nothing.

"Computer says your mother has dementia. Who is her power of attorney?" I asked as I looked at the family.

"I am," the woman stated. "I'm her daughter."

"Nice to meet you. The paperwork from the nursing home shows that she requires complete assistance for all of her needs. Is this correct?"

"Yes."

"And she's a full code?"

"Yes."

I struggled to hide my emotions. The woman was ninety-four years old and completely dependent on others for every aspect of her life. Why in the world were they keeping her a full code? I struggled to keep the words from bursting out of my mouth. At some point, I needed to advocate for my patient, right?

"Is your goal for her to remain alive or for her to live?" I was trying to be nice like AnneMarie asked me to.

"What?" the son asked.

"What is your goal for your mother. Do you want her to live or to be alive?" I repeated.

"I guess I don't understand your question," the daughter said.

"Well, your mother is ninety-four, completely dependent on everyone for every thing she does, she cannot communicate due to her dementia, and you want me to perform CPR if her heart chooses to stop? Seems kinda selfish." Shit. My mouth was going to earn me another visit with AnneMarie in the morning and she might just fire me.

"I don't think that's any of your business," the daughter said, anger rising in her voice.

"Okay," I said as I finished my charting and left the room.

I smiled as I left the room. I knew I should have kept my mouth shut, but I didn't care. I thought it was time families knew how ridiculous their requests were. How horrible doing CPR on someone that age is.

"Wanna go to lunch?" Mia asked when she saw me emerge from the patient's room.

"Absolutely," I quickly responded. "Let me go tell Amber so she can cover my rooms."

With Amber filled in, I met Mia in the break room for lunch. Instead, she motioned for me to follow her. We hadn't talked about what had happened at the bar and other than a few innocent texts since then, we hadn't talked at all.

"Where are we going?" I asked as I followed her through a maze of hallways.

"You'll see," she said with a grin.

Then, we stopped in the middle of a hallway, in front of the only door. There was no label on the door to indicated what it was, but Mia pulled a key from her pocket and placed it into the lock. *Click.* The door unlocked and she pushed the door open.

It was a small storage closet filled to the brim with old furniture, broken lamps and office chairs, shelves filled with old medical equipment, and cleaning supplies. I realized it was a dingy environmental services closet, but I couldn't figure out *why* Mia had brought me to this cramped closet in the first place. The door closed behind Mia as the light flickered overhead.

"Uh... Mia?"

Mia didn't let me say anything before she covered my mouth with hers and forcefully pushed me backwards into the stack of shelves behind me. As she kissed me, I felt her hand tug at the bottom of my scrub top. Her silky soft hands were cool against the bare skin of my abdomen as they made their way toward my breasts.

Chapter 20

I felt my guard drop and I began to return the passionate kiss. Sparks flew inside causing my body to feel electric. I didn't know what to do with my own hands, so I placed them around Mia just as I would have done if the person kissing me were Parker. Her cool hand squeezed at my breast now cupped in her hand while her other hand toyed with the nipple of my other breast.

Electric shocks pulsed up and down my spine and I realized that I liked what was happening inside me. The urge to pounce all over Mia was growing stronger with each squeeze of her hand around my breast and a flick of her tongue in my mouth. My eyes had been closed, but as the desire grew, I opened them and began to look around the room for a more comfortable spot. Suddenly, Mia pulled away from me.

"I'm sorry," she said as she adjusted her own scrub top. "I couldn't help myself. I've been wanting to do that since the night at the bar."

"I'm sorry too," I said realizing that the warmth inside me was gone the moment she had pulled away.

"What are we doing here?" she asked. "You're married still."

"And straight," I added with a nervous smile.

"And straight," she repeated with a frown. She paused before asking a serious question, "What do you want?"

I paused to think about her question. What *did* I want? Was I attracted to women? Or was I attracted to attention? Was all of this because I wanted to get back at Parker? I had a lot of things to think about and the last thing I wanted to do was lead Mia on or hurt her feelings. Being honest was going to be my best policy.

"I don't know. I need to really think about everything. I'm pretty sure I want to make my marriage work, which means we can't meet in this closet again," I said with a frown.

"That's what I was afraid of," she said quietly.

I took a deep breath and decided I needed to get out of this closet before my body made a different decision. My mind, my heart, and my body all had different opinions, but they needed to come together and make one decision. I felt the familiar throbbing return behind my eyes ever so slightly. I looked at Mia, gave her a peck on the lips, muttered a thank you, and then left the closet.

When I got back to the department, three of my rooms were empty, but my elderly woman from the nursing home remained. I hadn't been gone as long as I'd thought. In the closet, the clock had stood still and Mia and I were the only people in the world. Back in the emergency room, people buzzed around me everywhere.

For a moment, I felt like the world was going on around me, and I was just watching it. The throbbing behind my eyes became more intense, but I brushed it aside. I sat down at my computer when my pager sprung to life with an alert that the ER had received a call that a methamphetamine lab had exploded, and we would potentially be getting patients. Having three empty rooms meant I'd be getting at least one of these potential patients when and if they arrived.

It was the scream from the ambulance bay that caused my ears to perk up and a shiver to run down my spine. The blood-curdling cry was from a woman in pain, that much I recognized. Several of the nurses working the trauma team ran towards the ambulance entrance but I stayed put.

Miraculously, the woman was able to walk and held her arms out in front of her, bent at the elbow with her fingers pointing toward the ceiling, her skin melting away from the muscle. The smell of burnt flesh made my stomach turn and I knew that the sight and smell would be forever etched in my mind.

How had she gotten here? Had she actually driven herself? I watched as she was moved into the nearest trauma room, too burned for one of my rooms. I couldn't unglue my eyes from the entrance to her room. Had she been cooking meth or just in the wrong place at the wrong time?

My head swirled with questions and the pounding behind my eyes intensified the more I thought about it. But everything stopped the moment I heard the baby crying from the ambulance bay.

Another set of nurses and I sprinted for the set of double doors in the back. The sound of an infant wailing was intense and ripped at my heart. Anytime I'd heard a baby cry like that, it had never been a good outcome.

As we reached the door, a single infant car seat sat just outside the doors and the closer we got to it, the stronger the smell of burnt flesh became. I wanted to close my eyes. I wanted to pretend this was just a joke and this was just a life-like doll, but I knew the reality.

Some pathetic-excuse-for-parents had been cooking meth in their trailer with their baby nearby. The meth lab had exploded, catching both the mother and infant on fire. All I felt was my shattered heart as I grabbed the handle of the car seat and began to race with it back to one of the available trauma rooms and began to unbuckle the harness.

I carefully lifted the infant from the seat, a beautiful baby boy. Shock overtook my body as I scanned the infant from head to toe. Not even a tiny bit of the child was burned. He was perfectly intact. Why was he screaming? And where was the smell coming from? I moved the blanket around in the car seat and found several chunks of burned flesh, but not from him.

Relief flooded me. Then worry. Then sorrow. It was a rainbow of emotions. I paged social work and left the infant in the capable hands of my coworker as my pager had just buzzed and I needed to receive my own new patient.

The elderly man assigned to my empty room was there for chest pain. He was a frequent flier. I was pretty sure that he intentionally "forgot" to take his medicine most of the time. He refused to follow our discharge instructions or make any lifestyle changes. He was lonely at home and about the fourth time he came to us for chest pain over the course of one month, we were fast friends.

I wasn't in the mood for him right now. The questions and lack of answers from the meth lab situation continued to replay in my head and I felt the familiar surge of anger rushing through my body. I was angry at the world. I wanted to throw something, to smash something. To inflict hurt on something.

I closed my eyes for just a moment and took a deep breath. One thing I knew about the chest pain patient was that he was also an annoying, demanding jerk. He liked to flirt with the female staff, use his call light, and ask for a zillion things he actually didn't need. His favorite was asking for a bed bath. Despite being told time and time again that I wasn't going to be washing his genitals for him, he continued to ask.

This wasn't the day to mess with me, but he was worse than usual. His EKG wasn't looking the best, his blood pressure was extremely elevated, and his oxygen levels were low. Somehow, actually being sick this time around made him more needy, crude, and difficult to work with.

"No, Sweet Cheeks, you ain't putting that piece of plastic in my arm," he said as I came in with supplies for the IV.

"Oh yes I am," I replied with authority.

"No, no you aren't. I don't want that shit anywhere near me."

"Look, we do this every single time you come in. I'm going to start the IV, we're going to give you fluids and medication. Then, when things look better, we'll admit you or you'll be discharged. Can we for once just work together instead of butting heads?" I begged him.

"Hell naw," he said with the most serious face I've seen.

I rolled my eyes. "Do I need to get security in here? I'm really not in the mood to fight you."

"I don't know how to make it more clear. I'm not letting you put anything in this body. I'm a masterpiece just as I am."

"Oh God. Please tell me you're kidding?"

"Hell naw."

"Okay, well let's put the IV in your arm and then discuss that masterpiece you've got going on," I said, trying to sound persuasive.

"Listen, I love you. You're my favorite, but I'm *not* letting you put that shit in me anymore," he said.

"Okay, I don't have time for your bullshit. Why did you bother coming to the ER if you aren't going to let us take care of you? I don't fucking get it! Never mind, I'll be back," I said as I set the stuff on the counter and headed out of the room as my tolerance for his bullshit reached it's peak.

I expected him to stop me, but he didn't. Instead, he let me get to my computer, sign in, and then pressed his call light.

When I got back into his room, he again refused the IV but insisted I bring him a glass of water. I obliged for the sake of trying to make things easier, but it was not working. As if he had things timed, the moment I sat down at the computer and logged in, he'd press the call light.

"I have to use the urinal. Can you hold it for me?" he asked with his crooked smile, showcasing his gold front tooth.

"No. You hold it just fine at home, you can hold it yourself here too," I said through gritted teeth.

"Where's the fun in that?" The anger and aggression I was feeling surged and I wanted to scream.

"What is your goal here?" I finally snapped at him.

"To die. To have you kill me," he said with startling truth.

"That isn't going to happen. If you wanted that, you should have gone to the hospital across town."

"Nope, I want to die with *you* holding my hand. That's why I came *here*."

"I don't want to hold your hand. You smell and you're annoying," I said with a smile.

"And you love me," he replied with a toothy grin.

"Fuck that. I'm not coming back here unless you're actually dying," I finally said.

"As long as you promise to hold my hand."

"Fine, but just do it already. I need to go to lunch," I said hastily.

In one of the oddest situations of my career, it was as if he had control over everything. Just as I said it, he smiled his toothy grin again and went into ventral fibrillation! My pager alarmed and staff came rushing into the room, but as he was rolled to the side so our code team could place a board under his back for chest compressions, we found his "Do Not Resuscitate" paper lying on the stretcher, signed, witnessed, and notarized.

He had come prepared. He hadn't wanted anyone to fix him this time. He wanted to die with the only people that showed him they cared. How had he known that tonight was his night?

Instead of chest compressions, I held his hand and gently told him it was okay to go, that everything would be okay. After watching him take his last breath, I listened with my stethoscope to his heart, and confirmed he had done exactly as he'd said.

I took a deep breath and whispered under my breath, "Rest in peace, asshole."

I smiled thinking that he would have loved this scenario, but I still couldn't wrap my head around the situation. Would it have been considered a miracle or were miracles strictly good things that happened? It wasn't often that something really shook me, but this was one of those times that I would never forget.

"Mom, Brenden wants me to go to the lake with him today," Kamdyn said the moment I walked in the door.

Why was she awake so damn early? It was summer break, and she didn't have to get up for anything. I stared at her for a minute while I thought it through in my head.

"Excuse me?"

"Brenden. You know, my boyfriend. He wants me to go to the lake with him and his family," she repeated.

"I'll have to talk it over with your father."

"Mom! That's not fair," she screamed.

"I'm not worried about being fair. I'm worried about my teenage daughter wearing hardly any clothing around a boy I never even knew existed."

"Ugh. If you ever paid attention, you'd know who he is," she continued yelling before she gave up and ran up the stairs to her bedroom, slamming the door.

I couldn't do anything but shake my head. Where had my sweet Kamdyn gone? It wasn't long ago she was happily confiding in me about boys and now she was acting like the teenager she was. I wasn't sure if I could handle another teenager at the moment, but I knew I didn't have a choice.

That evening, there was no dinner on the table. I was still fast asleep when the pizza arrived, too. When my favorite show began at 08:00 p.m. that night and no one had heard from me, Kamdyn came and knocked on my door.

"Mom?" she called as she opened the door.

"Huh? What?" I said as I bolted upright.

"Are you okay? You've been asleep all day. Your favorite show is on. You never miss it. Everything okay?" she said carefully.

"I'm sorry. I'm okay. Was just exhausted. Did you guys have dinner?"

"Yeah, Dad ordered pizza for us."

"Is he home?"

"Yeah, he's in the kitchen cleaning up from dinner," she said, waiting for the shock factor.

"Alright, I'm getting up. Is he sick?"

"No, just wanted to do something nice for you. Do you work tonight?"

"Yeah. What time is it?"

"Eight."

"Okay, I needed to get up anyway. Thank you honey."

She smiled, gave me a kiss on the cheek, and then skipped out of the room. It was a total one hundred eighty degrees from when I went to bed. Had the mood swings already started?

When I emerged in the living room, I was showered and much more awake. I went straight to the coffee pot. Parker pretended to clean, but was actually watching me carefully. I guarded my body language carefully in response.

In the living room, Kamdyn was watching our show. Carter was in his bedroom doing whatever it was teenage boys do in their bedrooms. Finally, the coffee pot signaled it was finished and I poured myself an extra large cup and immediately took a sip. I practically spit the hot liquid into the sink. It was a little hotter than I had imagined it would be straight out of the pot. Ooops. Instead, I headed with my cup to the living room to catch the last part of the show with Kamdyn.

When the show ended, I went back to the kitchen to make my lunch. Parker had finished cleaning and on the counter sat a lunch made for me. He wasn't anywhere around, so I peeked inside and saw that he had taken care to not only pack a decent lunch, but to write out a note and attach it to my sandwich. Lovely. I didn't read it. I closed the lunchbox, grabbed another cup of coffee for the road, kissed Kamdyn, and headed into work.

Unfortunately, the chaos at work had been ramping up, and I was arriving at a moment of insanity. Holidays were always a busy time in the emergency room and the fourth of July was no exception. With a waiting room full of patients, a multiple car pile up on the freeway had overloaded our rooms beyond capacity and patients now lined the hallways. I sat my lunch in the refrigerator and immediately took my assignment and jumped right in.

I was extremely thankful I didn't have to work triage that night. The last thing I wanted was to have to deal with my least favorite spot. About an hour into the chaos, we received a call that a local fraternity had an issue with their furnace during a party, and we would be receiving multiple patients with carbon monoxide poisoning. Drunk patients. I rolled my eyes and prayed that at least they would be civil, but knew that they wouldn't be. I was irritated long before they even began arriving.

We discharged patients who were able to be discharged, diverted incoming patients stable enough to make it across town to the other hospital, and hurried to get every admission to the floor. Of course, that meant that the floor was irritated with us, but it had never bothered me before and wouldn't start now. I had too much other stuff to do than care about pissing them off. It was thirty minutes of absolute craziness, adrenalin, and teamwork. When we were finished with that, the frat boys began arriving.

A new form of chaos overtook the emergency room. Personally, I took in four of those drunk jerks. A little carbon monoxide wasn't going to stop them from having a good time apparently. They were easily making my life a living hell. And at the current moment, that was saying a lot.

"I must have died because it looks like you're an angel," drunk frat boy #1 said when I entered the room.

"How original," I said, irritated.

He laughed and then grabbed my butt as I typed information into the computer.

"Get. Your. Hands. Off. Me." I said slowly and clearly.

"Whoa, you don't have to be all offended."

"Don't violate me, and I won't be."

"Whatever."

"Have some fucking respect. When you get some, let me know and I'll come back and help you breathe," I said as I slammed my pen on the counter and abruptly left the room.

"You okay, Kate?" Sam asked when I walked out of the patient's room looking pissed off.

232

"Yep. Just some punk grabbing my butt again," I said as I rolled my eyes.

I had other patients to see and honestly, drunk frat boy #1's pulse ox showed a blood oxygen level well above normal, so he was the least of my concerns. The other three frat boys weren't *as* bad with their behavior, but mostly because they weren't trying to get handsy with me. Sure, they had inappropriate comments, but I could handle those. It was when they tried to get busy with their hands that I had a major problem. Why men thought they could touch any woman they wanted was beyond me and who were these mothers who allowed their sons to think this behavior was okay?

"Hey babe, can you get me some water?" drunk frat boy #3 called at me as I walked by his room.

"You wanna try that again?" I said as I stuck my head in his room.

"Hey babe, can you *please* get me some water?"

I rolled my eyes. "Wrong answer."

I kept on walking to my newest patient who was stationed on a stretcher in the hallway. Also drunk, the guy had been playing a game with his friends called who-could-perform-the-stupidest-trick-with-firecrackers. He had stuck a bottle rocket in his butt and his friend had lit it. He clearly wasn't the sharpest crayon in the box. Now he was facing a literal hole in his ass and burnt skin.

"Are you having any pain?" I asked, even though I knew the answer.

"Uh, duh! My ass feels like it's on fire!"

"As it should since you pretty much lit your butt hole on fire," I said bluntly.

"Can you just get me some ice? Or pain medicine? Something to make it stop?" he begged.

"Hey, I can't fix stupid, but I *can* medicate it." I gave him a little wink as I headed back to my computer.

Besides having a summer holiday, the other part of July that I dreaded the most is when a fresh wave of new emergency medicine residents started their rotations and I had to triple check orders and try to explain to them how to do their jobs.

Although we regularly hosted medical students, I didn't recognize any of the new residents listed in this month's rotation. There were four of them starting this month, I'd learned. Three men and a woman.

Usually I jumped at the opportunity to work with the residents, but lately I had zero patience for dumb. I liked to train them in the real world situations that we deal with versus their textbook ones. I liked to help them become the future generation of doctors who might be caring for me some day. But now, I just wanted to smack them in the back of the head like my father used to do when my brother said something stupid or had a smart mouth.

The new residents also meant it took longer for an ER visit. I had too much going on to be patient while they learned what the hell they were doing. I felt the familiar throb behind my eyes calling my name and for a brief moment, I closed my eyes and tried to imagine sitting on a beach.

I finally got a chance to pee about six hours into my shift when I finally discharged the last of the intoxicated frat boys and things had settled down some. By that time, I wasn't sure which would explode first: my head or my bladder.

Chapter 21

Waking up that afternoon, I was craving coffee, which was pretty much normal for me. Making my way to the kitchen, I saw Kendall sitting at the table reading a stack of papers. She wore pajama pants and a t-shirt, even though it was four in the afternoon. She dragged her hand through her hair and sighed heavily before acknowledging I was watching her.

"What's all that?" I asked, pulling out the chair next to her and sitting down.

"Paperwork I got from a legal help office. I have to go through it all and figure everything out regarding Sally," she said with a stressed look.

"Sally?"

"Yeah, I thought that would be a good name for the baby," she said, finally putting a smile on her face.

"Where did you get the name Sally?"

"Wasn't it Gran's name?" she asked.

"Uh, nope. That would be Celine," I said with a smile.

"Oh."

"What is the paperwork you've got?" I asked, leaning towards the stack and trying to sneak a look.

"It's information about parentage, and legal custody. An application for assistance and stuff."

"Well, I've been wanting to talk with you anyways. What are your plans?"

"What do you mean?" She began to fidget with her fingers.

"Well, what are your plans for after the baby comes? Where will you live? Will you get a job or go to school? Or even both? How are you feeling? Do you need anything?" All my questions came out in a pile of word vomit.

She paused, then said, "I don't know."

It was honest. I appreciated that. I had feared she wouldn't take any of this seriously, but I was glad to see she was really making an effort to figure things out on her own and not expect everyone to do everything for her.

"That's understandable. Your dad and I will be here to help you. But I don't want to tell you what to do. You're going to be the mom now," I said with a smile.

After another pause, she looked up at me and said, "I'm scared."

"I know you are, baby girl."

My heart melted into a million pieces and I pulled her close to me. I had an uncontrollable urge to laugh suddenly and as much as I fought it, a little giggle erupted from my mouth. Kendall pulled away from me and gave me a confused and angry look.

"Why are you laughing?" she asked.

"This seems to happen a lot lately, but I honestly don't know. I can't control it. It just happens. And always at the wrong times," I explained.

Kendall was upset and I was laughing. It wasn't funny. Not only was it not funny, this wasn't how I had imagined this conversation would go. She got up from the table, collected her papers, and quietly went to her room. She turned and gave me one last look as I continued to laugh at the table before she entered her room.

Why did this keep happening to me? What in the hell was wrong with me? Could stress really be the cause or was something else going on? If I were honest with myself, I was scared to know the answer. A lot of things had been happening in my life, but a lot of changes within me had also happened. Sometimes it felt good and other times I found my heart breaking when I reacted inappropriately, like right now.

First, I picked up my phone, called my family physician, and scheduled a physical for next week. I was sure this was all nothing, but it was truly starting to bother me. Not to mention, the constant throbbing behind my eyes was enough to drive me insane. I finally collected myself, then made my way down the hall to her room. I knocked. I heard a quiet answer and let myself in. I sat down next to her on the bed.

"I'm sorry, Kendall. Lately, a lot of strange things are happening to me — like laughing when we're having a serious conversation. I have zero control over it. And honestly, it scares the crap out of me," I confided in her.

"Really? Like being super moody lately?"

"Yeah, and daily headaches. And I've been getting in trouble at work," I admitted.

"Really? That's not you, Mom."

It was hard saying those words to her. A parent never wants to admit when things aren't going well. I hadn't told anyone that things hadn't been going well at work, but I knew I needed to put myself out there if I was going to help break down the walls Kendall had been building around this entire pregnancy.

"Aren't you worried?" she asked.

"I'm not worried. I'm scared. But, I just called and made an appointment to go see my doctor next week. Hopefully, we can get to the bottom of all of this. I don't know how much more of these throbbing headaches I can tolerate."

"Mom, I didn't realize it was that bad," she said with a concerned look.

"I have wanted to deny there was a problem for a long time now, but at some point I have to face it."

"What could be causing it?"

This was the scariest question. In all of my nursing knowledge, I knew what type of things caused these changes, but I didn't want any of the to be happening to me. Admitting I had a problem meant admitting that one of the medical problems *could* be happening to me.

"Well, that's a long list. I'll leave it up to the doctor," I said, skirting around the answer.

"I'm sorry, Mom."

"Don't be. Why don't you tell me more about the baby? We haven't had a chance to talk about everything since you announced you were pregnant. I'm sorry about that."

"Well, what do you want to know?" she said as her entire demeanor changed to something more upbeat.

"Start at the beginning. Tell me about her father," I encouraged.

"Okay, so I didn't do well on one of my exams and my roommates wanted to take me out, right? So we went to the bar..."

"You went to the bar?" I interrupted.

"Yeah, but not to drink, Mom! Anyways, we met up with some friends and I noticed this guy kept looking at me. He had a gorgeous smile. He was tall and dark. Ah... Such a nice body," she said with a dreamy look in her eyes.

"Hey, I know how babies are made. I don't need *that* much detail," I said as we laughed.

"When I went up to the bar to get a glass of water, he approached me. We chatted for a bit and then, I left with him," she said, fearing my reaction.

"I'm not going to comment," I reassured her.

"Okay, good. In the morning, he was still asleep and I just... snuck out. I was ashamed! You guys always told me to be smarter and I wasn't," she admitted.

"I feel like I'm missing a part of this story though. You are smarter than sleeping with a stranger, or at least I think you are. So, what made you do it? It doesn't seem like you."

"Ugh... I may have gotten toasted before going to the bar..." she sighed.

"Now it makes more sense. So why don't you know his name?"

"Well, if he told me, I don't remember it," she admitted.

"Do you remember what he looks like?"

"Oh yeah. I see him, I feel him, in my dreams every night. I mean these dreams are *so* vivid," she said with the dreamy look again.

I laughed, "Oh pregnancy."

"Yeah, pregnancy." She laid back on the bed with a plop.

"So did you try to find him?"

She bolted upright and stammered, "And say what? Hey, I don't know your name but I'm having your baby?"

"Well, not how I'd word it, but it would do the job, don't you think?"

"I can't do that!"

"Yet you slept with someone and don't even know his name?" I joked.

"Mom!"

"Sorry!"

"Ugh, I don't know what to do." She laid back down with another plop.

Finally, she understood that *something* needed to be done. This guy, whoever he was, deserved to know he had a child on the way. I somehow needed to get Kendall to find him, but the idea had to be her own. She would never do it because I said she needed to.

"He ought to know," I pushed.

"You can't be serious!" she exclaimed before running her hands through her hair. "But you're right."

"Now what?" I secretly encouraged.

"I guess I start at the bar, right?"

Internally, I smiled and for the first time in many months, I felt I'd finally done something right. Unfortunately, instead of feeling elated or some other happy emotion, all I felt was irritated and the familiar throbbing behind my eyes.

I needed an escape from everything around me. I thought I would do something I hadn't done in quite some time — go running. I strapped on my tennis shoes, grabbed my keys and cell phone, and took off running. At the end of the driveway, I put the earbuds in my ears and turned the country music up loud enough to tune out my thoughts.

The fresh air felt good as it entered my lungs. My feet pounding the pavement created a rhythmic cadence that flowed with the beat of the song in my ear. And for once, I didn't feel a throbbing behind my eyes.

First, I went around the neighborhood. It felt good. I felt good. I decided to keep on going, so I ran down the street to the next neighborhood. When that one was done, I decided to just begin running down the main street. Was this a Forrest Gump type run?

I kept on running for what seemed like forever, until I didn't recognize my surroundings anymore. I wasn't sure where I was, but I wasn't worried since I'd just followed the one road and had only gone straight. Or had it come to a tee and I'd turned? I was so into my songs and the pattern of my feet on the pavement that I had lost track.

The surrounding houses were in disrepair. Yards had grass that was long overdue for mowing. Trash was littered around the houses and along fences. The windows on some houses were broken. Driveways had large, deep cracks and broken down cars. People sat on porches, watching the cars pass. Where was I?

Not recognizing anyone or anything, my anxiety began to grow. I didn't recognize the name of the street. Ahead of me, I saw two men standing on the street corner. Ordinarily, I wouldn't have thought anything of this, but I wasn't in my neck of the woods anymore.

Should I cross the street? Do I just keep going and ignore them? Will they leave me alone? The two men were easily twice my size and were carefully studying me. I was sure I looked like a fish out of water. I reminded myself over and over that I had dealt with sketchier situations as an emergency room nurse plenty of times, although it wasn't comforting since I'd had security to back me up in those situations.

In the few moments I had to make a decision, I chose to just push forward and ignore the men and pray that they ignored me as well.

A woman on a porch a few houses from the end of the block called out to me, "Honey, where you from? You don't look like you b'long round here."

Was it that obvious I was lost? I didn't answer her. I put my head down and kept a slow jog.

"I wouldn't go that way if I was you," the woman cautioned with a low hum.

As I got closer to the men, I heard them whistle at me and begin making comments about being a "foxy lady" and a "fine specimen sent from God." I could feel my pulse quicken. Maybe I should call Parker. I knew he was probably in the operating room, but someone usually answered his phone. Maybe Kendall could come get me? Did I even need to be rescued?

"Excuse me gentleman, just out getting a run in," I said, trying to be nonchalant.

"Honey, you don't belong here. Someone could easily take a tiny thing like you and do whatever they wanted," the first guy said as he eyed my body from head to toe and took a step closer to me.

"Well, I'm just out for a run. I took a wrong turn," I said, keeping my shoulders back and putting my key between my fingers in my pocket.

I was now flanked by the men and could smell the alcohol on their breath. I could see the flecks of dirt under their fingernails and I wondered what they had under their baggy clothes.

"I suggest you turn around and run right back to where you came from, sweetie pie," the second man said with a southern accent as he placed his dirty hand gently on my butt.

"Don't touch me!" I yelled as I tried to move away from him but backed into the first man. "Do you know which way is Iroquois Boulevard?" I asked, trying to redirect the conversation to a safe place.

"Sweet cheeks, you're a long way from there. I'm going to let you go back the way you came. Next time you come this way though, I'm not going to be so friendly," the first man said as his gold tooth peaked out from his smile and his hand brushed against my cheek.

I made a quick judgement that these men meant what they were saying, turned on my heel, and began to jog back in the direction I'd come from. The woman on the porch yelled out that clearly I was smarter than she thought and I'd made the right decision. I didn't feel so tough anymore, and I pulled my phone from my pocket. I quickly dialed Parker's number as I continued to run, casually looking behind me to see if I was being followed.

"Hello beautiful," Parker said as he answered his phone.

"So I went for a run..."

"Good for you!" he said, cutting me off.

"Well... I'm lost. And I'm definitely not somewhere I want to be. Can you come get me?" I asked, my voice shaking more than I wanted it to.

"What? Of course. Do you see *anything* you recognize?" he asked as I could hear panic beginning in his voice and shuffling of papers in the background.

"Well... no... Wait... It looks like I'm on Bernard Street? Maybe?" I said with hesitation.

"Bernard Street? You need to keep running. I don't care which direction or how you got there, but you need to get away from there. And now."

"I'm trying. I just don't know which way to run. Everything is fuzzy looking."

My vision chose that time to begin blurring? Perfect. I had no clue where I was and now I wouldn't be able to see to direct my own rescue. I was screwed. I was in full on panic mode at this point. What was happening to me? How did I not know how I got here?

"I'll be there as quick as I can. If you have to, call 911 and a police officer can come get you."

He had a point there. Why hadn't I thought of that? Why had I thought that going for a run would be a brilliant way to clear my head? Clearly my head wasn't functioning correctly. I was scared, but I still wouldn't admit to anything being wrong.

I kept running along Bernard Street until Parker pulled up beside me. By the time I was safely in his passenger seat, I was absolutely exhausted from running. How long had I been running exactly? I didn't remember what time I'd even started my run. I prepared myself for the lecture that never came. Instead, Parker wrapped me in his arms.

"Are you okay?" he asked.

"I think so," I said as I began to cry softly now that I was safe.

"Everything is okay," he said compassionately. "Let's get you home."

We rode in silence the short distance back home. It had seemed like so much further when I was running, but it was actually only just a few miles.

When we got home, Parker helped me to the couch and sat next to me. He picked my feet up and began massaging them.

"So, are you ready to tell me what you were doing running in that neighborhood?" he asked quietly.

"I wish I had the answer. I took off for a run and just kept running. I kinda snapped out of a funk when those men began talking to me. I was totally freaked out," I said with a whimper.

"Hun, I don't know what's going on with you, but new rule: you tell me or text me where you're going so I know."

"You got it," I said as I snuggled into his arms and fell asleep.

I found myself stuck in triage again the following night. I was too tired to care, honestly. I'd grown to just accept my assignments lately. But when a woman arrived with her six-

244

month-old baby who was sporting a temperature of 100.0 degrees, I wasn't sure I was the right person to have in triage.

"Did you give her anything for the fever?" I asked.

"No, I wanted you to be able to see what she's been like," the mother said.

"How long has the fever been going on?"

"About an hour."

Was she kidding me? If I pinched myself, was this real life? An hour of a mild fever, and she's rushing the kid to the emergency room? People were in rooms facing life or death, and she's in a panic about a mild temperature for an hour?

"Any changes in the baby's diet or anything else you've done differently the last few days? Has she been exposed to anyone who's been sick?" I asked in rapid fire succession.

"Well, we did go to the doctor two days ago for her well-child check and there was some sick kids in the waiting room," she said with a concerned look.

"She got shots?"

"Yeah."

"I'll be right back," I said as I stood from my stool and headed straight for the door before my mouth could get me fired.

Chapter 22

It was a Friday morning when Parker and I loaded Kendall, Kamdyn, and Carter into the car and drove a few hours away to the beach. It was the first time we'd done something together since our cruise in April, and it was long overdue. The thought of an entire day doing nothing but reading and taking in the sun sounded fantastic in theory, but I had a lot of reservations.

The day had started off with another raging headache. Kendall and Kamdyn were fighting over who got which seat in the minivan and Carter was irritated that he was being "forced" to go at all. The only person in the family happy and healthy was Parker.

Of course, the moment the chairs were set up on the sand, Carter fell asleep, Kamdyn chose to read her book rather than socialize, and Kendall complained about how fat she looked in her bikini.

"You're not fat, Kendall. You're pregnant. There *is* a difference," Parker pointed out.

"I know that, Dad. But right now I look pretty fat. Have you seen me from the side?" she asked as she turned her body to give Parker a side view of her growing bump.

"Whoa, wouldya look at that! A baby is hiding in your belly!" he teased.

"You aren't funny," she said as she flopped down on her towel. "And how am I supposed to tan my back exactly?"

"Dig your fat belly a hole. Duh," Kamdyn said to her sister without even looking up from her book.

At thirty-two weeks pregnant, Kendall's small frame was struggling to cope with the shift in weight. While the rest of the family liked to pick on her about it, she was insanely irritated about it. Despite her balance issues, her little stomach protruded in a cute round basketball shape from her torso. I had gained fifty pounds when I had been pregnant with Kendall, and I was a little jealous at how well she was moderating herself.

Carter excused himself to go find some food, Parker offered to join him, and Kamdyn had fallen asleep. When I was alone with Kendall, I decided that there was no time like the present to push her again towards finding the baby's father.

"Have you made any progress?" I asked.

"No, but the doctor says I could start to see signs of things happening and an increase in these fake contractions over the next few weeks as my body prepares for birth," she answered casually without opening her eyes.

"What? That's not what I'm talking about, silly. I mean with finding her father!"

"Mom, you need to stop. I can't just go trying to find a guy looking like this to tell him it's his. I'll try after she's born so that the mere sight of me won't give everything away."

"Kendall..." I began before she cut me off.

"Mom, now you're giving *me* a headache." She put her headphones on and turned her music up.

Effectively shut out, I watched the swimmers for a few minutes and then opened my book. I wasn't going to win this battle with Kendall. Somewhere though, was a man who deserved to know the truth. Maybe I should go try to find him myself? It would all be so much easier if she at least had his name.

Parker and Carter returned with plates of fried food and continued their father-son time as if us ladies weren't even present. But when Kendall let out a high-pitched yell and instantly was reduced to the fetal position, everyone stopped what they were doing and all eyes were on Kendall.

"What's wrong," Parker asked as he moved towards her.

"Cramps," she muttered.

Before Parker or I could even suggest it, Carter and Kamdyn began to pack up the items spread on the blanket and prepared to leave the beach. I was sure she was having the Braxton-Hicks contractions, and she just needed more water, but Parker insisted that she be checked out "just in case". The thought of sitting in the emergency room, or even the doctor's office, for the rest of the day made my head hurt even more.

Parker dropped Kamdyn, Carter, and me off at home and proceeded to Kendall's doctor's office with her for further assessment. I tried hard not to roll my eyes, but I hadn't been successful. I could see the look in Parker's eye that was telling me to keep my mouth shut, and luckily, that I had some control over.

"They were able to stop the contractions, but she'll have to stay the night tonight as a precaution," Parker said over the phone.

"Is everything okay with the baby?" I asked, slight worry in my voice.

"Yeah, they said she looks great. And yes, Kendall was a little dehydrated, but everything is fine. A liter of fluid tonight, and she'll be ready to come home in the morning," he reassured me.

"Do I need to come up there and stay with her tonight?" I offered.

"Naw, I've got it handled. You need to get some rest. You have a big stretch of work coming up," he said and I could hear him smiling through the phone.

As I ended the call, I realized, yet again, that Parker was absolutely worth fighting for. I'd heard enough horror stories in my career to know that Parker was definitely one of the good guys. The fact he was staying the night at the hospital with Kendall so she wouldn't be alone absolutely melted my heart.

That is until I realized that Renee might also be working at that very same hospital at the very same time. Was this the reason he had quickly shot down my offer and insisted he be the one to stay with her? Was he really just masquerading as one of the good guys? Putting on a good show for the sake of appearances?

The damn throbbing began behind my eyes the moment my brain flipped the switch from good to evil. If I'd have been connected to a blood pressure cuff, I'm sure my pressures were escalating by the second. I could feel my pulse quicken and the anger and hatred take over my impulses.

What in the hell was happening to me? I was completely aware of it happening but completely unable to prevent it or change it. When I'd gone to the doctor a few weeks back, she had been unable to find anything and had me go to the lab for blood work, which came back beautifully. I was falling apart for no apparent reason?

I had so many questions and zero answers. And now, I was waging war with myself between reality and my imagination. I took a few deep breaths and tried to reassure myself. Parker was staying the night at the hospital so Kendall wouldn't be alone, not because he wanted to go screw the OR nurse.

At some point, I fell asleep, but not before I'd gone to the kitchen and had a snack because I found a fork laying on my chest when I woke up. I wanted to stab myself in the eyes with the fork to relieve the pressure already building behind them, but I fought the urge. I took more pills and went straight to the coffee pot as I checked my phone for any updates.

I had no text messages and no missed calls, but just as I began pouring the first cup of coffee, the door to the garage burst open and Kendall and Parker appeared.

"How are you feeling?" I asked.

"Tired. I was up most of the night as they kept coming in to adjust things and just waking me up," Kendall answered.

"I second that," Parker said as he carried a small bag in from the car.

Parker looked like he'd been run over by a bus. His hair flew in every direction, he had a bit of stubble on his face, his clothes were wrinkled, and by the way he was walking, his back was bothering him.

"Those couch beds haven't improved in the eighteen years since Kendall was born," Parker announced when he returned to the kitchen from dropping off the bag.

"Yeah, they spent all their time advancing the medicine of birthing the babies, not focusing on the father's comfort," I said with a laugh.

Parker shot me a glare before adding, "Hey, I did my time."

Kendall looked from me to Parker and then scurried like a mouse before she would have to get sucked into another conversation about the father of her unborn child. This time, I gave Parker a glare.

I was thankful we'd made the trip to the beach that last week of the summer. The summer was over before I knew it and school activities were starting. Carter, in his senior year, was excited to return to football practice. It always seemed like the one thing that he and I had in common. I like to think he gained his love of football from me, but he claims it was from watching his favorite quarterbacks on TV instead.

One of the things I had always enjoyed was watching his practices. It wasn't exactly something most parents wanted to do, but the coach allowed it. I wasn't always able to get to the football games themselves because of work, but I hoped this year would be different since I was working night shift again.

The first day of August was a Wednesday, and I was sitting in the bleachers during Carter's morning practice. He'd been having two-a-day practices for over a week now and I could see the boys beginning to get back into shape and mentally preparing for the season, which would begin in a few more weeks. The temperature, despite being so early in the morning, was already eighty-three degrees and I almost felt bad for the boys as they ran suicide sprints. Watching them run to each five-yard line and back to the end zone, increasing by five yards with each sprint, my own body ached and I took another sip of my cool water.

When one of the boys collapsed on the fifty-yard line, the coach began to yell for him to get back up, to not be a "pussy" as he called it. I hated this part of practice, but I had been forbidden by Carter from ever intervening or saying something about it. I sat watching as the boy continued to lay there. I watched his limbs fall weakly, and he laid there sprawled out while the other boys continued their suicide sprints and feared what might happen if they stopped to help him.

It was when I began to watch his chest that I realized he wasn't breathing as I would expect if he had passed out from being hot or out of breath or out of shape. With twenty plus years of emergency nursing under my belt, I was a well oiled machine for events like this and I sprung from my seat and took the steps of the bleachers two at a time as I raced to the field.

The other boys slowed down their sprints when they saw me racing toward the field, but did not stop completely. The coach moved to stand in my way but I yelled at him to get out of the way and I reached the kid in seconds as the coach chased after me, yelling profanities the entire way.

"What's his name?" I yelled to the field of players.

"Kevin!" one of the boys yelled in reply.

I called his name but got no response. I confirmed he wasn't breathing, and he didn't have a pulse. I looked at the coach and yelled for an automatic defibrillator, or AED, that I knew was on the sidelines. The athletic association had been mandated to carry and train coaching staff on its use for situations just like these. I knew that because I had been on the subcommittee pushing for the regulation.

I wasted no time trying to remove his clothing and unbuckle his shoulder pads. One of the assistant coaches arrived with the AED just as I ripped at the last buckle and began to pump the boy's chest. The assistant coach applied the pads while I continued. The head coach stood in shock, not moving.

"Someone call 911!" I yelled to the crowd of boys now forming a circle around us.

"Stand back. Analyzing rhythm," the machine mechanically stated. After what felt like forever, the machine said, "Shock not advised, resume CPR." And I did.

After barely five minutes of CPR, I felt a fog come over me. I felt weak, nauseous, and somewhat dizzy, but I kept on. I demanded someone needed to take over for me as I felt my pace slowing. The assistant coach practically pushed me out of the way and I collapsed on the turf next to him, breathing heavily.

"Mom, are you okay?" Carter said as he pushed his teammates aside and knelt next to me.

"Yep, just tired," I said breathlessly.

The AED came to life again and began analyzing the boy's rhythm. This time, a shock was advised and everyone stood back. I forced myself onto my knees next to him and prepared for the shock. The machine made a punching type noise and the boy's body jerked in response as the electric impulse moved through him. The machine began to re-analyze his rhythm just as he sputtered to life.

"Ahhhh," he moaned as he rolled onto his side and clenched at his chest.

"Hey there, Kevin," I said pleasantly, my ears ringing and my eyes with blurry vision.

"Ughhh," he continued to moan.

I heard the sirens growing louder as they pulled into the parking lot. Soon, Kevin was not-so-comfortably lying on the stretcher in the back of the ambulance and headed to the hospital. Finally, I stood up, just as the boys around me began to clap.

"Way to go, Mom!" Carter shouted above the noise.

I shrugged my shoulders and began to walk back to the bleachers when the head coach wrapped his arms around me in a tight embrace. I wasn't exactly sure why since he hadn't bothered to help one bit. He had just stood there watching like it was a movie instead of real life. I wanted to smack him. *This* was the man responsible for my child's safety in one of the most dangerous games on the planet, and he couldn't even react to something he was trained to react to.

"I'll see you at home, Carter," I called over my shoulder as I pushed the coach's arms off me. Then, looking the coach straight in his eyes, I whispered, "Don't you *ever* touch me again, you worthless piece of shit. That boy died on the field and you did absolutely nothing. I don't care how good at football you may be, you will never coach my son again. Get your ass off this fucking field."

I broke eye contact and headed towards the bleachers to collect my things. My words had been hateful and full of venom, but at least they were honest.

"Thanks, Mrs. C," one of the boys called.

I just waved. My arms ached and felt heavy. My eyelids were barely staying open and I felt extremely exhausted. And then that pesky throbbing began behind my eyes once again. I popped Motrin into my mouth as soon as I got in the car and swallowed as I shifted into drive. I wanted a nice long nap before I had to go into work. The adrenaline wasn't enough to keep me "high" for long.

After pulling my car into the garage, I threw my keys on the floor and removed my shoes. The throbbing in my head hadn't stopped, so I went straight to the cabinet in the kitchen that I knew held "the good stuff" and took an Imitrex that I tried to reserve for the worst of days. Straight to my bed, straight into pajamas, and I went straight to sleep.

The house was quiet when I finally woke up. A quick glance at the clock told me it was eight o'clock. Kamdyn was in her room working on homework and Carter left a note that he was going with friends for pizza after practice. I wasn't sure that eating pizza after twice daily strenuous activity was a good idea, but I also wasn't a teenager anymore either. Parker was on the couch asleep, remote in hand. The throbbing in my head bearable again, I packed my lunch, grabbed my keys off the floor, and headed to work.

I sat down at the computer and slowly sipped my coffee. Despite having such a rough time over the last few months, I really did love my job. It was nice to come into work and have another family. But just as the thought crossed my mind, the phone next to the computer rang.

"Hello?"

"Hi. Is this Kate?" the person on the other end said.

"Yes."

"This is Georgia. I'm not feeling well and I won't be able to make it in tonight." I rolled my eyes.

"What's wrong?" I asked as I grabbed the call in slip and began scribbling her information down.

"Well, I've been having diarrhea all day."

"Are you serious or is this just a bullshit excuse?"

"What? I'm serious," she said quickly.

"Okay fine." I hung up the phone.

As I met up with Tyrell to get report on the "yellow" team patients, I drank a second cup of coffee. The throbbing in my head was now compounded with some ringing in my ears, but I brushed that off as well. I was going to make it through this night, I kept telling myself. I'd already saved one life today and I wouldn't quit on any others.

Of the four rooms, I had three patients and an empty room. The first patient was being seen for generalized pain, the second was about to be discharged, and the third had a sprained ankle. I sat down at the computer and checked for any pending orders. The first patient was due for new vital signs and I knew that my PCA was helping in another room, so I went to take them myself.

Entering the room, I introduced myself and the patient smiled and attempted to introduce himself in return. The smile on his face was big and bright on one side while the other side remained unchanged. I noticed the difficulty he had while trying to say his name, something that most people can do easily.

"Are you having any pain?"

"Not really painful, but my right hand is numb," he mumbled as he tried to raise his right hand to show me.

"Can you squeeze my hands?" I said as I crossed my arms and held out my pointer and middle fingers for him to squeeze.

His right side was barely able to reach up and grasp my fingers while the left side had zero issues giving my fingers a tight squeeze. Instantly, I was confident he was having a stroke and excused myself to get the doctor. Within a few minutes, he was shipped off to a CT scan to verify what was going on.

I returned to my computer to document what had taken place and I looked over the patients in the waiting room. Besides the standard coughs, ear aches, and stomach pains, I saw a name that stuck out to me instantly. A name I recognized well. This particular gentleman was well known for going to the bar, getting completely trashed, and then trying to beat his wife. In the past he'd been brought to us to have lacerations sewn up, broken bones stabilized, and even once, drugs removed from his anus.

I went straight to the triage nurse and requested he be sent to my room. I was in no mood for his shenanigans and I didn't want to put that on anyone else either. I'd spent plenty of time dealing with him, and I was feeling ready to battle if he began to act up.

I went to the waiting room and called his name. Instantly, I knew this would be an interesting visit as he limped towards me, face red with anger, and some sort of white powder dusted his black hair. I could smell the alcohol on his breath, he hadn't shaved in three or four days based on the stubble on his face, and he wore tattered work jeans with a ripped t-shirt.

"How are you today?" I asked casually as I walked him toward the room.

"Oh shut up," he blubbered and I stopped talking.

Once in the room, I asked, "What are you being seen for today?"

"My wife threw a knife at me," he said as he lifted his shirt to reveal a small paring knife stuck in his lower abdomen.

"Wow," was all I managed to reply before helping him remove his shirt the rest of the way and helping him onto the stretcher.

"Yeah, that bitch should be arrested for her behavior," he seethed.

I don't know what came over me, but I began to laugh uncontrollably. I knew it wasn't appropriate, but I couldn't stop it. He shot me the death stare but I kept on laughing. I watched as he tried to determine if I was laughing at him or with him before he responded.

"What the hell are you laughing at?"

"Everything," I said with a snort.

"Well stop, you're giving me a headache," he said with a deep sigh.

I tried to straighten up, but couldn't, so I just left the room. I didn't really want to aggravate him further considering he had a knife within reach. I could only imagine the scene that would be if he removed the knife to threaten me further while blood squirted everywhere from the gaping hole left in his abdomen. I was already headed straight for hell.

"What's so funny?" Mia asked as she approached me.

"I'm not exactly sure, but this dude's wife stabbed him with a paring knife and I can't stop laughing."

"You're funny," she said, shaking her head and walking away.

Finally, I took one last attempt to settle myself and when it worked, I headed back to my other patient who had returned from his CT scan. Confirming he was having a stroke, I had a slew of orders to complete in a short amount of time and I quickly forgot about the stab wound and began the work at hand.

The problem was, I suddenly couldn't remember how to do them. I stood in the room holding the syringe to administer the ordered medicine, but stopped short as I racked my brain trying to figure out how I would get the liquid from the syringe inside the guy. I'd never had this problem before. I knew that I knew the answer, but for the life of me, I couldn't make myself remember it. It was as if the program called "nurse" had been deleted from my brain. I instantly began to panic.

Rushing straight to Sam, I begged, "Look, I'll explain later but I need your help with my patient *now*."

He didn't bat an eyelash and followed me to the room. I handed him the syringe and explained what needed to be done. Without having to think, he took it from my hands and administered it. Unfortunately, not a single thing he did registered in my brain with recognition. Instead, it felt like I was seeing the skills performed for the very first time.

"Okay, are you ready to explain?" Sam said as we headed back for the computers to chart.

"I blanked. I totally and completely forgot how to do anything," I explained bluntly.

"How do you forget? It's like second nature to you," he pleaded.

"That's the scary part! Even when you did it, it was like I was seeing it for the very first time. No part of me recognized what you were doing," I said, feeling scared as I said it out loud.

"What the hell? Are you okay?" he asked, concerned.

"I'm not sure."

I left Sam to go assist Dr. Moon with removing the knife in the next room, but felt my mind racing as it tried to recall even the simplest things I had done for over twenty years. What was I supposed to do if I couldn't remember? I was supposed to be the preceptor. I was supposed to be the one that was a leader. I fought back the urge to cry and tried to focus on the task at hand instead.

"Alright, hold still. I'm going to remove this knife and see what we're working with, okay?" Dr. Moon said to the patient.

"You do you, I'll do me," he said as he rolled his eyes and laid his head down on the pillow behind him.

As Dr. Moon began to pull at the knife, a grotesque growl emerged from his mouth and *crack.* His left fist landed on the side of Dr. Moon's head. I lunged forward, grabbed the knife and pulled it the rest of the way out of the wound before the patient had a chance to do so himself. I frantically called for help to the room STAT and paged security.

Dr. Moon crumpled to the floor, groaning, and grasping at her head. When other staff members charged into the room, I was standing there holding a bloody knife while our attending lay on the floor. I quickly realized that the first impression probably wasn't the best. I pointed at the patient, who was

attempting to stand up and had his fist ready for round two.
Not today.

Chapter 23

One moment I was standing still holding the bloody knife and the next I had dropped the knife on the floor and was yelling profanities at him in his face. Fearing the patient would attempt to punch me as well, Sam wrapped his arms around me, lifted me off the floor, and carried me from the room, all while I was kicking and screaming. Mia rushed to help Dr. Moon off the floor as a swarm of security guards stormed the room and detained the patient.

Fearing further complications with his wound, Dr. Moon was helped from the room and another attending entered to try to assess the patient, who was now strapped to the bed circa 1950s style. Sam kept walking, carrying me with his arms around me in a bear hug, until we reached the break room, my screams echoing off the walls and down the hallway as we went.

"*What* has gotten into you, Kate?" Sam finally asked when I stopped screaming, and he'd set me down.

"What do you mean? That jackass just sucker punched Moon in the head. You think I'm gonna just stand there quietly and not defend her? Not to mention the jackass had access to a knife!" I said, louder than necessary and still somewhat breathless.

"Kate, calm down," he reassured me.

"How am I supposed to calm down?" I asked as I began to pace back and forth.

"I've never seen you this worked up. In all the situations we've been through... In some of the craziest drama I've seen... You've always been the level-headed one. The leader of the group. The one to calm everyone down and get our focus back on the job at hand. So, *what* has gotten into you lately?"

"I... I... I don't know," I admitted truthfully.

"Well, you need to figure it out and fast. What happened out there was absolutely unacceptable and you know it. You can't do that to a patient, even when they sucker punch the doc in the side of the head," he scolded.

I didn't say anything. I knew he was right, but at the same time, no one deserves to get treated like that. Who did the patient think he was? Mr. Invincible? My anger continued to boil and I continued to pace. My heart felt like it would pound out of my chest at any moment.

"Kate, why don't you go home," Sam finally said.

"What? I can't go home!" I argued.

"Yes. Yes, you can. And yes, you will," Sam said firmly.

"Bullshit. I have patients to take care of."

"Not anymore tonight. Go home, Kate," Sam repeated.

He and I locked eyes in an epic battle for rightness, but he won when I realized I was too angry to work anyways. I went to my locker and grabbed the few things I left there and stormed out. I went straight to my car, threw it in drive, and peeled out of the parking lot five minutes later.

When I got home, everyone was still asleep. I threw my keys on the island counter top, threw my shoes across the kitchen, and then stormed off for the bedroom. I turned on every light as I went. I was mad and everyone was going to know about it. I didn't care if it was the middle of the night or not, the adrenaline was surging through my body.

"What the hell, Kate?" Parker said as he ran his hands through his hair as he came out of the bedroom.

"What?" I shrugged my shoulders, pretended not to know what he was talking about.

262

"For starters, why are you turning on all the lights. And why are you home so early? Is everything okay?" he asked, becoming alarmed at my odd behavior.

"No, everything is not okay," I yelled defiantly.

"Okay. What is wrong then?" he said irritated.

"Everything!"

"Will you please lower your voice?" he asked as he held his hands out in front of him at shoulder height and lowered them slowly.

"No!"

"Kate, there is no need to wake everyone up. You have my attention. What the hell is wrong?" he said as he took a few hesitant steps toward me.

"Forget it. You clearly don't get it!" I shouted as I brushed past him on my way to the bedroom, slamming the door loudly.

A moment later, Parker opened the door and sat down on the bed. Then, he stood back up, walked towards me, and put his arms around me tightly. I wanted to fight. I wanted to scream. I wanted to run. Instead, I crumpled and the sudden shift in weight caught Parker off guard, and we both fell to the floor with a thud.

Parker let go of me and brushed the hair out of my face. I was out of breath and I could feel my heart pounding in my chest. Beads of sweat lined the back of my neck, the pounding behind my eyes strengthened, and I felt dizzy and weak.

"Kate, what is wrong with you?" Parker whispered as he looked into my eyes.

I didn't answer. His eyes were soft and I could see he was genuinely concerned about me as we lay tangled on the bedroom floor. I rested my head on the floor as the rest of the fight within me left my body.

Finally, I spoke the only answer I had, "I don't know."

"I'm worried about you. One minute you want to jump my bones, the next you want to murder me. You laugh at things you never would have before, your head always hurts... And..." he paused and I saw him thinking, "AnneMarie pulled me aside the other day to ask if you were alright. She said you've been acting out of character lately."

"She did?" I asked, feeling betrayed.

"Kate, I'm really worried about you."

I took in what he said before formulating my response, "I'm worried too."

I was in the library reading a new book when I heard Carter screaming at the top of his lungs. I had been enjoying a moment of silence and dreaded having to move from my comfy place. When I got to the kitchen, Carter was holding my phone and looking at the screen. I grabbed it from his hands quickly and looked at it.

To my horror, the video of Parker having sex with Renee was staring back at me. Despite the pounding in my head, I was now screaming at the top of my lungs as well. Kendall waddled in from her lounge chair outside where she'd been sunbathing and Kamdyn came rushing from her room.

"What's going on?" Kendall asked urgently.

"Yeah, everything okay?" Kamdyn asked quickly.

"No. No everything is *not* okay," Carter managed to stammer.

I said nothing. I just kept staring at the phone. If I wished hard enough, maybe it would just disappear. Why had I kept the video in the first place? Was it for self-torture? I hadn't watched it since the day I filmed it. I had those images etched in my memory forever. I wasn't sure what I had intended to do with it, but now I had my own homemade porn of my husband cheating on me tucked away on my phone.

"I'm gonna puke," Carter announced.

"What? Gross, Carter!" Kamdyn said as she stalked back off towards her bedroom.

"Well, what has you both all freaked out?" Kendall asked, irritated that no one was answering her.

Kendall grabbed the phone from my hands before I had a chance to react and immediately dropped it to the floor and began screaming at the top of her lungs. Parker came running in from the backyard to see what was going on and I knew things were only going to get worse from here. I could feel the pressure in my head building.

"What is everyone screaming for?" Parker asked innocently.

"What the fuck, Dad?" Carter managed to get out.

"Watch your language!" Parker demanded.

"Really? You've been cheating on Mom?" Carter said as his face went red with anger.

"What?" Kamdyn asked from her bedroom doorway.

"I need to go wash my eyes!" Kendall said as she rushed to the sink and wet a rag.

"What the hell are you talking about, Carter?" Parker asked as he looked at me.

"I saw the video."

Parker's face changed from pale to red and back to pale. I saw the emotions flow through him as everything registered in his brain. He was clearly going to be the martyr and I was going to be the victim. My head throbbed more than ever and my own urge to vomit was more than I could contain. The mix of bile and dinner erupted all over the floor and Kamdyn, who had come out rom her room to witness everything first hand, barely backed up in time.

"Kate, are you okay?" Parker asked, concerned.

"No, I don't feel well."

"Don't touch her!" Carter commanded when Parker began to move towards me.

Parker ignored him and moved closer to me. Was the room spinning or was it just me? I began to feel light-headed as the pounding grew so intense that I thought my head might explode. As I stared at Parker and the kids, everything went silent and I felt myself falling but was unable to respond. I had passed out. Everything went black.

Parker knelt next to me and checked my vital signs. Before Parker had a chance to do anything, Kamdyn had picked up the phone, called 911, and was frantically yelling into the phone that her mother was on the floor. Chaos continued to erupt when Carter decided that it was time to defend my honor and told Parker to back away from his mother. Parker hadn't taken to that well and the two of them began to exchange words in a heated battled over me.

When the ambulance arrived, I was beginning to arouse but since I didn't want to deal with reality, I kept my eyes closed. I'm sure the entire scene was entertaining to some, but the stress was overwhelming and I felt that it was all because of me. Parker and I had been working hard to rebuild our marriage and our children seeing the video was the last thing either of us needed.

There was so much going on and I didn't want to deal with it. I couldn't deal with it. My head hurt and I felt sick to my stomach. Suddenly, I began to laugh. Uncontrollable laughter filled the room. Everyone around me stopped and stared. What had become of our picture perfect life?

Kendall offered to ride with me to the hospital and I didn't stop her. Just having her with me felt comforting, but we didn't talk. I didn't want to talk. I didn't have anything to say. I knew that things had been spiraling out of control, but I hadn't said a word about it to anyone. Sure, people were noticing small things, but no one did anything about it. Everything could be explained away as something else and the things that couldn't, I kept to myself.

I was a popular patient in my own emergency room. I had a CT scan and blood work done. When the doctor came in to give me the results, Kendall was conveniently in the bathroom. It was then that the doctor first told me there was a suspicious lesion on my frontal cortex and asked if I'd have an MRI done. I said I would, but I wasn't sure I wanted to know more.

When Kendall returned, I told her that everything had checked out well and I let them discharge me without another word about a tumor. For now, it was my little secret. I would decide what to do with my own body and when. I didn't want anyone pressuring me into anything.

At home, the tension was so thick it could be cut with a knife. I was afraid to ask what had happened with Parker and Carter after we left, but as I laid in my bed, Parker quietly knocked and came in.

"Kate, how are you?" he asked tenderly.

"I'm okay. I was just dehydrated is all," I lied.

"Dehydrated?"

I often wondered if it's possible to fool a doctor with these types of lies, but sometimes Parker is just a husband and believes what I say if the lie is believable enough. We both knew dehydration was a stretch, but how could he argue with me? My only fear now was that he'd go above me and seek my medical charts. I'd always given him permission to see my medical charts and I knew the hospital had that permission on file, but now I prayed he wouldn't be too nosy.

"I'm okay, I promise," I reiterated.

"I'm so sorry all this has happened."

"Well, we just fight to make sure it never does again."

"I know."

"How is Carter?"

He shrugged his shoulders, "I wish I could say. After you left, he stormed off again. I don't know what's gotten into that kid lately. He's going to give me a heart attack if I don't watch it."

"Tell me about it. He stresses me out. I don't know what to say to him anymore."

"Have you said *that* to him?"

"I should," I said with a sigh. "I didn't mean for the kids to see that video."

"I can't believe you *took* a video," he said under his breath.

"I thought you'd deny it. Well, actually... I don't know what was going through my head. Lately, I've had strange thoughts and done things I never would've in a million years. Between you and the kids, I'm a giant ball of stress."

"I'm worried about you," he said as he looked into my eyes.

A light switch flickered inside me and I went from feeling exhausted to feeling super charged. One look into Parker's eyes and my body responded. I knew I needed to rest, but I couldn't control my body. I could tell it to do what I wanted, but it wouldn't listen. It acted of its own accord.

"Don't worry about me. I'll be fine," I said as I reached for him. "I always am."

I spoke softly and trailed my fingertips down his chest. I expected his face to crack into a look of desire, but instead it turned into a look of sadness. It wasn't the reaction I wanted nor the one I expected.

"Kate, we shouldn't," he said softly as he grabbed at my hands and held them from further exploring his body.

"Why not?" I asked, pleading.

"Seeing that video... You should be angry with me. You should be turned off. I'm ashamed of me. I'm embarrassed. I'm hurt. I've let myself down. When it first happened and you agreed to work past it with me, I felt we could just pretend it never happened. I realize now that that isn't possible. It *did* happen. I need to make sure it never happens again. You're my one true love and the only woman I want to be with for the rest of my life. I want to build our emotional connection, our friendship, back up first. I want to earn your trust again," he finished as his head hung low.

"I understand. I don't know what else to say. I don't feel myself lately. My sex drive has gone from park to overdrive in the last few months, my moods have been riding a roller coaster, and I'm so damn tired all the time. I'm forgetting things I've done almost daily for twenty-something years. And I have a throbbing behind my eyes daily," I complained.

Instead of replying, Parker pulled me into a hug and rubbed his hand up and down my back. Without warning, tears began to fall from my eyes and Parker just held me tighter. He had been right. I should be angry at him. Who the hell was this new Kate? Where did she come from?

By the following week, I was back to work. I couldn't drive, but Parker had offered to drive me. I was nervous that rumors would be flying about the spot on the CT scan, but I also knew that HIPPA would hopefully protect me from said rumors.

Besides, I was waiting for an MRI, right? Until then, it was just a blip on a screen. An unknown.

I found myself working a float position. I was pretty confident whoever had made the assignments had done that to make sure I wouldn't be directly responsible for any patients on my own. Welcome back, Kate. I was fine. I didn't need a babysitter.

Around midnight, the phone rang, and we were informed of a fight at a local bar. The fight included several patrons who were injured from things such as bar stools and fists but also included at least one gunshot victim from the parking lot. Handling the injuries was second nature for us, but the drama that comes with these types of patients, such as being intoxicated and still angry at whoever, would up the ante.

I took a patient to the floor for admission to clear a room and when I returned, we already had a few of the patients from the bar fight. I offered to take one to help out as Sam went to lunch. The man was probably six feet five inches, built like a football linemen, and had thighs about as big as my waist.

He had a laceration above his right eye that appeared pretty deep and would most likely need stitches or glue, a laceration to his forearm, and bleeding knuckles. Despite these injuries, he rated his pain at zero. I rolled my eyes instinctively. It seemed like everyone was coming to our ER in search of drugs, but this guy was so macho he wouldn't even admit to pain.

"Look lady, please just get the doctor in here to do his thing so I can go," he said bluntly.

"That's the plan," I replied with a smirk.

When Dr. Moon stepped in to assess his injuries though, he became irate.

"Who the hell do you think *you* are? Don't touch me!" He yelled, his voice naturally booming.

"I told you. I'm Dr. Moon. Please let me look at your arm," she said firmly, standing her ground.

"Like hell! I'm not an idiot. You're not a doctor. You're just another nurse who wants to *play* doctor!"

With a deep sigh, "I'm Dr. Moon. I went to medical school, not nursing school. I'm the one who's going to fix you up and get you out of here. We can do this the easy way or the hard way, your choice."

"Get the hell out."

"Listen badass, I'm your nurse. She's your doctor. Let her do her damn job because we don't want to be here taking care of your tough ass any more than you want us to be. Let's all just admit it and get it over with," I said before I could stop myself.

Dr. Moon shot me a dirty look and the patient narrowed his eyes and studied my face. I didn't move a muscle as I stared back. Like a lion in a fight, I wasn't going to back down. Finally, he relented and held out his arm for Dr. Moon to look at. Mark one in the win column for Kate, I thought.

With his wounds cleaned and stitched, I was able to discharge him without further incident. None of these so called tough guys scared me anymore. This was my home, and they wouldn't come in and treat my family the way he had. The problem was, I'd never been like that before. While I commanded the respect and didn't have fear, I never lost my cool and spoke to patients as I had been lately.

The rest of my shift was spent starting IVs for other nurses, running errands to anyone who needed it, and trying to look busy when no one needed help. I was the person that used to love this type of assignment. I'd always felt it was a luxury to be the float nurse. I enjoyed teaching newer nurses skills and allowing them the time needed to learn something. Tonight, it felt like a punishment.

When the night was over, I hurried home and looked forward to being cozy in my bed. I tossed my keys on the kitchen counter and took off my shoes. In the kitchen was a note from Parker that he'd be home late. He would be having dinner at a learning seminar with a drug representative, and my gut told me it could all be a lie.

I was supposed to trust my husband, and yet I was doubting him. Isn't this what husbands said they were doing when they were really meeting their mistresses? Was I one of the gullible wives or had I spent too much time watching Hallmark and reading romance novel?

We still had a lot of work to be done. Could he ever regain my trust? Could I ever stop having these things? Maybe I could find a book on how to get past this type of thing. I didn't know, but I was still willing to try.

The following night, while I made my way to the triage area to double check something, I heard a woman screaming for help from the front door. Running at a sprint, I was the first one to the door. The woman was hysterical and it was difficult for me to understand exactly what the problem was.

I did a quick assessment of her as she screamed at me in words I could not understand. She had all her limbs, I didn't see blood, and clearly her lungs and heart were functioning well. I then noticed she kept looking at the car parked in front of the door and took off. The front seat was empty but I quickly saw a rear-facing car seat in the back.

As I flung the backdoor open, I saw what she had been trying to tell me. In the car seat was an infant and that infant was blue. I wasted no time unbuckling the harness but then my brain froze. No matter how hard I tried to think, I didn't know what to do now that I had the infant in my arms.

Luckily, the triage nurse was now at my side. Noticing my lack of immediate action, she grabbed the infant from my arms and took off sprinting back into the emergency room. Attempting to cover up my "error", I went to the mother and gave her a hug. I encouraged her to park the car and I would wait for her. It was only then I realized she didn't speak English!

Luck was on my side since the receptionist spoke fluent Spanish, and was able to help her. Feeling as though I had failed the infant *and* the mother, I sulked back to the break room to hide the remainder of the night. What was wrong with me? Why had I frozen?

The more I thought about it, the more sick to my stomach I became. Then, the blinding force behind my eyes started again. I slowly made my way back to the department from the break room. My balance felt off and I'm sure it had everything to do with the fact that my eyes were playing tricks on me, I had a pounding headache, and I felt sick to my stomach.

Almost to the bank of computers by the gray team, I stopped, reached for the wall to steady myself, and began to lower myself to the floor. Sam and Mia, standing nearby, rushed to my side as I collapsed the rest of the way down. With a hard crack noise, my head hit the floor as I blacked out.

My body began to jerk uncontrollably as Sam pleaded for help. As soon as Dr. Moon arrived, Ativan was ordered in an attempt to stop the grand mal seizure that was overtaking my body.

Chapter 24

I was whisked off to a room of my own and Mia undressed me and covered me with a gown. I'm not exactly sure what order things happened, but I know that Sam called my husband and I had another CT scan. When I finally began to arouse, Parker was by my side, gently rubbing my arm.

"Hey, what are you doing here?" I asked.

"You had a seizure," he said.

"A seizure? Damn."

"Yeah, gave everyone quite the scare from the sounds of it."

"I remember freezing up with the kid that was blue. I went back to the break room and then had another one of those blinding headaches. I remember feeling weird, so I started to make my way into the main ER. I remember vaguely that my legs were weak and I think I was trying to lower myself to the floor maybe?" I was uncertain about that last part.

"Oh hun, I'm so sorry," he said as he stood up and gave me a tight hug.

"So what next? EEG?"

"Well, you had a CT scan, and we're waiting for the results of that first," he said bluntly.

"Got it. Man, my head hurts," I said as I rubbed at the back of my head.

"From what I heard, you hit it pretty hard on the ground when you went down before the seizure," he said as he moved my hair aside to look at the spot I was rubbing.

Having a physician for a husband really is great, but at this moment, a small part of me wished he was a neurologist rather than an orthopedic surgeon! I could see the worry in his face as he tried to patiently be a family member and not the physician.

"Hey there pretty lady," Dr. Moon said as she entered the room.

"Back at ya," I said nervously.

"I got the results of the CT scan. They were less than ideal," she said with a frown.

"What does that mean," Parker asked quickly.

"Kate, there is what looks to be a mass on your frontal lobe," she said without dramatics.

"A what?" I choked out.

"Frontal lobe?" Parker asked quickly.

"Yes. We need to do an MRI to get more information and I want to set up a neurology consult. At this point though, with the recent seizure and the headaches you've been having, I need to admit you to the neuro floor tonight."

I groaned. Parked squeezed my hand and assured me everything would be alright. He asked Dr. Moon to order the MRI STAT, to which she replied that she'd already done so. A tumor? It would explain so many of the things I'd been feeling lately but hadn't had the courage to say out loud or that I'd brushed off as just having a bad day or assumed to be from working night shift or all the drama in the family lately. A freaking tumor.

I laid back and closed my eyes. Then, I opened them abruptly and asked Dr. Moon if the blue infant was okay.

"He's upstairs in peds ICU as we speak," she said softly. "Try not to worry about anything right now. You need to rest," she reminded me.

"Can I get some Zofran and Dilauded then?" I asked with a smile, only half-joking.

"Wow. Dr. Cordova, I wasn't aware that our patient was a drug seeker," she said with a laugh. "I'll see what I can do."

I was resting peacefully when I heard a soft knock at the door, the kids come in and begin talking with Parker, and then my mother's voice on speaker phone. As I opened my eyes, I had chairs set up all over my room. My kids were each on their phones playing games or something and my husband was reading some medical magazine.

"Hi," I said with a weak voice.

"Mom!" Kamdyn said as she dropped her phone and launched herself on me.

"Whoa there superstar," Parker said as he moved out of the way. "Be gentle."

"Sorry. I was worried about you," Kamdyn said.

"Kate, maybe now would be a good time to tell the kids what is going on?" Parker suggested.

"You haven't told them?"

"Not yet," he admitted.

"Yeah, Mom. What's going on?" Kendall asked as she came to the other side of the bed and held my hand.

"Well, I had a seizure at work last night," I began quietly.

"Wow! Are you okay?" Kendall asked.

"I have a tumor on my brain." There was silence in the room.

"Are you going to die?" Kamdyn finally said quietly.

"We don't know. Tomorrow they will attempt to get a piece of it, and then they will send it to the lab to be tested to see if it's cancer or not," Parker said, pulling Kamdyn into a hug.

"This is bullshit," Carter said, stood, and left the room.

"Carter," I called after him, but it was no use.

"Mom, it's going to be okay," Kendall said.

"Why only a piece? Why not just get rid of the whole thing?" Kamdyn said, her voice rising.

"Well, they need to know what they are working with before they can attempt a major brain surgery," Parker began to explain.

"I don't want you to die," Kamdyn said as she hugged me.

How does a parent respond to that? What was I supposed to say? Before I had a chance to say anything though, the neurologist came in. Dr. Rachel Tudor had been a neurologist at McKinley Baptist for years and was the only one I trusted if anyone was going to operate on my brain.

"Well, I reviewed your previous CT scan with the one you had done now as well as the MRI. Kate, that mass has grown a slight bit, but the fact that it's not grown much is a good sign," she said hopefully.

"Wait, what CT scan are you comparing it to?" Parker asked, confused.

"The one Kate had done last month during her ER visit," Dr. Tudor said.

"You had a CT scan last month and it showed this thing and you didn't say anything?" Parker said with a flash of anger.

"Well, at that time we weren't sure if it was anything at all. We scheduled an MRI, but Kate cancelled it."

Clearly Dr. Tudor wasn't on my side since she was hanging me out to dry. I thought there was a girl code or patient confidentiality or something that would prevent her from telling my secrets, but I was wrong. I felt another headache boiling behind my eyes.

"She *what?*" Parker raged.

"Dr. Cordova, please go easy on her. There wasn't much concern last month, so I understand the lack of urgency in getting the MRI," Dr. Tudor explained.

"No excuse. I didn't want to do it. I didn't want to know and I didn't care," I said flatly.

"Mom!" Kendall shrieked.

"Sorry, not sorry," I mocked back.

She rolled her eyes, but Parker hadn't found it very funny. He was very upset to learn that I'd know *something* wasn't right last month and I'd ignored it. I'd know something was wrong for at least the last three months. If I was going to receive a death sentence, I didn't want to know a timeline and just knowing what kind of tumor it was would mean knowing a timeline. I wasn't stupid.

Dr. Tudor continued on explaining the process for the biopsy the following day and what we could expect after that. Everything in my entire life hinged on this biopsy and I hated letting something run my life like this was. I just wanted the damn thing gone now that everyone knew about it.

"So this would explain some of the odd behaviors you've had over the last few months," Parker said quietly.

"Most likely. I guess I'm not the bitch I thought I was."

"You aren't a bitch," Parker added.

"Well, kinda," Kendall said with a little laugh.

I looked at her and together we both began to laugh.

"I don't understand you girls," Parker said, laughing at us and shaking his head.

Kamdyn hadn't stopped clinging to me the entire time and I wasn't sure if she was even still awake until she released her own little laugh. Carter returned just as Dr. Tudor left and apologized for running away.

"Carter, you can't run from problems. I wish I could say that I don't do it either, but I've learned over the last few months that it's better to stay and face the music and battle a problem head on," Parker said to him before pulling him into a hug.

"I'm just scared," he admitted.

"We all are," I said.

"I'm so sorry," he said as he broke down and began to cry.

Seeing my children hurting broke me. The walls crumbled down and all the control I was clinging to was gone. It started with small tears rolling down my cheeks, but they grew bigger and within moments, the flood gates opened. Big fat, wet tears streamed down my face as I sobbed and the weeks of fear that had been building inside me released.

Finally, when the sob fest ended, I was left with a soaking wet gown, red, swollen eyes, and a massive throbbing pain behind my eyes. I silently hit the call light and asked for pain medicine. My kids looked at me with shock. I pretty much had refused to take pain medicine and I had an extremely high pain tolerance. They had heard the stories of the three times I gave birth naturally and without pain medications. Asking for it now meant I was hurting.

"Mom, it's going to be okay," Kamdyn assured me.

"I know. But sometimes we all have weak moments," I said quietly, trying to make myself believe it.

"Mom, you aren't weak," Carter said. "You're the strongest person I know."

"Yeah, I second that," Kendall added.

"Me three," Parker said.

"We love you," Kamdyn said sweetly.

"You look tired. Why don't we let you get some rest. I'll be up here tomorrow in the morning, and we will face this thing together, no matter where it leads us, alright?" Parker said, giving me a kiss on the lips.

And with that last kiss, I was left with only my thoughts for company. When the nurse came in a minute later, the pain was practically blinding me. When she sweetly asked for my pain score, I tried to remain calm and answer, but I ended up shouting far louder than I'd planned.

"Okay, let me go get the doctor to order something and I'll be back."

"He hasn't ordered pain medicine yet?" I barked at her.

"Um, no."

"What the fuck?" I said as I rolled my eyes and pounded my fists down on the bed.

She didn't answer but instead scurried from the room like a mouse. I hadn't meant to react that way and I felt guilty. I knew apologizing would be pointless. I was feeling so many things, and I was sick of it. I wanted to be Kate again.

The next morning, the neurologist was in my room before the sun had even risen. I was barely awake, still feeling groggy. She smiled at me and explained that I'd be headed off to have the biopsy done in a short time and asked if I had any questions. I knew she didn't have any answers to give, so I didn't bother with any questions. I let her do her thing and just closed my eyes. I was ready to get it over with. I was ready to return to being me.

A warm hand touched my arm and without looking, I knew it was Parker's. My body instinctively relaxed and I closed my eyes.

"Kate," he said, waiting for me to open my eyes and look at him, "I don't want to fight with you anymore. I just want to love you," Parker said sympathetically.

"I don't want to fight either. I need us to be strong. I need you, tumor or not," I admitted.

"Can you ever trust me again?"

"I'm going to have to, aren't I?"

He nodded and pulled me into a deep hug. It wasn't a poetic answer and it didn't mean I'd forget everything. I could forgive him and work on trusting him again.

And just like that I felt a stack of bricks lift from my shoulders. I felt like a floating feather. While I knew there would definitely be moments that I would hesitate and my mind would venture to the "what if" game, deep in my soul I knew that everything that had happened had been an awakening for both of us. Our lives had been changed. Despite everything that had happened, there was no one else on this planet that made me feel the way Parker did. He was *my* person. My one true love. My happily ever after.

The next thing I remembered, Parker was holding my hand, and I was waking up. Biopsy completed, now the fun part was beginning. Everything was a waiting game. Waiting to find out if the mass growing on your brain is going to kill you or just drive you insane is the worst wait. To cry or to celebrate. To live or to die.

I spent the rest of the day resting and being monitored, but by the next morning, I was released from the hospital and Parker took me home. I had exactly one week until my follow-up appointment, which is when I'd learn my fate. Until then, I had to take things easy. I was aware that this might be the most difficult week of my life.

"Are you having any pain?" Parker asked as he tucked my blanket around me on the couch.

"Not too bad," I admitted.

Carter jumped up from the couch and went to the kitchen to fetch my medication. Kendall sat cuddled at my feet and Kamdyn was reading her book on a pillow on the floor. I accepted the pill Carter handed me and a glass of water. After the pill was swallowed, I closed my eyes and sighed.

I sat in the stands next to Parker as we watched Carter take the field with the football team. I sat anxious while Parker sat playing a game on his phone. I was the one who screamed and cheered from the stands. Parker just attended for the supportive father role. He had never been a big football fan, instead he'd spent his time with his nose in medical books studying for exams.

As the band took the field to play the national anthem, the announcer asked the crowd to stand and remove their hats. It always amazed me that an announcer would even have to remind people still. Wasn't that taught to kids anymore? I saw the football team moving onto the field and standing between various band members who remained in formation. Then, the cheerleaders took the field and stood in front of the band. During this silent moment, the crowd began to buzz as everyone was trying to figure out why they were doing pregame differently.

"Ladies and Gentleman, before we honor our nation with the playing and singing of the Star Spangled Banner, I'd like to introduce you to a very special guest at today's game. Senior defensive back, Kevin Parsons, experienced a medical emergency this summer while at practice. Unable to join the team this season, he has been named a special captain for today's game. Please join me in welcoming Kevin to the field," the announcer said as the crowd went wild with a standing ovation and applause.

My heart warmed as I watched the boy, dressed in jeans and a jersey, proudly walk to the field. I'd forgotten to ask Carter how he'd been doing, but clearly he was recovering well. Parker squeezed my hand and I snuggled closer into him as I felt the cool breeze blow through the stadium.

"Appreciative of the honor bestowed upon him, Kevin has proudly chosen to recognize someone else in attendance today. On that fateful day when Kevin's heart stopped beating, a mother in the football stands stormed into action without hesitation. Always a nurse, she quickly got to work performing CPR and was able to bring Kevin back. Without her, Kevin would not be with us today," the announcer continued and everyone began looking around at each other.

"Nurse Kate Cordova, it would be Kevin's honor for you to join him on the field today as honorary co-captain," the announcer said cheerfully and the crowd went wild.

Hearing my name, I froze. I couldn't go down there! I began to panic. I was still missing a chunk from my skull, and I was supposed to go in front of thousands of people? Was there somewhere I could hide and pretend I wasn't really at the game? Why wasn't the assistant coach being mentioned at all?

"In Kevin's words, Kate, you're a real life hero. Instead of a cape, you've got a stethoscope."

Parker stood and began to clap. I tried to tug at his shirt, hoping he would stop and no one would notice he had done it. But it was too late. The people around be also stood and began clapping and I noticed two of the football players at the bottom of the stairs waiting for me.

I conceded, stood, and began carefully walking down the stairs. Each of the boys held an arm as they escorted me towards the field. With each step, I noticed the applause grew. I still wanted to hide. Instead, I made a small wave towards the stands and forced a smile. I wasn't good at being recognized for what I did. I did it because I loved it, and it made me feel good.

Standing on the field next to Kevin on the field was his mother and one look at her tear streaked face caused the tears to begin flowing from my own eyes. We embraced for a long time before she finally whispered a thank you into my ear and I moved on to hug Kevin. The band played the national anthem and then the football players escorted me back to Parker.

"Can we go home?" I asked when I reached my seat.

"Everything okay?" Parker asked, concern written across his face.

"Just another headache. I'm tired. And it's loud here," I complained.

Rather than answer, he helped me back down the steps again. Cuddled on the couch, Parker and I received constant updates of the game from Kamdyn.

Chapter 25

I sat alone in the waiting room. I had asked if I could do this alone. I didn't want the pressures from anyone in my family trying to tell me what to think or feel. I was anxious as I waited to see the doctor, but that trusty gut of mine told me everything would be just fine.

The office was plain. There were many plastic cushioned chairs and benches, an assortment of magazines, and a television showing advertisements. A soft classical music could be heard if quiet. It felt sterile.

"Kate?" a medical assistant called as she peeked her head out of a door along the far wall.

I took a deep breath and stood up. I demanded my legs to walk but they hesitated. This was worse than walking down the aisle at my wedding. In only a few short minutes, my entire life would be changed in a matter of mere seconds. I would have to make a decision, but at least I knew the decision would truly be mine once I'd made it. I wouldn't have regret that someone asked me to do something I didn't want to do.

"Please have a seat and Dr. Tudor will be right in," she said with a smile.

I sat in the empty room staring at the pale green walls and playing with my hands. I needed to puke. I wanted to run. But most of all, I craved answers.

"Good morning Kate," Dr. Tudor said a few moments later as she came into the room and took a seat next to her computer.

"Good morning," I managed to say.

"How are you feeling?"

"Anxious, scared, nervous. I have a headache too," I said as the truth spilled out.

"Well, no need to be anxious or scared. Your results show that the tumor is *not* cancerous," she said with a big smile on her face.

I felt a wave of relief as a surge of tears threatened to storm from my eyes. She noticed this because she gave me a hug immediately.

"There are still some serious discussions we need to have, but that was the good news. Where is your husband?" she asked, looking around the room.

"I came alone."

"What? Why did you do that? Where is he?" she asked with confusion.

"I wanted to do this on my own. I wanted to make the decision about what we do next without anyone telling me how to feel or what to think." She nodded understanding.

"I feel it's important to have someone else here with you so that when you go home, you'll have someone who may remember something you've forgotten. Especially in your situation considering you have had some memory issues." She continued to watch me.

"Nope. I don't need that. If it's okay with you, I'd like to record our talk to help remind me."

"That would be fine."

I turned on the voice recorder on my phone and nodded for her to continue.

"Kate, the biggest decision, and maybe the easiest, is whether you'd like to remove the tumor or not," she said.

One by one, she explained the options to me and answered all of my questions. When she was done, I told her my decision with 100% confidence. I knew what needed to be done and I didn't need to discuss it with anyone other than her.

She returned a few minutes later with the information necessary for the next step and told me she would be in contact, presumably to make sure I felt the same way as I did now. I thanked her and checked out. My confidence dissolved after I left her office and I needed to sit in the car for a few moments to think. Had I really done the right thing by blocking everyone from coming to this visit with me?

While I knew that this entire experience had changed my relationship with Parker, I also knew that it would eventually emerge stronger than ever and not weaker. But the hole had already been poked in the damn and bubblegum was only a temporary fix.

Would Parker return to another woman if I wasn't able to have sex with him while I did the treatments? Wasn't it he that said he'd slept with Renee because I hadn't been meeting his needs? This and many more thoughts crossed my mind in a continuous loop. Would this always be in the back of my mind?

I closed my eyes to think when my phone rang. Startled, I answered it.

"Are you serious? Oh my God. I'll be right there!"

I hung up the phone and promptly forgot all about those options as I put my car in reverse and sped across the hospital campus to the building that housed the maternity ward. Kendall was in labor!

I practically ran through the doors and straight to the desk where expectant mothers were triaged. The woman was young with an oval face and long blond hair.

"Can I help you?" she asked.

"Kendall Cordova, please."

The woman picked up the phone and dialed a number. She got permission from the nurse, gave me a room number written on a sticker, and applied it to the front of my shirt. She then unlocked the door and pointed out the directions.

"Mom!" Kendall exclaimed it when she saw me walking through the door.

"Oh baby girl," I said as I ran to her side and begin to caress her cheeks. "Are you okay? How are you feeling? How far apart are they?"

"Mom, calm down. I'm just beginning. My water broke when I was at the store, and they called an ambulance and sent me over here, but I'm not having a lot of contractions just yet."

"I didn't want to miss anything."

"You haven't missed anything that was worth it," Kendall said.

I was admiring her beautiful blue eyes when they turned a shade of gray and closed tightly as a contraction took over her entire body.

"Breathe. Breathe," I reminded

When the sensation passed she opened her eyes again.

"That was intense," she commented.

"Yeah I bet it was. And yet you've only just begun," I said with a little laugh.

"Why did you do this three times?" she asked me. "I haven't even started and I don't think I ever want to do this again."

I laughed, "Just wait. The moment you look in that baby's eyes, you'll wish you could do it all over again."

Over the next eight hours, as I talked to Kendall through contraction after contraction after contraction, I realized that the choice I had made earlier in the day at the neurologist's office was most certainly, without a doubt, the right decision. I was going to have the tumor removed and do whatever it took to ensure that it would not return.

Because I wanted to be here for everything. For my grand baby. And all the other grand babies I knew I would eventually have. And I wanted to go back to work. I wanted to save more lives and help people and their most traumatic time of need. But most of all, I did not want to leave Parker.

When the baby was finally born, I was overwhelmed with joy watching Kendall snuggle her newborn daughter. I didn't care that I had a slight headache and I didn't care that I was missing a chunk of hair from my head. All I cared about in that moment was that bundle of joy wrapped in a pink flannel blanket.

And once things calm down, and I was sitting on the couch Kendall asked me if I would like to hold my grand baby for the first time, and I realized she was right, I wanted nothing more than to hold that baby.

"What's your name?" I asked the baby hesitantly.

"Sally Kate Cordova," Kendall said with a smile.

Chapter 26
The Present

I'd made my decision, the day had arrived, and my surgery had gone perfectly. At least that's what the surgeon had said into my ear as I was waking up from the anesthesia. I still feel groggy, but I am still trying to wake up. I am laying on my back in recovery and praying that Parker will be allowed to come back here soon. I hate laying here alone.

My wish granted, Parker appears next to me with a smile on his face. He's gorgeous and I'm glad he's with me. I feel a calm come over me. Everything is going to be okay.

"Don't try to talk, Hun. They'll be taking you to the floor soon. Evan said things went extremely well so you should only need one night," Parker says optimistically.

"Evan?" I ask with confusion.

"Yeah. My partner, Evan Moringa. You've met him plenty of times. If I couldn't do your surgery, he's the only other one I'd want operating on you," he says confidently.

"Where is Dr. Tudor? Why would you do my surgery?" My confusion increases.

"Why would Dr. Tudor be here?" he asks, taking his turn at being confused.

"Nevermind," I say, too tired to care.

"Okay. Well, how are you feeling?" he asks.

I just nod. Hadn't he told me not to talk? Honestly, I don't feel anything other than being tired anyway. I close my eyes and drift back to sleep. When I open them again, I am in a different room. The curtains are pulled back and it's light out. I look around the room and see Kendall, Carter, and Kamdyn sitting next to Parker. I smile, pleased they are all here.

I don't know what day it is or what time it is, but none of that really matters. I am here. I am alive. I'm going to be the old Kate again.

"Hi, Mom," Kendall says with a kiss on my cheek.

"How are you feeling?" Kamdyn kisses my other cheek.

"I'm okay. I'm happy to see all of you," I reply, my voice cracks due to not using it much.

I continue to look around. The room is plain. It has a TV, a bathroom, a sink, and a little couch that converts to a table with chairs or a bed. I rub my eyes and see that dinner is sitting on the over the bed table.

"Can I have something to drink?" I ask.

"Of course, here is some water," Parker says as he hands me a Styrofoam cup with a straw.

His smile is genuine. He brushes a stray strand of hair from my face and my body warms with his touch. The gentle tilt of his head, his warm tone when he speaks, and the way his eyes communicate with me all put me at ease.

"How are you feeling Kendall?" I ask.

"I'm fine. Why do you ask?" she says with a look of confusion.

"Where's the baby?" I ask as I continue to look around the room to gather my surroundings.

"The baby?" Kendall looks at Parker and then back to me.

"Yeah, I can't remember her name. Isn't that awful?"

What kind of grandmother can't even remember her grandchild's name? Her only grandchild.

"Mom, what baby are you talking about?" she asks, now looking concerned.

"You had a baby! Where is the baby?" I ask with more determination, more insistence.

Kendall looks at Parker again before adding, "I haven't had a baby. Dad, is she okay?"

Now I am concerned. What had happened while I was asleep? Why was my family playing jokes on me? Had I missed something crucial? I had only been put asleep for a short time, not enough to miss something like this.

Parker says, "Kate, why don't you get some more sleep, and we can talk again in the morning."

He stands and comes to my bedside, reaching for my hand. He is warm and soft. He places a kiss on my forehead. It is sweet and tender, like the old Parker I remember.

"No, I want to know what is going on!" I insist.

Parker rubs his hands over his face. He is saved from having to answer when my nurse walks in with a handful of pills in a cup. She smiles when she sees that I am awake. I look at her but I don't recognize her. I look at her name tag and it says her name is Renee.

"Renee?" I ask in horror, my pulse quickens.

"Yep, that's me. It's nice to meet you," she says with a smile.

"Have you been here all day?"

"Yep, since seven this morning. I'm about to give report to the oncoming nurse though," she says nonchalantly.

"Parker, what the hell is going on?"

The panic is rising inside me. I can feel my pulse in my eyeballs, but I don't have any pain in my head. I reach for my head and there are no bandages. None of this is making sense.

"I'm not sure I know what you mean," he says as he lets go of my hand and sits back down in the chair.

"This isn't right. Why are you guys playing a tricks on me?" I ask seriously.

292

"Mom, we don't know what you're talking about," Carter says before he returns to a text on his phone.

"Kate, are you having any pain?" Renee asks pleasantly.

"No, I'm just very confused," I reply.

"You can say that again," Carter mumbles under his breath.

Kamdyn giggles.

"Okay, why do you think that?" she asks kindly.

"Well, nothing makes sense right now. Parker, what is going on? Please tell me the truth."

I move to get out of bed, but as I work to swing my legs over the side, I realize that my right leg won't move. Am I paralyzed? What happened during surgery? I feel a shooting pain move up my right leg and I let out a cry.

"Kate, you need to stay in bed unless someone is helping you," Renee reminds me as she pushes my leg back on the bed gently.

I feel the pain subside. I wiggle my toes and know that I am not paralyzed.

"No, I need someone to tell me what is going on," I say with more urgency. "What happened while I was in surgery? What happened before surgery?"

Everyone looks at each other and appears confused. The panic is surging through my body and I make another attempt to climb out of bed. Shooting pain up my leg stops me yet again.

"Kate, you can't get out of bed right now," Parker says firmly.

"Why not? I had my head worked on, not my body!" I say defiantly.

"Kate, you had a knee replacement," Parker says, tilting his head to the side and staring straight at me.

"My knee? What are *you* talking about? I had the brain tumor removed."

"Brain tumor?" Parker says as he begins to laugh.

"Why are you laughing?"

"What are you talking about, Kate? You don't have a brain tumor."

"I don't have a brain tumor because I just had it removed. Again, what are *you* talking about?"

"Why don't you tell me what you think has happened to you?" he says with a grin.

Is he trying to mock me? Are they all recording this for some television show? I'm ready to kick them all out of my room except I need to know what has happened and why they are all acting so strange.

"Well, I started having issues. Headaches, being rude to the patients, trouble making decisions, forgetting things... You know... I had a seizure at work and that's when they found the tumor. The biopsy said it isn't cancer. I decided to have it removed since it was causing so many problems. Right?" I ask for reassurance, but instead, they all stare at me like I'd just told them Donald Trump was President of the United States.

"Kate, let me review everything for you," Parker says when he stops laughing.

"Please. That would be helpful."

"You went for your daily run yesterday but got tripped up on a root or something and fell. You hit your head on something, which caused a concussion, and screwed up your bad knee. Your knee had already been giving you trouble, so it was an easy choice to replace it. Early this morning you had the knee replacement. You're just now recovering from that. We will be going home tomorrow," he says with a smile.

My entire world is flipped upside-down. I have no idea what he's talking about. Nothing makes sense. A knee replacement? Daily running?

"Really? So what about my brain tumor?" I ask, expecting an answer.

"Kate, you don't have a brain tumor. You never have, but I'm thinking we should order a CT scan for you now," he says as he looks to the nurse and chuckles.

"What? I didn't have brain surgery?" I look at everyone again.

"Nope." They all shake their heads in confirmation.

I look down at my right knee and see it's bandaged up. I try to move it but it hurts so bad that I stop trying. I let out a little groan and Renee immediately looks up from her charting on the mobile computer station in front of her.

"Painful?" she asks.

"Yeah."

"On a scale of zero to Jesus being nailed to a cross, what would you rate your pain at?" she asks with a mischievous smile.

She hands me a cup of pills and uses a syringe to put some medication into my IV. I feel my eyes begin to well up with tears. That was my line. I used that all the time in the emergency room. How had she known that? Had I really imagined everything?

"So, Kate didn't have a baby?" I ask with hesitation.

"No way, Mom." Kendall says.

"Parker, did you have an affair with... Renee?" I ask, then look at Renee and shrug my shoulders.

Parker begins to laugh uncontrollably, "Of course not. Kate, I would never do that to you! I come home every night to you and only you. You're the woman of my dreams and have been for over twenty years. You make my life complete, even if you are a little confused," he teases.

As I ask questions, I learn that everything was just a freakishly realistic dream while I was out cold! I still work day shift in the emergency room downstairs, Parker never cheated on me, Kendall was never pregnant, Kamdyn still finds boys to be irritating, and Carter was never caught having sex in our house.

"Carter, did I really save a boy at your football practice?" I ask, still struggling to believe all of this.

"Mom, you don't even come to my practices," he says, shaking his head.

I softy cry. I hated the "new Kate", but not knowing who I really am bothers me even more. What was real and what was all a dream? I close my eyes and wish it all away. I wish for clarity and healing. I wish for the old Kate that I love to return. I wish I knew myself again.

"You must have hit your head harder than I thought," Parker says with a smile as he pulls me close for a kiss.

What Did You Think of Heroes Wear Stethoscopes?

First of all, thank you for purchasing Heroes Wear Stethoscopes. I know you could have picked any number of books to read, but you picked my book, and for that I am extremely grateful.

If you enjoyed this book, I'd like to hear from you! I hope that you could take some time to post a review on Amazon, and share with your family and friends by posting to Facebook, Twitter, or Instagram.

I want you, the reader, to know that your review is very important and so, if you'd like to leave a review, all you have to do is visit:

https://www.amazon.com/dp/B081LQFDY3

Want even more? Follow me!

Facebook: www.facebook.com/jmspadewrites

Instagram: www.instagram.com/jmspadewrites

Goodreads: JM Spade

Or sign up for my mailing list:
https://forms.gle/jfXn5RyNW2YxJG4fA

Love always, JM Spade

Made in the USA
Middletown, DE
31 January 2020